The Undergrounders
&
the Flight of the Falcon

C T Frankcom

Book 1 in 'The Undergrounders' Series.

First edition: November 2018
Second edition: July 2019
Third edition: April 2021

Front cover design by Sam Waters
Explosion image from www.textures4photoshop.com
Images from www.pexels.com
Inside cover illustration by C.T. Frankcom

Special thanks to J. Shardlow, M. Agrasut,
A. Okonkwo and T. Frankcom

For Francesca and Jessica x

The Bird of Prey

From: T77
To: J21
Re: Bird of Prey {Encrypted}

<u>Update 23.7</u>

In response to the information given by our Turkish
source, we have continued surveillance at the
aforementioned site.

As of this morning, we have completed a successful
search, as instructed.
The nest was vacant, but there were significant signs of
recent activity.

We continue to follow new leads but wanted to give you
immediate visibility of the evidence found.

I attach a copy of the communication that we uncovered
at the site.

We believe that the bird had been resting here mid-flight
and is, possibly, moving northwest.

End.

I am Victor Sokolov.

Seven years I have been waiting.
Waiting to get my revenge,
Waiting to take back what they stole from me,
Waiting to re-build that which they destroyed.

Abandoned by my mother country,
Abandoned by my captors,
Abandoned by my allies.

I will send the Falcon to flight,
I will hit them where it hurts the most,
I will snatch the thing they hold dearest,
I will make them beg for lenience.

I am Victor Sokolov.

From: J21
To: T77
Re: Bird of Prey {Encrypted}

Response to Update 23.7

This is great progress; the best we could have hoped for.
We need your source to keep his eyes and ears open.
We must have more information about the flight path
and whether the bird flies solo.

End.

Chapter 1: Stranger Happenings

George Jenkins lumbered around the corner of Oak Lane with his bag full of papers tearing at his shoulder. His mind wandered and all he could think of was how much his life sucked. Two days into a new school year and he'd already failed at his mission to stay off the radar. Not only were Liam and Connor, his constant tormentors, already on his case, but the new form tutor, Mr Jefferson, seemed to have taken an immediate disliking to him. The two days had been a total disaster. In fact, his whole life was a disaster, and the last thing he needed right now was to be trudging through the dark on a paper-round that wasn't even his.

Dark, grainy driveways; rustling in the bushes, terrifying dogs: George hated everything about it. Walking alone down the empty lanes just reminded him of all the things he wasn't: brave, strong … brave.

As he pushed on towards Mrs Hodge's house, his least favourite on the round, the jitters crept over his skin and he cursed himself for not going out earlier.

Just get it over with, George.

Old, decrepit and buried deep in an overgrown plot, Mrs Hodge's house felt like a death-trap. The drunken front porch looked like it might collapse at any minute, the letterbox was finger-snappingly stiff, and however hard George tried to silently tiptoe up the long, nettle-ridden path, Mrs Hodge's dogs always threw themselves at the letterbox like rabid wolves.

George hesitated at the gate and peered down the driveway. It was dark – darker than usual – and things seemed to move in the shadows. Flexing his shoulders, he slid the paper from his bag and carefully placed his toe onto the cobbled path, hoping not to wake the dogs.

Edging closer, he tried not to look up at the fractured windows. Even though he rarely saw Mrs Hodge, George couldn't help imagining her pale face peering out at him from behind her tea-stained net curtains. But tonight, the curtains didn't twitch and the dogs didn't bark. Silence. Far worse.

His heartbeat pulsed at his throat as he took the final step towards the porch. He was half tempted to hurl the paper and run, but he couldn't stomach another complaint from Mr Holmes at the newsagents, so he leant forwards and reached for the door handle.

Thud! The undergrowth on the other side of the pond quivered, and George froze. The pulse in his neck turned into a thump.

Jeez, it's probably just one of her flea-bag cats.

Taking a deep breath, he gently pushed down on the handle ...*squeak!*

Something screeched overhead, and out of the corner of his eye, George swore he saw a shadow dash between the conifers that cocooned the house. He strained his ears, but all he could hear was the thundering of his own pulse, so he threw the porch door open and shoved the paper halfway through the jaws of the letterbox, before spinning on his heels and racing back down the path and out into the deserted lane.

Maybe if she's away, she won't complain!

He kept up the pace as he dashed towards the centre of the tiny village, where the cottages were nestled together in rows of five, and he rapidly fired a Chiddingham News through each door before sprinting for home.

Reluctant to take his usual shortcut through the alleyway that by-passed the cricket ground, he skimmed around the green's perimeter with his empty bag slapping at his back, but as he approached the other end of the alleyway, he spotted a man standing half-hidden in the shadow of the trees. He was hunched over what looked like a phone, although no light shone up from its screen. George could just make out his dark jacket and tattered jeans, but his hood obscured his face, and his back was partially turned on George.

George chewed at his cheek. He was only a few hundred yards from home, so he mustered up some courage and attempted to casually saunter past. Crossing the street for extra caution, he pushed out his chest and tried to look bigger than he was. He wasn't tall or well-built for his age, and something about the stranger made him feel even smaller.

He tried not to glance over as he came up opposite the alleyway but couldn't stop his feet from speeding up as he neared the end of the street. Just as he was about to turn the corner, he gave in to temptation and stole a look over his shoulder. The man looked up for a split second and then turned, swiftly ducking into the darkness of the alley. In that miniscule moment, his shadowed eyes had somehow pierced right through George. Shaken, George turned and ran the last hundred yards home.

"Nice one, George," he muttered to himself. "No wonder everyone thinks you're a total loser."

George was disappointed to see that his dad wasn't home. However embarrassed he was of his dad's old beaten-up van, it's absence meant that his dad was working late … again. Sam Jenkins was a self-employed plumber. He was regularly out on call at all hours, which meant that George spent most of his time at home with his gran and her schizophrenic cat, Marshall.

George's shoulders eased as he headed up the front path and was welcomed by the familiar sound of the TV resonating from behind the lounge window.

Gran's home.

Gran had a habit of having the TV on at the same time as the radio and spent most of the day cranking them each up in turn as she pottered between the lounge and the kitchen.

As he turned the key to open the door, he took one last look over his shoulder to make sure that the hooded guy hadn't reappeared. There was no sign of him, but he could hear the growl of an engine coming down the lane.

Dad?

Slowly, a small van glided past. The driver turned to look at the house, then seeing George, sped up and disappeared from view. George shoved open the front door, slipped inside and slammed it shut behind him. He stood for a moment, his ear pressed to the cool timber of the door, listening for the van to return, but all he could hear was the distant rumbling of thunder.

It's nothing, he told himself, shaking off his nerves.

Happy to be safe inside, George flung down his bag, kicked off his shoes and let himself be led down the long, thin hallway by the heart-warming smell of Gran's cooking.

"Ah, how was it?" Gran asked, as George pushed open the kitchen door.

"Er … yeah, fine," George replied.

Gran looked up over her spectacles and George shifted his eyes to the oven. "What's cooking?"

"Cheesy pasta," Gran replied, giving him a sideways glance. "You OK, boy?"

George thought about the guy by the alley. "Yup, I'm fine."

Five minutes later, they sat together at the breakfast bar and ate. George silently shovelled. He could still feel Gran's eyes on him.

"How was school?" she asked.

"Hmm, yeah OK, I guess," George mumbled through a mouthful of pasta.

At that moment, Marshall appeared from behind the kitchen door and saved George from Gran's scrutiny. He was one ugly-looking cat. White with a splattering of grey, he was longhaired, but he had several patches of fur that were sparse and stubbly. That, and his one wandering eye, made him look trampled on. He hissed at George and glared at him with his good eye, before leaping up onto the counter and swishing his puffy tail in George's face.

"Get off," George grumbled.

"Oh, Georgie, when did you and Marshall fall out?"

Gran had let George name the cat when she first brought it home. It wasn't that long after George's mum had died. She was right that they used to get on, but since George had become a teenager, the cat had turned quite vindictive towards him. Marshall hissed once more and George took it as his cue to leave. He thanked Gran for the pasta, added his plate to the pile of dishes in the sink and disappeared upstairs to change.

George's shoebox of a bedroom was at the back of the house overlooking the long, thin garden. It was a mess. His cluttered desk was covered in school books and the balled-up remnants of failed homework; his wardrobe doors gaped open, limp arms and legs drooping out at all angles; and the one picture he owned of himself with his mum had toppled off the windowsill and was lying face-up at the foot of his bed.

Carefully, he picked it up and rubbed his sleeve across the glass. He was a toddler, sitting on a seesaw with his mum crouched down beside him, steadying him with both her hands. You couldn't see much of her face, but you could tell that she was smiling and looking at George in a way that he imagined all mums did when they loved their child. His dad had taken the photo from the other end of the seesaw. It must have been a wonderful family day out, or that is how George liked to picture it.

Ping!

George dug around in his pocket and pulled out his phone. It was a text from his one and only friend, Felix.

'How was the paper-round?'

George started typing: *'There was some guy…'* but hit delete. He didn't want to appear like a wimp, but then again … this was Felix.

Felix Patterson was a self-confessed coward. He tried everything to avoid any danger or conflict, although he regularly drew the attention of the school bullies, with his thick glasses, mouth full of braces and unusually tight, curly, blonde hair.

George started the text again, but the crunch of tyres on the drive stopped him short.

Dad!

Leaping up from his bed, George pulled off his sweaty t-shirt and searched through the pile of clothes on his floor for his favourite hoodie. He could hear the front door close and the muffled rumblings of Gran and his dad talking, but by the time he'd managed to get his hoodie on the right way around, the back door had slammed shut and the garden floodlights had sprung to life.

Lifting his blind, George watched his dad disappear up the garden path and into his shed.

Typical!

"Georgie, come down and watch the news with me! I hate watching it on my own!" called Gran.

George slumped back downstairs and joined Gran in the lounge.

"How was Dad?"

"Oh, you know; tired, busy…" Gran said, shrugging.

George collapsed into the faded armchair. The news had started and there were several mundane reports about end-of-holiday traffic incidents. His mind drifted, until one article caught his attention. There had been a shooting in south Kent. A fuzzy CCTV image of a man's face, shrouded by a hood, filled the screen.

George leant forwards to get a better look, but a sudden flash of lightning lit up the night sky, silhouetting sharp shadows against the lounge window. Marshall hissed and dived under Gran's footstool, and George leapt from his seat.

"What the…" George swore he saw a figure by the gate, but before he could make anything out for sure, the light had vanished, and the driveway had returned to black.

"What's the matter?" Gran asked. "You're not yourself."

George bit his lip, then folded and told her about the man on the street. Gran stood, shuffled across the lounge and drew the heavy curtains.

"Never liked you doing that round," she sighed. "When are you handing it back to the usual boy?"

"This week."

"Good," she said, heading for the door. "Time for some apple pie, I think."

George let her go before peeking out of the curtains and scanning the front drive, but there was nothing.

Get a grip, George.

By the time he made it into the kitchen, his dad was leaning up against the counter, devouring a slice of Gran's pie.

"Hi," George said, sliding past him.

"Hi," Sam mumbled back, not lifting his eyes from his plate.

"Help yourself," Gran said, winking at George.

She took her slice and made her way back to the lounge, leaving Sam and George alone. George stood on the opposite side of the breakfast bar and stared at his dad. He looked tired, but then he always did.

George looked nothing like him. Sam was tall and well-built with dark hair and even darker eyes, which were regularly shrouded by the faded blue cap he wore. He rarely smiled, not that you could tell through his untrimmed beard. He had never really recovered from the death of George's mum. There were few pictures and even fewer spoken memories. And if George ever asked, Sam's eyes grew even sadder and darker.

George grabbed a knife and sized up a slice of pie.

"How was school?" Sam asked, placing his empty plate down on the counter and finally looking up at George.

George was pushing some stray pie crumbs around the counter with the tip of his knife. "Fine."

"Great." There was a long pause, and George could almost hear his dad's brain churning; desperately trying to think of a suitable topic of conversation. "Gran told me you'd been followed by someone on–"

"It was nothing," George said, his head snapping up. "Just some idiot outside the village hall."

"Right, fine," Sam said, dumping his plate in the sink.

George hated feeling weak in front of his dad but hated the silence between them even more.

Sam's phone buzzed and George watched the creases in his forehead deepen as he read the message.

"I've got a job," Sam said, as he went to leave the kitchen.

"At this time of night?" George asked.

"It's all money, George."

With that, he left, leaving George on his own in the kitchen. George grabbed a slice of pie and headed to the lounge, but just as he reached the end of the corridor, the front door flew open and Sam stormed back in.

"Someone's slashed my tyre!"

He marched up the corridor, out of the back door and up to his shed. Seconds later, he returned with a handful of tools.

"C ... can I help?" George asked.

"No," said Sam, bluntly. "I don't need any more hold-ups."

"But ... shouldn't we call the police?"

"No, that's the last thing I need!"

George peered through the open front door and out into the driveway. "But what if it was–"

"I said, 'No', George!"

With that, Sam slammed the door and left. Gran had come out into the hall where George stood with his plate of pie in his hands.

"What did I do wrong?" George asked.

"Nothing, boy. He's not a big fan of the police … not since all the nonsense with your mum's death and all."

"What nonsense?"

"Don't you worry about it, Georgie. Come and eat your pie."

But as Gran shuffled back into the lounge, George just stood glaring at the back of the front door; his chest deflated, his shoulders heavy, and the slice of pie slipping from his plate.

From: J21
To: Group - BOP
Cc: Chief
Re: Bird of Prey {Encrypted}

Update 23.8

Urgent. Our asset in protection has been shot at his safe house on the south coast. We do not have confirmation of the identity of the shooter.

We must assume that there is a link between this and the movement of the bird.

As soon as we have a positive identity on the shooter, we will release a network wide alert.

End.

From: Chief
To: J21
Cc: Group - BOP
Re: Bird of Prey {Encrypted}

Response to update 23.8

How has this happened?
I expect a full investigation.

Move the flock to the agreed top security location. Need-to-know basis only. The circle on this must be extra tight.

End.

Chapter 2: Familiar Foes

Wednesday morning arrived, and George reluctantly peeled himself out of bed. He washed, brushed his teeth and tried to impose some control over his hair. There was always one section in the middle that just wouldn't sit down.

As he traipsed downstairs, he could hear Gran in the kitchen making pancakes, so he made his way towards the sweet smell and decided to delay the inevitable misery of his day by filling his gut in complete abandonment.

"Shouldn't you be getting going?" Gran asked, when George reached for his sixth pancake.

The school's old double-decker would be passing through the village at half past eight, and George couldn't afford to miss it. He dumped his cutlery on his plate and dragged himself from the kitchen, out of the cottage and towards the bus stop; his legs heavy and his bags even heavier.

The streets were quiet and the previous night's events were still playing on his mind, so he strengthened his stride and made it to the bus stop early.

When the bus eventually pulled up, George's eyes instinctively met the pavement. The bus was always heaving with boisterous, over-confident teenagers, but if he kept his head down, he could go unnoticed and avoid the usual barrage of banter and abuse that was often hurled his way.

Climbing aboard, he noticed an empty seat next to Lauren James. He faltered half a second and pulled at his collar, which suddenly felt a little too tight. But before he could compose himself, Lauren glanced his way from beneath her tumble of curls, sending his legs to jelly and making him trip on the step and crash to his knees.

Mr Steckler, the school bus driver, peered down at him from the driver's seat. "You OK, George?"

"Fine, thanks," George grunted, the heat spreading up his neck and flushing across his cheeks.

He didn't look back up. He just gathered up his bags and slunk into the single seat behind the old bus driver.

Great one, George!

His day didn't improve. None of his morning lessons were with Felix, so he had to brave them alone. By lunchtime, he was ready to bury himself in a hole.

Begrudgingly joining the end of the long line of hungry students, he slid his tray along the counter and wrapped his blazer around his growling stomach, trying to stifle the sound.

"You should really eat a more sustaining breakfast." He turned to see new girl, Francesca, beaming at him with her perfect smile. She was impeccably well groomed, with long glossy hair and smooth, honey skin.

"Right," said George, suddenly very aware of his wayward hair and off-centre tie. He tried to flatten down his involuntary mohawk and slid further up the counter.

"My mother says it's the only important meal of the day," Francesca continued.

"Right," George repeated.

"Jenkins, you're holding up the whole queue!" It was Mr Jefferson.

George clamped his fingers around the edges of his tray.

Great!

Mr Jefferson had only been at the school for three days, yet it didn't seem to matter what George did or where he went, the new teacher was always there, scowling at him with his icy eyes and making him centre of attention. A few people sniggered, so George edged forwards and grabbed a plate, aware that the teacher's eyes were still boring into him.

As quickly as possible, George piled up his plate, then trying to look nonchalant, he turned to find a seat, but in his haste, he slammed his tray right into Francesca's elbow and showered the nearby row of students with red-hot soup and a melee of sausage and fries.

"You idiot!"

Rising up like a fortress from his bench was Liam Richardson.

Oh, no!

He was the size of a grown man with oversized ears and what looked like a broken nose. No one argued with him, especially on the rugby pitch.

"S…sorry," George stuttered, his empty tray trembling in his hands.

"You're gonna' pay for that!" Liam snarled.

By now, every student in the room was staring at George, including Lauren and her friends. Red blotches threatened to swamp his cheeks, so he threw himself to the floor and buried his face as he attempted to scoop the remnants of his meal onto his tray.

"You're an utter fool, Jenkins," Mr Jefferson bellowed. "You will stay down there until you have cleared up every last drop of this mess!"

Mr Jefferson stood over him; his focus not shifting once. By the time George had finished, most people had cleared out to break, tossing jibes at him as they passed.

"You need to know," Mr Jefferson said as he left. "I'm watching every move you make."

George stood up, grabbed two bread rolls and ran from the hall. He didn't fancy seeing anyone so hid himself in the boys' bathrooms and ate his rudimentary meal alone.

Perched on the sink with his legs dangling down, he sat in silence, waiting for break to end, but just as he was about to lower himself to the floor, there was a murmur of footsteps. In the distance. Coming his way.

Damn!

George glanced at his watch. Break was over, but he was pretty sure that no one would need to pass this way. That's why he chose these bathrooms, that's why he always chose them: tucked away and forgotten, even by the cleaners.

Leaping off the sink, he dived into the nearest cubicle, pounced onto the toilet seat and rammed his feet against the door.

Leave me alone!

But the footsteps kept coming, pounding against the wooden floor, faster and louder. And as the bathroom door crashed open, George gulped in a lungful of air and pinned his lips between his teeth, hoping that the intruder would just turn and leave.

George waited.

Nothing.

Whoever it was, they just stood mute, the wheeze of their panting echoing around the half-empty room.

George gripped the toilet seat and tried to stop his feet from sliding down the cubicle door as his legs began to cramp, but the thud in his chest threatened to make him gasp. He couldn't hold his breath much longer.

The intruder shuffled forwards, their shadow passing beneath the cubicle door. George's head began to spin. His lungs began to scream. His legs began to shudder.

"George, you there?"

And all the air came out of George's cheeks in one blast.

"Felix!" he gasped, as he tumbled from the loo and flung open the toilet door.

"Thought you'd be here," Felix grinned, his braces flashing in the harsh lights of the bathroom.

George stepped out of the cubicle and Felix grimaced. "Ah, I heard it was bad, but…"

George stared at his reflection in the mirror. His usual chestnut hair had tinges of red, his white shirt was sopping wet and practically baby-pink, and something green was clinging in flecks to his aubergine blazer. He looked like he'd had a fight with a giant tomato – which wasn't far from the truth.

George tried to force a smile. "You should have seen the other guy."

"Liam?"

George nodded.

"Maybe next time you get the urge to throw your lunch over someone," Felix said, throwing his arm around George's shoulders, "don't choose the one person who would happily break your neck."

George chuckled and the knot in his chest started to loosen. "I'd like to say it was intentional … but it wasn't."

"Still," Felix grinned, "I wish I'd been there to see his face."

George smiled and wrung out the hem of his shirt.

"Seriously though, he's on the war path," Felix said, stepping back and flicking some stray basil from his wrist.

"Why d'you think I'm hiding in here?"

The bell rang, making both boys jump.

"Come on, you can't hide in here forever," Felix said, heading for the door. "You better get changed for well-being."

George sighed and dragged his feet after Felix.

Wednesday afternoons were designated for student well-being, and George had Orienteering this term, which was the last thing he needed right now.

"What group did you get?" he asked Felix, as they peeked out of the bathroom door to check that the corridor was clear.

"Meditation," Felix said, screwing up his nose.

George laughed. "Sounds right up your street."

"Try to keep out of Liam's way, will you?" Felix said, as they reached the locker room. "No more accidents."

"I'll try, but I don't think my day could get much worse," George said, naively.

By the time George had changed into his PE kit, the rest of year nine had cleared out to well-being, but taking no chances, he loitered behind the curtains of ivy that hung from the schoolhouse walls and peered out towards the woods. The school lawns appeared empty, so he stepped out into the autumn sun, letting its warmth soak into his cheeks and ease his shoulders.

Sauntering across the rugby pitch, he sucked in the afternoon air and smiled at the view. He may not have relished school but he did agree that Oakfield Manor was pretty special. Sat upon a ridge and nestled amongst ancient woodland, it overlooked the rolling Kent countryside, and what it lacked in modern facilities, it made up for in impressive, sprawling grounds and fine sports fields.

George wasn't good at sport, unless you included his attempts at cricket. In fact, George wasn't really sure that he was good at anything. And even though he tried his best to keep his head down and out of trouble, trouble seemed to always find him. And at that very moment, the tall, lanky frame of Mr Jefferson came storming out from behind the sports pavilion.

Not again.

George was running late and didn't need to give his form tutor any reason to reprimand him again, so he ducked behind the team benches and watched as, flushed and dishevelled, Mr Jefferson marched up to the schoolhouse ranting to himself.

What's he up to?

George waited until the teacher had disappeared inside before creeping out from behind the benches.

"Hey, cockroach!"

George stiffened.

You've got to be kidding.

Outside and alone, he'd let down his guard and put himself right where Liam and Connor wanted him.

You idiot, George!

Refusing to look back, he straightened his spine and tried not to appear panicked as he picked up his pace, but the tremors in his chest soon trickled down to his legs, and by the time he'd reached the edge of the woods, he was running.

"Didn't know cockroaches could run so fast!" shouted Liam, who was coming up behind him.

"Yeah, they squish easily too," Connor yelled.

George was in the woods now; running down the snaking path towards the dell. His laces were coming loose but he didn't stop.

Just make it to the dell.

"You can run," Liam barked, "but you can't hide!"

George pressed harder.

"Run, cockroach, run!" Connor laughed.

But as George leapt over a fallen branch, the damp leaves slid from beneath him, and he tripped on his laces and fell to his knees.

Get up!

His heart raced. His head pounded. And his feet scrabbled against the slick mud. But before he could right himself, Liam's boot was at his back and he was shoved back down into the dirt.

"Going somewhere in a hurry?" Liam snarled.

"Get off!" George said, trying to squirm free, but Liam's weight was too much for George to throw off.

"You owe me an apology," Liam said in George's ear, and George's ribs screamed as Liam drove all his weight down.

"Stop it!" George spat.

"Stop it!" Connor squeaked, hopping around beside Liam like some over-excited jester.

George twisted in an attempt to dislodge Liam's boot, but he just ended up burying himself deeper in the mud.

"We only wanna' have some fun, Jenks," Connor said, glaring down his long, pinched, freckled nose at George.

George wasn't afraid of Connor. He was a flimsy-looking kid with spiked, ginger hair and a mouth jammed full of tiny teeth – his friends called him Sharkie, but his bark was worse than his bite.

"Leave me alone," George growled.

"Why? What you gonna' do? Tell your mummy?" Liam teased. "Oh, wait, you don't have one!"

That was it. Everything inside George erupted. His chest ballooned, his muscles screamed and the heat ran up his neck and seared through his jaw, setting it like stone.

I've had enough!

He filled his lungs, buried his fists into the mud and pushed, but Liam was a pro, and as George thrusted upwards, Liam pulled aside, leaving George to flail about as he tumbled backwards into a puddle, his head colliding with the nearest tree trunk.

Ow!

The damp soaked into George's joggers, but before he could lift himself from the puddle, Liam was back on him, his fingers at George's neck, pinning him to the tree.

"I wouldn't try that again if I were you," Liam sneered. "Cockroaches aren't meant to fight back; they're only supposed to run and hide."

"Yeah, or play dead," Connor added.

Liam pushed harder and George gasped for air.

"If you want to survive…" Liam growled.

But before he could say anything else, Will Carter and Jess Stone appeared on the path ahead.

"Hey!" Will said. "If you want a fight, I'm happy to take you on!"

George's body sagged as relief washed over him.

Will wasn't George's friend but he was alright. Short but all muscle, he had inherited his mum's soft Jamaican looks but his dad's fiery temper, so you could easily misjudge him. When he wasn't tampering with technology, he was boxing or training in Taekwondo, and

George knew that he was the only guy in year nine who could go toe to toe with Liam.

"You and some girl, Carter," Liam said, glaring at Jess.

"You wanna' try me?" Jess scowled.

She was braver than George realised. She stood stock still with her arms folded, and with her short, mousey hair tied back, she looked pretty severe. Some of the kids at school tried to tease her for being a chemistry nerd and a teacher's daughter, but she was a pretty tough cookie and took no nonsense. George wished he had half her brains and at least a measure of her courage.

"I'll happily lay you out," Liam said, releasing his grip from George's neck. "Both of you."

"Yeah, yeah, yeah!" Connor clapped. "Bring it on!"

George shuffled to the side and pulled himself up.

He felt like he was on the sidelines of some surreal fighting contest. Will and Jess had the upper hand, he figured. Will could probably lay them both out with one move, and Jess could quite easily overpower skinny-legs Connor, but a sudden whistle broke up the foray.

"What are you lot up to?" It was Mrs Stone, the art teacher and Jess' mum. "We are all waiting for you in the dell. I hope there's no nonsense going on here."

"No, Mum," Jess mumbled.

"Then get moving!"

"Saved by Mummy," Liam whispered in Jess' ear, as he shoved past her.

"You're the one who got saved," she snapped back.

I'm the one who got saved, George thought.

From: T77
To: J21
Re: Bird of Prey {Encrypted}

Update 23.9

Urgent.

The bird has flown. Evidence had suggested that it had crossed the Black Sea, but we now believe this to be a decoy.

It is headed your way.

There have been several sightings on the path to the French Capital but the trail has gone cold.

We do not have confirmation of whether the bird has crossed the channel. Our source in Paris will send an update as soon as we know more.

End.

From: J21
To: T77
Re: Bird of Prey {Encrypted}

Response to Update 23.9

Message received. We will alert all border agents.

End.

Chapter 3: Out of Bounds

They all trudged down to the dell where the rest of the group sat waiting around the campfire site. George plonked himself down next to Will and Jess and attempted to wipe the mud from his knees.

"Thanks for helping me out, there," he said.

"No problem," Will said. "I'm sure you'd do the same for us."

"Er, yeah, of course."

Mrs Stone talked them through the afternoon's challenge, but George was too busy trying to avoid Liam's death stares to take anything in.

"… map reading and teamwork skills … three groups."

George crossed his fingers behind his back.

Please don't put me with Liam and Connor. Please. Please.

"Rules: you must stay together as a group and return as a group. You must stay within the school boundary, which is marked by the orange rings around the boundary trees. You are all well aware of this rule."

"Miss, will we be getting dirty at all?" Francesca had raised her hand, making Jess roll her eyes.

"Quite possibly, Miss Brown."

"Er, it's actually Bonacci-Brown, it's–"

"Right, let's get started." Mrs Stone blew her whistle again, obviously not interested in hearing the story of Francesca's double-barrelled name.

She listed off the first group that included Connor and the twins, Hayley and Annie Fox. George was relieved not to be in that group; they were all as bad as one another. That only left Liam to avoid.

"Group two will be Zac, Izzie, Lucy, Gavin and Liam." George felt the jitters in his legs dissolve into the woodland litter at his feet. "That leaves Joshua, Francesca, Will, Jessica and George in group three."

"Great," George mumbled under his breath.

He'd managed to avoid the school hit squad but had been left with Francesca (who George hadn't yet worked out); Josh Palmer (who was the under-fourteens' rugby captain and far too handsome and confident for his own good); and Will and Jess (who were practically joined at the hip).

Francesca beamed at Josh and skipped over to join him, and Will and Jess were already deep in conversation, so that left George floating on the outskirts.

This day officially sucks.

Each team was given a compass, map and set of instructions.

"Your first job is to choose a leader. The first team to retrieve their nominated flag and return here will win. Good luck," Mrs Stone said.

Team three huddled together, which made George feel a bit sweaty. He wasn't really a huddling kind of guy, so he loitered at the edge of the circle looking at his toes.

"I should be leader, obviously, as I'm Rugby Captain," Josh said, gliding his fingers through his short, sandy hair and breaking out his trophy-accepting smile.

"Yes, and we know how much brainpower that takes," Jess said, glaring at him.

"Oh, yeah. What mad scientist skills have you got to offer then, Professor Stone?"

Jess was used to being named after her famous father. It didn't bother her. "More skills than it takes to dump a ball over a line."

"I think Josh is right, he's got the most experience," Francesca said, glaring back at Jess and raising one of her perfectly shaped eyebrows.

"Ooh, no surprise there, then."

George stood silently on the sidelines of the match watching the insults volley back and forth.

"Right, well, George, you have the deciding vote," Jess said, taking him by complete surprise.

"Me? Um … I, I don't know really," he said, stuffing his hands in his pockets and avoiding eye contact with either candidate.

"Great, well if we can't decide, then it should be George," decreed Jess.

"Oh."

He was stumped. That was not his intended outcome. He had never led anything in his life, not even a conga line. He was by far the least qualified, but it seemed the others had made peace with their decision and had moved on to collecting their gear.

"I know where that old rope swing is," Josh said, as Jess read out their first instructions, and he headed off with Francesca in tow.

Jess and Will grabbed the map and compass, and they all started to wind their way through the ancient oaks and up towards the easterly ridge.

They hadn't been going long before Francesca started to complain.

"I'm too warm in this awful kit. It is utterly non-breathable. God knows what it's doing to my skin."

"It's a school PE kit," Jess said, pushing ahead. "We're not on the catwalk now, so suck it up,"

George hung back. Francesca was sulking. He tried to break the tension by asking her about her name. "So, how come you've got two surnames?"

"It's half my mum's," she replied, her eyes brightening at the interest. "She's the model, Sophia Bonnacci."

"Wow, is she … famous?" George asked.

"Well, she was," she replied, coyly, "when we lived in L.A."

"I was born in Jamaica," Will butted in. "Didn't really live there though. We moved back here when I was six months old so my dad could take over my grandad's security company."

"Ooh, that's cool." Francesca said. "What does your mum do?"

They were sauntering along and not really paying much attention to where they were going. George loitered at the tail.

"She's a … um … performer, I guess," said Will.

"Ha! What like an exotic dancer?" Josh laughed, grabbing a tree trunk and dancing around it.

"No, you idiot! She's a singer. Plays at weddings and stuff."

Francesca tutted at Josh as if telling off a toddler.

"What about you, George?" she asked. "What does your mum do?"

The others stopped and fell silent.

Francesca looked around. "What did I say?"

George felt the dull ache in his chest that always came at the thought of his mum. "My mum died when I was young."

He could hear his own voice inside his head. He hardly ever uttered the words, but when he did, they felt so alien; like it wasn't his pathetic life he was talking about but some other unlucky kid. He could see the pity in their eyes and wanted to shout at them, 'I never really knew her, so it's no loss!' But he didn't, because it wasn't true. He felt the loss every day.

Out of nowhere, Baxter, the school caretaker's dog, barrelled in, scattering acorns everywhere. He jumped up at George in pure joy.

"That dog loves you," Jess said, glad to have something else to talk about. "You got treats in your pocket?"

"No, I swear, I don't know what gets into him."

With that, they heard a sudden noise in the trees to their left and George turned a full circle, scanning the woods.

"It's probably just Mr Hill," Will said. "Don't need him on our case." He looked down at the map and up at the path ahead. "So, is that the tree we're looking for?"

A long, frayed rope hung from the lowest branch of the nearest Oak. It didn't look much like a swing to George but maybe it once was.

"Must be it," George said, still looking over his shoulder.

"Well, we're supposed to go northeast from here," said Jess, fiddling with the compass and pointing out towards the ridge. "It's that way."

"Are you sure? That's towards the boundary," Francesca warned.

Another argument broke out, so they turned to George. He didn't want to question Jess' abilities, as she was easily the brightest amongst them, so he let her take the lead and they steadily climbed up the bank.

Baxter was bouncing around their feet, frustrating Josh, so Josh picked up a stick and threw it as hard as he could. It ricocheted off the base of a mangled tree stump and cartwheeled down the escarpment with the dog in hot pursuit.

"For God's sake, Josh! He's probably injured himself!" Jess yelled.

"Well he didn't have to go after it, did he!"

George peered over the edge of the decline. He couldn't see the dog anywhere but could hear him barking from far below. They all started calling Baxter's name; their voices echoing around the valley, but the dog's yelping just grew more urgent and more distant. They all glared at Josh.

"I'll go down and get him," he huffed.

"You can't climb down there, and anyway, it's outside the school boundary," Francesca said, peering over the edge. "And how on earth would you get back up?"

"No sweat," Josh said, as he started to feel his way down, sliding on the loose ground.

"Er, we're supposed to stay together," George said, wiping his sweaty palms down the sides of his joggers.

"It's not that hard. You're a bunch of wimps," Josh called up, practically skiing down the slope.

"I'm perfectly capable," Jess said, striding forwards.

Will shrugged and smiled at George. "I'm in. You coming, Jenkins?"

George hesitated. He glanced at Francesca, who just shook her head. And he glanced back the way they'd come. He didn't want to be left behind, and he wanted to help Baxter, but he could just picture himself being hauled into the Head's office for breaking school rules.

"Come on!" someone called up from below.

George looked down at his soggy joggers and thought about his feeble attempt to fight back against Liam and

Connor. He thought about the laughs that had bounced around the dining hall as he'd tripped and lost his lunch. And he thought about the many times he'd hidden in the bathrooms to avoid any danger.

"Wait for me," he said, his voice embarrassingly squeaky, and he took a deep steadying breath before sliding down off the ridge.

"Wait! What about me? I can't do that. I might fall and break something," panicked Francesca, as she was left staring down at them from above.

"What, like a nail?" Jess' voice was already muffled by the undergrowth. "You can always go back," she called.

"We're a team," Francesca said, stamping her foot.

She was leaning over, holding onto an orange rope that hugged the large tree stump when suddenly Josh reappeared and grabbed her by the hand. She screamed and jerked backwards.

"I'll help you down," he said. "It's not as bad as it looks from up here."

As they descended, George was amazed by just how steep it was. He could feel his heart fluttering and the blood pumping through his veins as his feet slid and his hands flew out to grab at the nearest branches for support. By the time he joined the others on the valley floor, his legs felt all soft and wobbly.

Will looked around. "Well, where's the dog?" They spread out and searched, but Baxter was nowhere to be seen. "Well, that's just great."

They were about to start arguing again when there was a crack of breaking branches from not far away.

"What was that?" Francesca said, clinging to Josh's arm.

George shuffled up closer to the others. "There can't be anyone else down here."

"Maybe it's Baxter," Will said, as he started picking his way towards the noise, whistling and calling.

George followed behind, nearly tripping in his haste to keep up.

"He's there, look!" shouted Jess.

Baxter's tail was sticking up from behind a large, upturned root ball on the other side of a small river. He lifted his head and started barking furiously at whatever he'd had his nose in.

The only way to get to him was by climbing over the half-rotten hull of the felled tree, and Francesca looked unsure.

"I'll give you a piggyback," Josh winked.

Jess rolled her eyes, again. "Seriously, I thought you were a gymnast."

"I am. I've won several—"

"Then cartwheel over the thing!"

"It's not quite the same."

"Fine, I'll go first," Jess said.

"No, I'm fine," Francesca said, climbing on after Josh, but as Josh leapt off at the other end, the whole trunk rocked and Francesca slipped. She managed to lunge for the bank but fell hard on her ankle. "Argh!"

"You OK?" asked Josh.

"No, I think I've broken it," she said, wincing.

The others clambered over and came to survey the damage. George knelt down in the mud. "It's scraped up pretty bad, but I don't think it's broken."

"My mum will kill me," Francesca said, burying her head in her hands.

"Guys, we need to hurry up," Jess said. "It's getting pretty late and we're well out of bounds. Let's just grab Baxter and go."

Jess was right. The light filtering through to the valley floor was starting to fade, and they still had to find their way back up the escarpment.

The Labrador was still barking and tugging at something half buried under a pile of leaves. Josh wandered over to see what he was harassing, but as he vaulted over another lying trunk, he landed on something soft.

"What the–"

"What is it?" Will came over to join him and grabbed Baxter by the collar. "It's just an old bag of rubbish, you duffus." But as he kicked it, the black plastic fell away and out flopped a pasty, wrinkled hand.

"Oh, God!" Will stumbled backwards, tripped and collapsed into a holly bush.

George took two steps backwards.

"Ahh guys, this is not good," Josh said, gagging.

"What! What is it?" Francesca asked, hobbling closer.

"We need to get the hell out of here!" Will said, scrabbling to his feet and pushing past Josh.

"Why, what is it?" Jess asked.

"It's a hand – like a human hand!" Josh said.

With that, Francesca screamed at the top of her lungs, making George flinch.

"Shut up! Will you just shut up!" yelled Jess, running out of patience.

"Let's just go!" shouted Will, as he and Josh grabbed Francesca and slung her arms over their shoulders.

George stood staring at the fallen tree; his eyes glazed over; his throat dry.

"George, grab the dog!" Jess ordered, snapping him out of his trance.

He hooked his fingers through Baxter's collar and heaved him away, still barking. They ran straight through the river, not stopping when Jess dropped the compass.

"Forget it. I know the way back," she said.

It was a slow, frustrating climb. They scrambled up on hands and knees, sliding back down as they lost their footing. Francesca was still sobbing by the time they threw themselves back up onto the ridge and collapsed in a steaming heap.

"Man, that was gross," Josh said, his eyes wide and distant. "I can't get it out of my head."

George sat up and pinched at the stitch in his side. "Are you sure it was a real human hand?"

"It looked pretty goddamn real to me," Will said, scowling at George.

"Yeah, maybe it was just a glove," Jess said, standing up and brushing herself down.

"No!" Will snapped. "It wasn't a stupid glove!"

"I was just saying. I mean, maybe you mistook it for–"

"You wanna' go back down and take a look for yourself?"

"Please stop shouting," Francesca said, wiping her face with her sleeve. "We just need to stay calm."

Will glared at her. "Calm! Seriously? We just saw a dead body!"

"But how could it have got down there?" Jess said, leaning out over the ridge.

"I don't care," Josh said, turning to Will. "I wish you'd left the stupid bag alone."

"Oh really – it's my fault, is it? Maybe if you hadn't sent the dog off the edge of the abyss, we wouldn't have ended up down there," Will fired back.

"Well, maybe if you'd done the map reading properly, we wouldn't have ended up on the ridge."

"That's' enough!" said Jess. She should have been the leader. George felt lost. "We know where the body is. We'll tell Mrs Hamilton; she can deal with it!"

With that, Baxter twisted in George's hands, slipped his collar and raced off into the woods.

"That stupid dog!" Will kicked the undergrowth, sending tattered leaves flying. "Forget him. He can find his own way back."

"Where the hell have you lot been?" They all jumped out of their skins. It was Mr Hill, the caretaker. "And where's my Baxter?" They all started talking at once. "Hold it, hold it. I can't understand a word you're saying. You can save it for the Head and Mrs Stone. You're in big trouble."

"You don't understand," George said. "There's a body down there! We found a body!"

"What? Nonsense! I walk these woods every day. If there was a body down there, I'd know about it."

"No, really. There is a body, like a real one, in a bag … just down there … we can show you," Josh said, grabbing Mr Hill by the arm.

"Get your filthy hands off me. You can tell Mrs Hamilton your story. You're late and out of bounds."

They exchanged glances. George opened his mouth to protest but realised it was futile. They all trudged back up to the school, filthy, exhausted and traumatised. Surely, Mrs Hamilton would believe them.

Chapter 4: Disbelief

Mrs Stone was the first to spot the bedraggled crew as they hauled themselves, heads hanging, across the lawn.

"My goodness me. What on earth have you lot been up to?" she said.

"Found them up by the ridge with some sorry story about buried bodies," said Mr Hill.

"I beg your pardon?"

"Mum, we went down the other side of the ridge looking for the dog and found this body – you need to call the police," said Jess.

It was probably best coming from her. George kept his mouth shut.

"What on earth were you doing up by the ridge? You know that is out of bounds. I would expect better of you, Jessica Stone."

"You're not listening!" Josh said. "We found a body – you know – like a dead person!"

"I know perfectly well what a body is, Joshua, and I would suggest you refrain from yelling at me. You are already in hot water and you, especially, don't need any more detention time."

"But –"

"That's enough – all of you – straight up to the Head's office. Your parents have been called."

By the time they got inside, the school day had finished and George had missed the last bus home. They could hear Mrs Hamilton's muffled voice through the door as they sat in a sombre line outside her office. She sounded infuriated. After a while, the great, heavy door swung open, and her squat, plump figure marched out and spun around to look at their pitiful faces. They must have looked like a criminal line up. Francesca's leg was smeared with blood and her cheeks were stained with muddy tears; Will's arms were punctured and scraped from his run-in with the holly bush; and the others looked like they'd been dragged through a hedge.

They sat in silence awaiting their fate.

"Firstly, I am happy to see you are safe, if a little battered." She looked them up and down. There was some sympathy in her eyes, but it was fleeting. "I am, however, very disappointed that you have abused the trust we had in you to behave sensibly and maturely."

George's teeth ground and his jaw bulged. He hated being unfairly reprimanded. "Miss we–"

"Let me finish, George. I would like to know why you thought it necessary to go up to the ridge?"

"The instructions sent us up that way," said Josh.

"Joshua, did you not stop to think that it was unlikely that Mrs Stone would send you in that direction?"

"Jess and Will were map reading," he grumbled.

He completely threw them under the bus. With that, the otherwise deserted corridor filled with the sounds of their remonstration.

"It was Josh who sent the dog flying down the cliff!"

"It was Josh that made us all go down there!"

"You guys made me do it!"

Francesca was crying again.

"Miss Brown, will you stop crying for one minute!" Mrs Hamilton was losing her patience.

George couldn't take it any longer. "There is a body in the woods," he blurted out. "We didn't mean to end up down there, but we did, and now we need someone to listen to us – to take us seriously – we need to contact the police!"

He stopped and felt a rush of heat to his face. He'd never spoken to a teacher in that way before, let alone the Headmistress.

"Is this true?" she asked, as she scanned the gathered faces. They nodded in unison. "Right, well, I will send Mr Hill down to investigate and—"

"We'll show him," said Josh.

"You will do nothing of the sort. Your parents are on their way. You will all wait here until you are picked up. Francesca and William, I suggest you go to the nurse and get cleaned up."

"But I've got rugby practice," Josh protested.

"You are on thin ice, Mr Palmer! You'll be lucky if I let you play in the team at all."

With that, she turned and scurried off down the corridor, leaving them sitting in silence. George couldn't help noticing that Mr Jefferson was absent. It wasn't like him to miss an opportunity to reproach his students. Mrs Stone ushered Will and Francesca down to the medical room after informing Jess to stay put until she returned. Jess immediately turned on Josh.

"This is all your fault and then you try to blame me and Will. You're so predictable."

Josh stood up. "What's that supposed to mean?"

"I thought captains were supposed to support their team, in victory or defeat. You quit and run the minute you see trouble."

"What? It was me that had the balls to go down that damn slope and save the stupid dog."

George had heard enough. His head pounded, his hands were raw and his stomach was aching with hunger. His two-roll lunch hadn't really prepared him for such an unexpectedly strenuous afternoon. He closed his eyes and wished for his gran to appear and whisk him off home for a warm meal and steaming bath, which was unlikely, as she didn't drive. With that, the front doors flew open and a whirlwind of a woman stormed in on towering heels with a small creature growing out of her armpit. In her wake was a grey shadow of a man who George could only assume was her husband.

Today couldn't get any weirder.

"Where is my baby?" the woman wailed.

It turned out that the creature was a rat of a dog with a gremlin-like face. George scrunched his nose up and blinked in disbelief. It was wearing a pink leather jacket. Maybe this whole day was one surreal dream – or nightmare. He half expected the dog to start talking. He was in definite need of sugar.

"You – scruffy boy – where is my daughter?" the tiny-dog woman asked.

"Um … who?" George's mouth was dry and the words stuck at the back of his throat.

"Francesca, of course."

"She's in the medical room," said Josh, who had no problem finding his voice. "I can take you there."

"Oh my goodness. Not her face, I hope; please not her face." She teetered off down the corridor with Josh, dog and her husband in tow.

Mrs Stone returned. "Time to go, young lady," she said to Jess. "We will talk about this at home."

George waited for over an hour. Shivering and exhausted, he tucked his knees up to his chest and rested his heavy head. He must have drifted off, because when he came to, his dad was standing in front of him holding his rucksack and a bundle of uniform.

"Dad!" He wanted to jump up and hug him, but he couldn't remember the last time he saw his dad hug anyone.

"You look like death," Sam said.

George rubbed at the back of his neck. "It's been a pretty rough day."

"So I hear."

"Dad, honestly, I don't know what Mrs Hamilton told you but–"

"Save it for the van, George. I've signed you out."

George took his coat from his dad and dragged himself out of the door and down to the car park where Sam's old, white van sat looking like an abandoned joy ride.

George lingered by the van door while Sam rummaged in his pockets for his keys. He peered across the lawns, towards the darkness of the trees and wondered whether Mr Hill was down in the valley right now, looking for the body. A shiver ran up his spine at the thought of being down there alone.

"Get in, George," Sam said, flinging open his door.

George pulled his coat around himself to ease the chill, but as he turned back towards the van, something caught his eye. There, peering down from one of the first-floor windows of the schoolhouse, was the stick-insect silhouette of Mr Jefferson.

Where the hell has he been?

"Dad," George said, his eyes struggling to pull themselves away from the heat of his form tutor's stare.

"What?" Sam said.

But George must have looked too long, because Mr Jefferson's outline quickly slid from view.

"Nothing," George said, sliding into the van.

As they trundled down the school drive, George couldn't help looking back to see if Mr Jefferson had reappeared, but he hadn't. George slumped down in his seat and sighed. He was sure that the teacher had been watching him, and that probably meant that the news of George's rule breaking had spread, which surely meant that he'd get it in the neck at form time tomorrow.

Great.

Sam didn't say a word the whole journey home. Pressing his face up to the window, George watched the world pass by instead: a couple strolling home, deep in conversation; a man, head to toe in lycra, pumping the pedals of his bike; a group of animated school children laughing and fooling around. He wondered what had happened in their day and how his had been such a catalogue of disasters. Maybe he could swap lives – for just twenty-four hours. Maybe if he was more like someone else. Maybe if he was just a bit braver, a bit stronger, a bit less … himself, then his life wouldn't suck so much.

As they crunched onto the gravel drive outside their cottage, George was reluctant to turn and face his dad. Sam didn't move; he just expelled a long, deep sigh.

"Are you going to tell me how you got yourself caught up in this mess?" he asked, looking over towards George, who was fiddling with his keys in his lap.

"We just got lost and ended up in the wrong place – that's all. It was no one's fault."

"Why didn't you turn around and go back to the school? You're more sensible than that, George."

George didn't shift his eyes from his lap. "I don't know – I wanted to stay with my friends, I guess."

"I'm not sure these kids are your friends," Sam said. George curled his fingers around his keys and the metal dug into his palms. "And what's this about a body? I hope it's not a joke. You're going to be in big trouble if you're wasting Mrs Hamilton's time." The tension in George's fists crept up his forearms. "You better think long and hard about whether or not you want to be involved with this nonsense."

"It's not nonsense," George said, the tension seeping across his shoulders. "There was a hand – a body – in a bag."

"Did you actually see this – with your own eyes?"

George's neck stiffened. "Well … no … but Will and Josh did."

"And what if they're messing you about; getting you into trouble? I think you've got very bad judgment if these are the kind of people you want to hang around with, George."

George snapped. "How would you know? You don't know any of them – in fact, you know nothing about my school or my life for that matter – you're never around!"

With that, he hurled open the van door, leapt out and barged his way into the house, almost breaking his key in the lock. Gran was peering around the kitchen door. He felt the urge to run and tell her everything – surely she would believe him, but Sam was on the threshold, so he threw down his keys, thundered upstairs and slammed his bedroom door. The whole house shook.

George sat stubbornly in his room, ignoring the call of his stomach. He could smell Gran's cooking but refused to go down. It wouldn't be long until his dad would either disappear out on call or hide himself away in his shed, so he would just have to sit it out.

He was just about to pass out with hunger when there was a soft knock at his door and Gran peeked in.

"I come bearing gifts," she smiled.

George practically drooled at the sight of the food. Gran had laden a tray with a steaming hot jacket potato, erupting with baked beans, followed by her mouth-watering, home-made chocolate fudge cake and a large mug of milk.

"You're a superstar, Gran. Thanks."

"Sounds like you've had a busy day – thought you might need it."

"Dad told you," George said, glumly.

"Yes, well some of it, I guess. You want to tell me your side of it?"

George could always rely on Gran to give him time – to listen. Bobbing around him, her little white bun toppling around on top of her head, she busied herself tidying his desk and waited until he'd finished his tea, before plopping herself down onto his bed. George told her everything. She sat in silence, not interrupting once, just nodding in all the right places.

"That is a very extraordinary day, my boy. No wonder you're exhausted. It's not every day you stumble upon a crime scene," she said, her soft eyes framed with creases of concern.

"Yes, I know, but no one believed us, Gran – not even Dad," he said clenching his jaw. "What if it's to do with that guy we saw on the news?"

"Don't you lose any sleep over it, Georgie," she said, patting him on the knee. "The police will deal with it. You've done your bit. Just promise me you won't go down there again … promise?"

"Yeah, of course. Thanks, Gran."

She picked up his tray and ruffled his hair.

"Shall I run you a bath?"

"No, it's OK. I'll jump in the shower."

As she made her way to the door, she paused for a second. "You know, your father just wants the best for you, Georgie. He was dreadfully worried when the school rang."

"He doesn't care or he'd take me more seriously," he grumbled.

"I'll prove him wrong," he said under his breath as Gran left.

Chapter 5: Truth or Dare

As the alarm clock brazenly announced the arrival of Thursday morning, George was heaved out of a turbulent, dreamed-filled sleep. The tangled bed sheets had him in a vice-like grip and his pillow had been flung aside. He had fallen asleep with damp hair after his shower so rose from the carnage like a titan from the deep. For a brief moment, he forgot all about the previous day's trials, until it all came flooding back in a wave of urgency. He must get to school and see what Mr Hill had found. Surely, the police would be swarming over the school grounds and beyond, searching for the perpetrator and everyone would applaud him and his friends for uncovering a heinous crime.

Rapidly, he threw on his uniform, showed his brush to his teeth and flew downstairs, two steps at a time. Gran had laid out a selection of breakfast bounty, but his stomach felt like a corkscrew, so he snatched a croissant, stuffed it in his mouth and dashed out of the front door before he'd even managed to get both arms into his freshly cleaned blazer.

The cool, damp air hit him like a wet flannel as he ran to the bus stop, but he didn't stop, even when the fine mist turned into a persistent drizzle. The school bus was running a little late, so he pressed his back up against the worn wood of the old bus shelter and bounced up and down with anticipation. He had to get to school and speak to Mr Hill, so he could prove his dad wrong.

By the time the bus arrived, he'd gone over the conversation that he planned to have with his dad several times in his head.

"Morning, George," Mr Steckler said, as he wrestled with the gearstick. George couldn't help staring and regretted it immediately.

"Ha! Not easy driving with one finger missing, eh?" he grinned, exposing his mouth full of half-broken teeth. "Got it chewed off by a rabid mutt when I was working as a road sweeper in Cambodia. Nasty business ... road sweeping ... very dangerous!"

"Um, I bet," George said, taking his seat and turning towards the window.

He was sure that Mr Steckler had told him a different story last term, but he wasn't in the mood for making small talk. He just wanted to get to school.

As Mr Steckler careered the double-decker down the school drive, George was on his feet, ready to leap off as soon as the doors flung open. He almost went flying as they bounced over the tiny speed bump that the old bus driver always seemed to forget. He darted straight to the locker room in the hope of finding someone who had news of the body, but instead he found Felix with his head stuck in his locker looking at something by torchlight.

"Er, Felix, what are you doing?"

Felix yanked his head up, smacking it on the doorframe of the locker.

"Ouch! Hi. What happened to you yesterday?" he asked, rubbing the back of his head.

"You're not going to believe it."

George told him all about the afternoon's adventures and the discovery in the woods.

"No way!" Felix exclaimed. "Did Mr Hill find it?"

"I hope so. I'm gonna' go and find out now. You want to come with me?"

"Absolutely!"

As they exited the locker room, the registration bell sounded and the rest of year nine started piling in. They fought their way against the flow of bodies, and had just made it out into the corridor when their path was defiantly blocked by Mr Jefferson. George's heart sank.

Great!

"Where do you think you're going? The form room is that way," Mr Jefferson said, pointing over their heads.

"Morning, Sir," George said, lifting his chin and forcing a smile. "We were just hoping to see Mr Hill to ask him about last night and–"

Mr Jefferson's thin lips puckered up on one side.

"There will be no need for that, Jenkins. That issue is closed. Mr Hill found nothing in the woods, and I suggest you drop the whole fabricated story unless you want to find yourself in detention."

George's chin dropped and his mouth fell open.

"What? But how? That's not possible. He can't have looked in the right place. He needs to–"

"Enough!" Mr Jefferson bellowed, his left eye twitching uncontrollably.

"Sir, I…"

"Move, Jenkins!"

Several people were stopping in the corridor to spectate, and George couldn't help shrinking a little. Reluctantly, he and Felix turned and headed to the form room with Mr Jefferson hot on their heels.

They were the first in the classroom, so they sat in silence waiting for the others to arrive. George was brooding.

How on earth has Mr Hill missed a whole body?

He looked up at his form tutor who was intently scribbling something down at his desk, his greying sweep-over flopping about as he moved.

George glared at him. He wished he could obliterate him with one intense stare: his stupid, pointy nose; his nasty, beady eyes; his ridiculous ankle-swinging trousers that hovered above his impeccably shiny shoes. Everything about him was agitating. But as George daydreamed about having such a superpower, he noticed that Mr Jefferson had a bandage on his left arm. It was obscured by his shirtsleeve, but George was pretty sure it hadn't been there the previous day.

His thoughts were interrupted by the rest of the class coming into the room. Liam and Connor were shoving each other through the door, but Mr Jefferson was too busy to notice, so George sat up and tried to make eye contact with Jess and Will.

"Face front, Jenkins!" Mr Jefferson was up from his seat, his insect eyes flitting back and forth. "You will all be aware, by now, that there was an incident yesterday where several students disobeyed school rules and went out of bounds. This issue has been dealt with, and I will not tolerate any more discussion about the subject. Those involved have, in my opinion, got off lightly, but I will not be so lenient if I hear another word about it. You have been warned," he said, staring straight at George with a look that made him slide back down in his seat.

The morning dragged, and George's frustration festered as he waited to steal a moment to speak to the others. After what seemed like hours, the break-time bell finally went. George dumped his stuff in his locker, grabbed his blazer and sped out to the ark, where most of year nine were sheltering from the depressing drizzle.

Francesca was sitting on the long wooden bench, whispering with Lauren and her friends. Her ankle was bandaged, and even if George wanted to approach the gaggle of girls, he didn't think that she was likely to want to talk about the previous day's events. Before long, Jess and Will approached with their blazers over their heads. He leapt up and ran out to intercept them.

"We need to talk," he said, urgently. "Mr Hill didn't find the body and–"

"We know, George," Jess said. "We're not supposed to talk about it. Mum said they don't need all the other kids getting upset and paranoid."

The three of them were huddled under their blazers and didn't see Liam, Connor and the Fox twins approaching.

"Oh, look," called Liam, "it's Detective Jenkins and his two stooges." Connor sniggered and the twins cackled in unison. "Uncovered any more fake crimes?" he asked. "I can get you a costume if you want to play make believe."

George scowled. He wasn't in the mood for being ridiculed.

Connor flopped his hand over Will's shoulder.

"Argh! Look! It's a dead man's hand! Run for your lives!" he screamed.

Without warning, Will grabbed Connor by the wrist, twisted, and before Connor knew what had happened, Will had pinned his arm behind his back.

"You're gonna' be the dead man," Will hissed in his ear.

Liam launched himself at Will, barging the twins out of the way, but Will had seen him coming and threw out his free elbow like lightning, catching Liam squarely on his, already misshapen, nose. He recoiled, stumbling into the twins, sending them careering towards Jess, who stuck out her foot, forcing Annie to her knees. The scene was rapidly escalating into a full-on brawl right before George's eyes, and a crowd was gathering. Connor eventually escaped Will's grip and came at Jess, who had Hayley by the hair. Liam and Will were now nose-to-nose, wrestling on the ground, just as Joshua arrived and attempted to pull them apart. The spectators were chanting and cheering.

"Teacher!" someone shouted from the back of the crowd, and the sea of bodies parted to reveal Mrs Hamilton, who stood at the opening looking like her head might explode.

"My office – now – all of you!"

George followed the sorry line of convicts even though he hadn't thrown a single punch. He thought his input might be needed, but somehow, he just managed to get himself signed up for lunchtime detention. It was the first time he had ever been given detention, and in a weird way, he wasn't upset. He wanted to stand by his new friends.

Felix was waiting for him by the lockers when he returned.

"What happened?" Felix asked. "When I got out of maths, everyone was buzzing about you guys having been dragged off by Mrs Hamilton for fighting." He had a look of utter shock and puzzlement on his face.

"Yeah, something like that," said George, shrugging. "I've got detention at lunchtime."

"What's got into you?" Felix asked, looking at his friend as if he didn't really know him.

George realised he'd let Felix down, but strangely he wasn't ashamed. He felt like he'd grown a few inches and was, somehow, no longer the big wimp everyone thought he was.

After lunch, George made his way down to the Head's library where he joined the accused for detention with old Mr Walters.

The room was a divided battleground. Liam, Connor and the twins sat defensively huddled together on the beanbags on one side while Jess, Will and Josh sat stoically on the bench on the other.

The room was silent, but vicious looks and deadly stares were being lobbed across the defence lines. George edged in and perched next to Josh on the low-slung bench. They were all supposed to be reading, so he grabbed the nearest book from the shelf behind him and flicked to a random page. Holding the book up high, to obscure his face, he whispered to Josh.

"We need to get back down into the woods. We need to find that body to shut this lot up."

Josh just shook his head. George was about to press him harder when he heard the opposition sniggering. Lifting his eyes above the book, he saw they were laughing at him but had no idea why. Josh nudged him and nodded towards the book. He'd managed to pick up a copy of 'A guide to growing up: you and your body'. He immediately flushed red, snapped the book shut and shoved it back onto the shelf. The others struggled to contain their laughter, to which Mr Walters slowly lifted his wobbly head and peered at them over his glasses.

They spent the next twenty minutes in silence, pretending to read, until eventually Mr Walters let them go a little early for good behavior. Bursting out of the room, they chased down the corridor, past the Head's office and out onto the damp lawn.

"Can't understand why you'd want to hang around with such a bunch of losers, Palmer," Liam taunted, as he followed them out of the door with Connor hopping around beside him.

"You their new babysitter?" Connor teased.

"Shut up, Sharkie," snapped Josh. "I'll sit on you – we'll see who's the baby then?"

"Ooh – big tough guy," said Liam. "I heard you cried like a baby when you thought you saw that corpse."

"That's rubbish!" yelled Josh, a vein pulsing in his temple. "It was me that went to check it out."

"You so brave – why don't you go back down there, drag it up that cliff and prove us all wrong," Liam dared him. "We'll see who's got balls then."

"Whatever," Josh said, steaming. "It was all a big joke anyway. We were just trying to freak out the others and now it's over so everyone can just drop it."

He glanced towards George and the others, before quickly striding off. George stood dumbstruck. Josh had just totally lied to get himself off the hook with Liam. He turned to Will and Jess for back up but with little response, as they both appeared to have lost the ability to speak.

"It's not a joke!" George yelled, balling up his fists. "And we'll prove it!"

Liam and Connor laughed. "Go on then, cockroach – we dare you."

From: P18
To: J21
Re: Bird of Prey {Encrypted}

<u>Update 24.0</u>

Our source in Paris was found dead.
The bird knows it's being watched.

End.

Chapter 6: The Vanishing

By the time Thursday was over, George felt thoroughly worn down by all the taunting he and the others had received as word of their escapade spread throughout the school. Mrs Stone's plan to keep the story quiet had not been particularly successful. His fleeting dream of being a hero had been utterly crushed, and Josh's complete denial had only made things worse.

George couldn't have been more relieved to escape the heckling on the school bus when he jumped off at his stop. Desperately trying to think of a way to prove them all wrong, he trudged home under the colourless sky. Somehow, he needed to convince the others to go back into the woods and retrieve some irrefutable evidence. He didn't fancy getting closer to a corpse than absolutely necessary, so the only way to silence the doubters was to get photographic proof and that meant smuggling his phone into school. It wasn't going to be easy as phones were banned unless you had special permission, and even then, you had to relinquish it to the school secretary every morning for safekeeping. It would be harder still with Mr Jefferson watching his every move.

There was no way Josh was going to agree to help, and Francesca was still hobbling around, making the most of the attention, so he would have to focus his powers of persuasion on Will and Jess. If all else failed, he could try to convince Felix to join him, which was definitely a last resort, as he was a stickler for school rules. He decided to put his plan into motion at first break on Friday.

The sun had barely emerged from its hiding place when George was woken from a bizarre dream in which he was suffering from an inexplicable amount of nose hair. However hard he tried to cut it, it just kept growing, thick and long and suffocating. He blinked open his eyes to find Marshall sitting stubbornly on his pillow with his over-poofed tail in George's face.

No wonder, he thought, shoving the unwanted intruder from his bed.

Marshall looked over his shoulder as he slunk from the room. George was sure he was smirking.

It was early, but George could hear Gran downstairs, so he washed, dressed and made his way to the kitchen, determined not to miss out on his breakfast feast this morning.

Gran was singing to herself as she trotted out of the bathroom wrapped up in her thick, bobbly dressing gown and wearing a pink, spotted shower cap.

"Morning, gorgeous boy. Why you up at the crack of dawn?" she asked. "I didn't wake you, did I?"

"No, Gran, it was … a dream," he said. He didn't have the heart to blame Gran's beloved cat even though he could see Marshall sneering at him from behind the bathroom door. Gran pottered around him, still in her shower cap, with her slippers flip-flopping on the kitchen tiles. She wasn't her usual chatty self, which puzzled George.

"You OK, Gran?" he asked.

"Yes, yes, dear – you?" she replied, peering over her shoulder from the sink. He didn't have time to answer. "Have you made up with your father yet?"

That's what was on her mind. She didn't like her two boys fighting and made it her mission to seal the peace.

"Haven't seen him," George huffed.

"Maybe that's because you've been avoiding each other. Both as stubborn as mules!" she frowned.

He sat with Gran and ate like a man before battle. He inhaled: two bowls of porridge with Gran's homemade jam; two eggs; four rashers of bacon; three slices of toast and took a banana for the road. Thanking Gran, he made his way out, growling at Marshall as he passed him in the hall.

Morning break arrived and George had prepared his rallying speech so cornered Will and Jess as they came out of the science lab after Chemistry. Jess was explaining some complex chemical formula to Will, who looked slightly baffled.

"Guys, we need to talk," George interrupted. "We can't go on letting everyone think we're total losers."

"Speak for yourself," Jess replied, smiling.

"I'm serious. They all think we completely made up the whole thing. Aren't you mad at Josh for lying?" he asked, turning to Will.

"Of course I am, mate, but there's not much we can do, is there?" Will said, shrugging his shoulders.

"Yes, there is," he whispered, leaning in closer. "I've got my phone stuffed down my sock, we can go and take a photo."

Jess laughed. "OK, secret agent Jenkins. I'm sure you could just carry your phone in your pocket. It's not like we get body searched every morning."

She obviously found the whole thing very amusing, which agitated George.

"Look, are you in or not?"

"How exactly do you plan to get back down there?" she asked.

"We'll go at lunchtime. We can get Francesca to cover for us."

"I think it's a bad idea, George. I mean, we've already been in trouble twice over it all."

"So you're just going to let everyone think you're cowards or that you made the whole thing up? I'm fed up with being picked on. I want to prove them wrong."

George spread his shoulders and jutted out his jaw – it was his best attempt at being forthright and compelling.

Jess and Will looked at each other. They obviously communicated in a way George couldn't understand because they both turned to him at once and nodded.

"OK, we're in, but we go straight there, take a photo and come straight back. No nonsense," insisted Jess.

"Deal," said George. "After lunch, we'll meet behind the sports pavilion. I'll speak to Francesca."

He was thrilled that they'd agreed, but once the reality hit him that they were heading back down to the valley floor, he felt more fearful than joyful. It was too late now, but he was determined to follow through with it. Jess was right, it would take no time at all to get one photo.

He went to track down Francesca. She had left Chemistry early for a singing lesson, so he headed up to the music block where he figured he'd catch her alone. He sat on the stubby wall that surrounded the little, wooden cabin that housed a handful of practice rooms. A cacophony of varying sounds drifted from the open windows.

After a few music-filled minutes, Francesca bounded out. Her ankle must have been feeling better, although she was still wearing the bandage, and when she spotted George, she seemed to redevelop a slight hobble.

"Hello, George," she said. "Are you waiting for a lesson?"

"No, actually, I'm waiting for you," he replied.

"Oh, how lovely. What can I do for you?" she asked, looking a little surprised.

"I need to ask a favour."

He explained his plan and that he needed her to cover for them if anyone asked where they were.

"Um … I'm not sure that's a very sensible idea," she said, frowning.

"Please, Francesca. I'm not asking you to come with us."

"Well, of course … I would, but I'm still injured you see. I … I'd only hold you up."

"Er, yes, I know," George said, looking down at her ankle.

"What would you want me to say?" she asked.

"We're in the sick bay … um … vomiting." George was thinking on his feet. His plan hadn't quite included all the details.

"OK. I'll do it, but if you get caught then I wasn't involved. I'm already in deep water with my mother."

"Thanks, Francesca. We owe you one."

"Good luck, George – be careful," she said with a concerned smile.

Lunchtime break arrived, and George was convinced that the other two would back out at the last minute; maybe he even hoped they would. However, as he came out onto the lawn, he could see them loitering by the edge of the rugby field. They made their way down to the sports pavilion, which was buzzing with year seven students all keen to take part in the rugby and netball trials. The timing couldn't have been more perfect. There was such a crowd gathered, that they managed to sneak off down the path to the woods without being spotted.

"OK," said Jess. "Let's make this quick. I can remember the way to the point on the ridge where we descend, and then it's not too far a walk to the tree bridge."

The other two nodded. George felt slightly more relaxed with Jess in charge and Will by his side, but he could feel his undigested bolognaise churning inside his stomach. He checked that his phone was still in its hiding place and followed close behind the others.

The sky was darker and heavier than it had been on Wednesday, and a gusty wind was blowing in George's face, but they made it to the tree stump with ease. The climb down seemed even harder, as the damp air and recent rain had turned the slope into a slide. They slithered their way down, aware that muddy uniforms would be difficult to explain, especially if they'd supposedly been in the sick bay.

The valley floor was dimly lit and rich with the smell of rotting foliage. All George's senses were on edge. The oaks groaned and creaked in warning, and acorns were pummelling them from above. Everything was telling them to turn back. George's heart was thumping in his chest.

"Right, who's going over to take the photo?" Jess asked. They both looked at George.

"It was your idea and your phone," shrugged Will.

George stared back. "Maybe we should all go … you know … in case..."

Will smiled. "Of course, mate – we wouldn't leave you hanging."

They carefully crossed the river and rounded the tree stump. George's heart was tearing at his rib cage, fighting to break out of his chest and run in the opposite direction. He could barely breathe and he desperately wanted to close his eyes. Will tentatively stepped forward.

"It's gone!" he exclaimed.

"What?" said Jess.

"It's completely gone. I swear, it was right there."

George let out the breath he was holding and peered around the stump. Will was right. There was nothing there but a patch of flattened mud and a heap of rusty leaves.

"Well, that explains why Mr Hill found nothing," George said, slightly relieved.

"Yes," said Jess, "but who the hell moved it?"

They all stared at each other as it slowly dawned on them that whoever dumped the body had probably been back to move it. George's temporary relief was crushed by a tidal wave of horror.

"What if they were here – you know – when we were here – watching us," he said, searching the surrounding woods in panic.

But before he could say anything else, the fallen tree trunk shuddered and they looked up to see someone leaping down at them. Jess screamed and George lunged backwards, toppling over a tangle of ferns. He looked up expecting to see the face of a murderer but instead saw Josh beaming down at them.

"Ha! Got ya'," he laughed. "You should see your faces."

"That was not funny!" Jess said, thumping him in the arm.

"It was a bit," he said, trying to look apologetic.

"What are you doing here?" George shouted, heaving himself up out of the sea of ferns. "I thought you said it was all a big lie!"

"Well, I had to save face didn't I, but when Francesca told me what you were up to, I figured, I couldn't leave you wusses down here alone."

"Well it was a complete waste of time because someone has moved it – look," said George. He glanced back towards the empty gravesite and noticed something behind Will's legs. "What's that?"

Lying on the ground, a few feet away, was a bright green slip of paper. George squeezed between Will and the holly bush and bent down to pick it up. It was a library ticket from the Pendleton Museum & Library and it was dated from the previous week. As he stood back up, something else caught his eye. Behind the holly bush was a trail of glistening, muddy tracks, as if a giant slug had hauled itself across the ground. It was as plain as day, someone had dragged something large and heavy through the undergrowth, exposing the damp, slick mud beneath the woodland litter. It led towards a thick tangle of branches and ivy that was pressed up against the side of a large mound of earth and rock.

"George, what is it?" Jess asked.

"Er, I think whoever took the body, took it this way," he said, pulling back the slicing arms of the holly bush and revealing the evidence.

"Whoa," exclaimed Josh. "You're totally right – let's follow it."

"No, let's not," said Jess. "This has gone far enough."

"Come on, Jess. Don't be a wimp," said Josh, as he pushed past George and followed the tracks no more than a dozen steps to where they stopped.

Pulling at the web of debris, he revealed, to all their shock, what looked like the entrance to a squat, stone tunnel. The temptation to move closer was too great. They edged forwards and Will tried to peer inside.

"Pass us your phone, George. It's too dark in there. I can't see a thing."

Hanging back, George flicked on the light from his phone and passed it down the line. Will and Josh leant in and shone the light into the opening. It was just about the height of George and about as wide again. The stonework at the entrance was smoothed by age but badly notched in places. Streams of ivy grew up and spilled out of its mouth like fleeing serpents. The beam of light barely made it a few yards before being swallowed up by the darkness. George could just make out the odd worn step descending into oblivion.

"Well?" said George. "Where the hell does that go?"

"I don't know, and I don't want to find out," said Jess, abruptly. "If that's where the body is, then good luck to anyone who wants to go in there and find it. I'm done."

"Any volunteers?" asked Will, looking at George and Josh who both shook their heads.

"Who's the wimp now?" Jess sneered at Joshua.

"We've got to get back up to school before the bell," said Josh, as if that justified his hesitation.

"But we didn't get any evidence," said Will.

"I've got this," said George, holding up the library ticket. "I'm guessing that whoever was down here dropped this ticket, so we just need to find out who it belongs to."

"And how do we do that?" asked Josh.

"We'll have to go to the Pendleton Library," George said, trying to sound assured.

With that, they turned and hurried their way back up to the school grounds before the afternoon bell.

They scrambled into class just in time for Mr Jefferson to call the register, but his high backed chair sat vacant. He usually moved about the school with military precision, so this was a first. They all sat unsure of what to do. The silence, that had already become customary in his form room, was slowly broken by rumblings of confusion. Before long, there were several full volume conversations gaining momentum. George was sure he would pounce out of a cupboard at any minute, giving them all detention for breaking his rules. As the atmosphere in the room slackened, a few people dared to wander about and perch on each other's desks, making idle chat. George sat still waiting for the punch line and noticed that Felix's backside was firmly glued to his seat too, although he was twisting about trying to survey the unfolding chaos.

Francesca had turned in her seat and was grilling Josh on the outcome of their lunchtime excursion. He was quite visibly enjoying the attention as he relayed the tale. She sat with her elbows on his desk, looking entranced.

It was nearly time for their next lesson, but as they began to make their way towards the door, it suddenly flew open and, a less-than-composed, Mr Jefferson stormed in. The whole room froze in various states of motion.

"Sit down!" he raged at the top of his voice, his trembling eye going into overdrive. "I did not dismiss you!"

A manic stampede followed, as people tried to get back to their desks; no one wanting to be the last. Mr Jefferson was breathing hard and slightly flushed. His usually pristine tie was loose, revealing a nasty scar just under his collar. The bandage on his arm was straying from beneath his sleeve, and his usually gleaming shoes were caked in mud. George had a very turbulent feeling in the pit of his stomach.

Has Mr Jefferson been in the woods? Did he follow us?

As quickly as he had burst in, he dismissed them.

"You can now go," he said, matter of factly. They cautiously got up from their seats. "Except you, Jenkins."

And the turbulence in George's stomach whipped up into a full-blown storm.

Chapter 7: Digging Around

As soon as the room was empty, Mr Jefferson strode towards George and stood towering over his desk.

"Where were you at lunchtime, Jenkins?"

"Um," George swallowed hard. Had Francesca told anyone that he was in the sick bay? Had his form tutor checked the sick bay? "I was … sick, Sir."

"Really? You look perfectly rosy to me; in fact, I'd say you look like you've been out for a jog."

George could say the same about him but didn't dare.

"Um … it's hot in here, Sir," George offered as an excuse.

Mr Jefferson didn't look convinced.

"I better not catch you being where you shouldn't be or it will be maximum penalty." George wasn't even sure what that meant, but he did know that Mr Jefferson was on his case, and he was now curious as to what the new teacher had been up to.

"Now go," Mr Jefferson said.

George almost knocked over his desk as he leapt up to leave.

"One minute, Jenkins – what's that in your pocket?" Mr Jefferson said without turning to look at him.

George gulped and looked down at the bulge in his back pocket. He'd forgotten to put his phone back in his sock.

"It's my phone, Sir," he said, sheepishly.

"I assume you have a very special reason to have it on your person, otherwise you would, of course, be breaking another school rule."

"Um … no, Sir … sorry, Sir," he said, feebly. "I … I forgot it was there."

"That is not an excuse. Put it on my desk. You can retrieve it at the end of the day." George placed the phone down on the polished wood. "And you can join me on Monday lunchtime for detention."

George nodded and dragged himself towards the door feeling a tonne heavier than when he had come in.

"You haven't got anything else in your pockets, have you, Jenkins?"

"No, Sir," he lied, as he slipped out of the door clutching the library ticket firmly in his fist.

The end of the day couldn't come quickly enough as far as George was concerned. It had been a long and turbulent week, and the freedom of the weekend felt well overdue. The dread of detention on Monday hung over him like a thunderous cloud, waiting to unleash its fury, but he tried to distract himself by actually paying attention to Mr Walters as he explained the pros and cons of child labour during the industrial revolution.

The lesson finally ended and it was time to escape, but George had two more things to do. He cornered the others in the locker room as they were gathering their belongings and loading up their backpacks.

"Is anyone up for coming to the Library tomorrow and helping me find out who this belongs to?" he said, holding up the ticket that was rapidly becoming crumpled and tattered from being squeezed into his palm.

He rarely spent time at the weekend with anyone other than Gran, Felix or his dad, and his dad hardly counted, as that was pretty infrequent. They exchanged glances.

"Not sure it would do much for my street cred' hanging out with you guys at the weekend," Josh grinned, but the others looked wounded. "I've got a match first thing, but I could meet just after lunch," he quickly added.

"Guess there's no harm in it," said Jess, shrugging. "Count me in."

"Shouldn't you just tell someone what you found rather than find yourselves in more trouble?" Francesca said, warily.

"Who am I supposed to tell?" said George. "And anyway, we'd have to admit that we went out of school bounds again. We'd get in more trouble that way."

"You're probably right," Will nodded, so the four of them agreed to meet at the library at one o'clock.

"What about me?" said Francesca, pouting.

"Didn't think you'd want to get your hands dirty," Jess smirked.

"I know exactly what you think of me, Jessica Stone," Francesca said, looking hurt. "You just think I'm precious and spoilt, but you're wrong."

Jess looked a little ashamed. "I'm sorry. I just … OK, well, you know what – come with us and you can prove me wrong." She attempted a sincere smile.

"Fantastic," Francesca beamed.

It crossed George's mind that maybe he wasn't the only one who struggled to fit in and make friends.

With that crossed off his list, he reluctantly made his way back to the form room to claim his confiscated phone. He prayed that Mr Jefferson had just left it on his desk, but it was wishful thinking. As he approached, the door was cracked open and he could hear Mr Jefferson mumbling something in French. George knocked timidly and nudged the door open. Mr Jefferson was on the phone.

"Fais-le," he barked at the person on the other end and then hung up. "I assume you've come to get this," he said, holding up George's phone like a piece of evidence from a crime scene.

"Yes please, Sir," George mumbled, with his eyes fixed on his shoelaces.

Mr Jefferson let out a low, rumbling growl. "I never want to see it again."

"Yes, Sir, thank you, Sir." George shuffled towards the teacher and leant out to take it without getting too close. As soon as he had his hands on it, he turned and sped out of the room as fast as he could.

It was Friday night, and George felt strangely light as he strolled home through the centre of Chiddingham. The breeze was pleasant and the clouds had lifted to reveal a watery blue sky. His phoned buzzed, making him jump. It was a text from Felix asking if he wanted to meet later. George replied and asked where they should meet. Felix couldn't come to George's house as he was allergic to Marshall, so they agreed to meet at the cricket ground.

He went home, changed and told Gran he was going to grab fish and chips from the van that stopped every Friday outside the village hall. By the time Felix arrived, George had gorged his way through a battered cod, large chips and a jumbo sausage. He felt like his jeans might explode at the seams at any moment.

"Did you leave any chips for me?" Felix asked, picking his way through the screwed up newspaper.

"Sorry, mate," George apologised, with a greasy burp.

Felix frowned. "So, what happened with Mr J today?"

"He confiscated my phone – he was acting pretty odd though don't you think? Did you notice he was all sweaty and covered in dirt?"

"Um, not really," said Felix, still absorbed in looking for chip scraps.

They wandered down to the cricket green and George told him about the missing body, the library ticket and the hidden tunnel. Felix seemed disinterested, but his attention perked up when George mentioned the tunnel.

"What kind of tunnel?" he asked.

"I don't know – like a stone one, I guess."

"Probably one of those old war tunnels," Felix said, casually.

"What? What war tunnels? How do you know about them?" Now George was alert.

"Oh, my dad studies local history. There's a whole network of tunnels under Kent. They start right down at Dover and run all over the place," said Felix, knowledgably.

"Seriously?" George said, astounded.

"Yeah, they had to close a shopping centre one weekend because the shops were slipping into a bunch of crumbling tunnels 100 feet below the surface; no one even knew they were there!" he said, his eyes opening so wide that his glasses nearly slid off his nose.

"How did no one know they were there?"

"Government cover up," Felix grinned mischievously. Conspiracy theories were his favourite reading material, even more so if it had anything to do with alien encounters. "The Government denied any knowledge of them, but several were used during the Second World War – you know, for running communications or as bomb shelters. I reckon there's no way the Ministry of

Defence doesn't know what or where they are. Some people say there are still secret military installations hidden down there."

"So, the one in the school grounds could lead anywhere?" George's brain buzzed.

"Well, yeah I guess, but most of the local ones were closed up a few years back after pressure from residents and the local MP."

"Why?" asked George, intrigued.

They had reached the green and plopped themselves down on a bench, watching a few old guys practicing their batting in the nets.

"Oh, it's quite cool actually," Felix said, his eyes lighting up. "There were rumours of the tunnels being haunted, and for a while some groups held meetings and parties in them. Then one day the MP convinced the local authority to shut them down. Most of the known entrances are heavily fenced off or closed up."

"No way?" George was enthralled. "Is there any way of finding out where they go?"

"Oh yeah," said Felix, swatting at a persistent fly. "There's loads of stuff about them at the Pendleton Library."

George sat up and grabbed Felix by the shoulders, shaking his glasses right off the end of his nose. "What did you say?"

"Man – George – calm down. I said you can see maps and stuff about the tunnels at the Library in town."

"You're a genius, mate," George said, unruffling Felix's t-shirt.

Chapter 8: Buried Truths

Saturday afternoon arrived and George was the first to arrive at the library, so he sat on the front step and fidgeted. Pendleton was a typical old Kent town with narrow streets, cobbled sidewalks and a picturesque high street that was taken over fortnightly by a bustling farmers' market. There was a small cottage hospital at one end of town and a deserted, old train station, buried amongst the overgrown oaks, at the other end. Several of the old buildings leant on their neighbours' shoulders like drunken revellers as their roofs sagged under the strain of the heavy slate tiles. The museum and library were combined in one such building. Blink and you'd miss it, but it was quaint, and as a child George had been there with Gran on numerous occasions for story time or the odd Easter egg hunt.

The gentleman that ran the library was as old as some of the relics but had enough energy and enthusiasm to make up for it. He had lived in the area all his life and bounced around in excitement whenever anyone wanted to know anything about its history.

Jess and Will arrived with Josh not far behind. They all looked so different out of uniform; it took George a moment to realise it was them. They were about to go inside when Francesca appeared looking frustrated.

"Sorry I'm late," she said. "I had to escape my mother."

A tinkling announced their arrival as they filed into the building. The hefty door creaked closed behind them and sealed them in the musty, airless room. The low ceilings and tiny windows made it feel like you were walking into a doll's house. Glass cabinets and warped wooden shelves filled the rooms to the left. Several displays contained pieces of iron-age tools and broken clay pots. At the far end was a giant stuffed bear. George was pretty sure no bears lived in Pendleton, but still, it was impressive. He scanned the exhibits but couldn't see anything to do with the old war tunnels. He wandered past a glass coffin that contained a human skeleton; its head was turned towards him and its jaw hung open as if it was uttering its final words. George shivered.

A small set of rounded steps descended into the library. It was only the size of an average living room but was stuffed full of racks upon racks of books, which looked like they'd topple over like dominoes if you sneezed.

"Hello!" called Josh.

There was a loud bang followed by a thud.

"Oh, damn it!" a voice proclaimed from behind one of the racks and out popped the head of an incredibly petite old man with the longest moustache George had ever seen. Snow white and sharply pointed at each end, it dripped over his lips and cascaded down past his chin.

"Hello, young folks," he said, leaping out and clapping his hands. "What a delight!"

He looked uncannily like a garden gnome, dressed in tweed dungarees, a well-pressed white shirt and a red and white, gingham bow tie.

"Er, hi," said Josh, trying to hide his amusement. "Are you the librarian?"

"I am indeed, young Sir – see," the little man replied, pointing at his gleaming ivory badge, which read 'Wilbur Cook, Head Librarian and Curator'.

"Excellent," said Francesca, striding forwards and taking him by the hand. "How delightful to meet you."

"Well, the same to you, young lady."

George thought Wilbur's face was going to crack, his smile was so wide.

"What can I do for you lovely folks, this fine day?" he asked. "Would you like the tour?"

"Um … actually we're interested in finding out about a book that someone took out last week," said George, hesitantly.

"Of course, what is the book's title?" Wilbur asked, trotting off towards the single computer that sat centre stage on his impeccably tidy desk.

"Well, we don't actually know," George said, "but we have the library ticket, so maybe you could look up what it is and … er … maybe who took it out – please?"

Wilbur had just managed to hop up into his seat and get comfy in front of the keyboard when his expression changed. He stared suspiciously at the green ball of paper in George's hand.

"I can't do that I'm afraid, young man, especially if that is not your ticket," he frowned.

"It's my uncle's," Josh chimed in. "He can't walk – and is very forgetful – he wants me to return it, you see, but can't remember which book he took out."

The others stared at him.

"Really? I don't remember anyone by that description borrowing a book last week, and why would your friend here need to know *who* borrowed it?"

There were obviously no flies on Wilbur, even if he did look like a gnome. Josh huffed.

"I may be old, but I'm not a nincompoop," Wilbur tutted. George wasn't sure what that was, but he was sure they'd hit a dead end.

"Of course you aren't. We wouldn't assume such a dreadful thing," Francesca said, sidling over to his desk. "We don't mean to pry. I would love that tour, though, if you still have time."

"Absolutely!" he cheered, springing from his chair. "This way Ma'am."

She winked at the others and skipped off behind the old curator.

"Well," said George, "what do we do now?"

"We set Will to work," smiled Jess, deviously. "He can hack this old thing right open in no time."

They all turned to look at Will.

"Right," he said, "so looks like I'm up then." He looked reluctant, but three pairs of eyeballs were on him, so he rounded the desk and got to work. "Should be pretty easy. You keep watch; make sure the old loon doesn't come back."

He pulled his glasses from his pocket and fired the computer screen to life. His fingers powered over the keyboard, and in no time, he had cracked the basic security.

"I'm in – what's the ticket number?" he asked, staring over his glasses at George.

George dictated while Will plugged the numbers in and waited for the results to load. There was a tinkling sound; someone else had crossed the threshold. George snuck over to the stairs to see who it was, but all he could make out was a pair of steel capped boots disappearing behind one of the displays. Francesca was, however, heading their way.

"You guys need to hurry up," George whispered.

"I've got it," Will cried, a little too loudly, as Francesca re-joined them.

They all crowded around the screen. "It's 'Buried Truths: A History of War Time Kent' by M. A. Peel, and it was due back today."

Will scrolled down through the details. It had been borrowed by Mr J Phillips whose picture was plastered next to the single entry. He looked like a Navy SEAL; buzz cut hair, thin intense eyes and a scar above his right eye that severed his heavy eyebrow in two.

"Doesn't look like a particularly friendly guy, does he?" Josh said.

Wilbur was raising his voice and coming their way. Will flicked the screen off and they all pegged it up the stairs and out onto the high street. As the door swung shut, George could hear Wilbur shouting. They ducked into the coffee shop opposite and collapsed into the well-worn sofas.

"So, what are we supposed to do now?" George asked, looking around at the others.

"We should give the information to the police," said Francesca, sensibly.

"What would we tell them?" said Jess. "There's a guy called Mr Phillips who took out a book from the library and dropped his ticket in the woods."

"Yeah, they could get him for littering," sniggered Josh.

"Alright, do you have a better idea?" Francesca said, glaring at him.

With that, the door to the library flew open and a man ducked out. He glanced up and down the street and fiddled with something at the door, before dashing over the road with a package bundled up under his arm.

"What's that all about?" Josh said.

"I don't know, but he looks like he's up to no good," said George, getting up from his seat and peering out of the window. For a split second, the man looked up, straight through the café window, revealing his face and his splintered eyebrow.

"It's him!" gasped George, as he raced towards the door, narrowly missing a waitress and nearly sending a tray of hot drinks flying.

"Where are you going?" yelled Jess.

"To follow him!"

George was already out of the door before the others could pluck themselves from their sunken sofas. They bundled out onto the pavement nearly barging George into the traffic. The suspicious figure was making his way up the hill at quite a pace.

"Come on then, what are we waiting for?" urged Josh. The others looked a little unsure. "It's broad daylight, in the middle of the high street – what's the worst thing that could happen?"

After some convincing, they weaved their way between their fellow pedestrians on the narrow side walk, up the hill, trying not to get too close to their target. It wasn't easy keeping an eye on him, and it wasn't long before he had stepped off the street and out of sight.

"Where did he go?" said George.

"He must have gone in there," said Jess, pointing up at the peeling painting of a 'Spotted Hog' dangling over the door to a historic looking pub.

"Well, that's great," said Will. "We can't go in there without an adult."

"We'll just have to find an adult then," said Francesca, looking around.

The others looked perplexed.

"Watch," she said, grabbing Josh by the hand and tailing behind an elderly lady who was just entering the inn.

She bent down and fussed with the lady's dog while Josh held the door for her. Flashing a cheeky smile at the others, they strolled into the pub making pleasantries.

"Ha!" said Jess. "That girl has more nerve than the rest of us put together. I'm starting to quite like her."

She grabbed Will and dragged him inside, just as a man and his wife arrived for a late lunch.

George was left standing solo on the pavement. Several punters came and went, yet he failed to pluck up the courage to fake any kind of relationship with a passing over-eighteen. Improvisation was not his forte. After a few minutes, Josh came charging back out, grabbed him by the arm and pulled him inside.

George had only ever been inside a pub once, when his gran took him to the 'Poacher' in Chiddingham for a celebratory lunch in honour of him passing his cycling proficiency test. It was the only exam he'd ever officially passed, so it was worth celebrating. They'd eaten steak and chips and 'knickerbocker glories' until they were as round as the beer barrels and had to roll themselves home. However, the 'Spotted Hog' was a very different kind of pub. The ceilings were so low you had to duck to avoid head-butting the huge worm-eaten wooden beams. A dim orange glow was emanating from several dusty old velvet lampshades that were hemmed with beads and hanging tassels. The open fire was ablaze, even though the autumn temperatures hadn't yet arrived in earnest. The whole place was dingy, hot and stifling.

Huddled in a far corner, trying to look relaxed, were the others. They hadn't managed to keep hold of their adult chaperones. George was sure it wouldn't be long before they were turfed out, especially if they didn't order anything. He peered around the poorly lit room but couldn't see the guy from the library. Will was waving furiously at him and pointing towards the toilets, just as Mr Phillips exited with the parcel still under his arm. He made his way towards the fireplace where he took a seat opposite a man in a long dark overcoat and shabby red cap. He had his back to them, but George could just make out a stubbly beard and a rather large hooked nose.

He joined the others. "We need to get closer," he said. "We need to hear what they're saying."

"We're already on borrowed time," said Jess, looking towards the bar where a very mean and manly-looking waitress was staring at them with a not very welcoming frown.

"I've got an idea," said Francesca. "Grab that – on the windowsill behind you, George." She was pointing at a charity collection box.

"I can't steal that," he said, horrified. "It's for guide dogs."

"No, George – start collecting," she said, nodding her head towards the suspects.

"Me?"

"Yeah," said Josh, "you look like a charity collector."

"What?"

The waitress was coming out from behind the bar and it wouldn't be long before her meat-cleaver hands were hauling them off the premises. George took a deep breath, snatched the tin and moved towards the sinister duo. He nervously asked a few people for donations and was surprised by how generous they were, but he needed to get closer.

Right behind the two men, sat the pleasant old lady with the dog. He made a beeline for her. She was over the moon to contribute and conveniently began telling George all about her Golden Retriever and how he was a retired guide dog. George nodded enthusiastically as she continued to delve around in her purse for all her buried pennies. He was close enough now to hear every word that was being said at the neighbouring table. The eyebrow guy, Mr Phillips, had handed the parcel over to his friend. At closer range, George could see it looked like a roll of parchment or papers, maybe even a large map, tied up in string.

"This is excellent work," said the man with the hooknose, in a strange accent that George couldn't quite pinpoint. "We will need to recover our stolen artifacts before we move to the next phase. Is everything in order?" Mr Phillips nodded. "Perfect. This Wednesday it is then. We will meet at the entrance to the Natural History Museum – 1pm – no later. You will make sure everything is in order before we begin?"

Mr Phillips nodded again. "Yes."

"And you will need to deal with the package you left at the library."

"Yes."

"Excellent work," he repeated.

"That's it. I don't have a penny more, young man," the old lady said, tapping George on his outstretched hand.

His collection tin felt twice the weight. He felt terribly guilty that he'd completely cleaned her out. Time had run out: the men were rising from their seats and his friends were being corralled out of the door by the, now extremely mad-looking, waitress.

"Thank you," he said hurriedly to the old lady as he turned to follow his ejected friends, but there blocking his path was Mr Phillips. He stared down at him with his bullet-like eyes.

"Out of my way, beggar," he growled.

George froze. His brain was telling him to move, but his body was completely paralysed. Mr Phillips bore down on him, snorting like a bull, his face only inches from George's.

"And you too, you little blighter!" yelled a booming voice from behind.

It was the waitress, and she had George by the scruff of the neck. Still frozen stiff, he was dragged out backwards like an old plank of wood with his heels bouncing off the carpet folds. Once outside, she let go and he teetered on the edge of the pavement as she slammed the door in his face. Just as he was regaining his composure, the door flung back open, she grabbed the collection tin from his grip and heaved the door shut once more. The last thing he saw was Mr Phillips' chilling stare.

"Blimey, she was a piece of work – you OK, George?" Will had appeared in his line of vision. "Hello, earth to George."

He sparked out of his trance. "I think it's time to go home."

"Yeah, I'm with you there, mate," said Will. "Come on, the others are around the corner."

They scarpered down the hill as George told them what he'd heard.

"Doesn't make any sense to me," said Francesca. "What artifacts are they after?

"No idea," said George. "But they are definitely meeting on Wednesday at the Natural History Museum to do something, and I don't suppose it's just a tourist trip. They are definitely involved in what we saw in the woods – I'm sure of it."

"Well, there's no chance we can follow them to London," said Francesca.

"Wait. Did you say Wednesday – this Wednesday?" asked Jess.

"Yes, why?" said George.

"Will and I are on a Science Club trip with my dad on Wednesday."

"Well, that's *jolly* nice, but what's that got to do with anything?" said Josh, confused.

"It's in London, you dummy. My dad is hosting a world science fair at The Imperial College; it's practically next door."

"Right," said Will, "so now we're expected to sneak out and chase bad guys, I suppose."

"Maybe we can come too," said George, excitedly. "All we have to do is sign up to Science Club and get permission from our parents." As he said it, he realised it was a little ambitious with only two school days before the trip.

"I guess so," said Jess. "I mean, the Science Club isn't exactly oversubscribed. I'm sure Dr Root would be more than happy to have some new recruits."

Dr Root was not a big fan of George. He had managed to set fire to his whole science folder in her lesson on combustible materials and had once caused an evacuation by adding far too much ammonia to his chemical reactions experiment. Science was another subject that he couldn't call a forte.

"I'm up for trying," he said, after some thought; however, it would mean having to talk to his dad.

"Hmm … I guess," said Josh. "But I'd need to be back for rugby practice at four thirty."

"We'll be back well before hometime, I'm sure," Jess said, reassuringly.

They all agreed to try to get in on the trip. If nothing else, it would get them out of the coming week's 'orienteering', which had to be a good thing.

Chapter 9: London Bound

Autumn made a fuss on Monday morning with howling winds and driving rain. The bus journey to school was like a roller coaster ride as Mr Steckler, quite excitedly, dodged flying branches and weaved past lake-sized puddles. The greater the challenge, the more he came alive, as if reliving some insanely exhilarating past. He bounced around in his chair, whooping and punching the air at every overcome obstacle. George watched, in intrigued awe, while clinging to his seat with all his might.

He'd never been more relieved to arrive safely at school and was even happier when Miss O'Donnell addressed the class at registration, telling them that Mr Jefferson was off sick. George was off the hook for detention, at least for now. He had an unusually relaxed and disaster-free day. All he had to do was make sure that he saw Dr Root at lunchtime.

Lunch was rarely the highlight of George's day, unless treacle tart was on the menu. It was never quite as good as Gran's, but it was better than fruit salad or lumpy yoghurt. Today was treacle tart day, and George and Felix were taking their time relishing every mouthful. It was the first he'd spoken to Felix all day.

"So, where were you on Saturday?" Felix asked, licking the sticky crumbs from the back of his spoon. "I thought you'd be up at the cricket nets as usual."

"I had to go into town," replied George, feeling a little guilty that he'd abandoned his best friend.

"Right – sounds fun," Felix said, his voice muffled by the inside of the bowl he was now cleaning.

"Um … no, it was a bit boring really."

George wasn't very good at lying; he knew his face read like a book.

Felix gave up on the bowl and looked straight at George. "You go with your new friends, then?"

George's tart sunk to the bottom of his stomach.

"Um … well we went to see if we could find any information about those tunnels, you know…"

"You're not still on about that body, are you?"

"Well, we think we know who moved it and–"

"It was probably abducted by aliens," Felix said, as he clambered off the bench, wiped his mouth with his sleeve and grabbed his empty tray. Obviously not interested in hearing any more, he left without another word.

Great, I've managed to upset my only real friend.

George finished his lunch alone and then went to find Dr Root. Getting himself signed up for the trip to London was easy enough, so he spent the rest of the afternoon daydreaming about how the trip might go. He couldn't stop thinking about the venom in Mr Philipps' eyes. And the longer he thought about it, the more convinced he was that he and his companion were up to no good.

I just need to catch them out – then I can prove that it wasn't all a big lie and everything can return to normal.

Lost in thought, George almost missed his stop as the school bus hissed to a halt outside the newsagent. Leaping from his seat, he just managed to squeeze through the rapidly narrowing gap in the folding doors. Unfortunately, his blazer wasn't so lucky. Without thinking, he heaved on the protruding sleeve just as Mr Steckler released the doors again, sending him flying backwards and crashing into a passer-by. Several of the remaining passengers looked thoroughly entertained, but

George was fed up with being the comedy act. He turned to apologise to his victim only to find it was his dad, who was standing in a milky puddle on the pavement.

"Dad!" George exclaimed.

Sam stared at the split shopping bags that hung from his hands. "Right, well, I need to get some more milk."

George grimaced. "Urgh, sorry."

George waited outside the shop while Sam restocked on milk. He was agonising about how to break the ice with his dad and ask about the science trip. But when Sam came back out, he was on the phone.

George scurried along behind him as he made his way back to his van, which was parked on the corner.

"Can you take this milk back to Gran?" Sam asked, as he hung up and pulled his keys from his pocket.

"Er, yeah … of course," George replied.

"Great, thanks."

"Dad, I need to ask you something," George said, as Sam opened the front door of the van.

"Can it wait?" Sam said, glancing at his watch. "I've got to be somewhere."

George frowned. "No, not really." He had no idea if he'd see his dad again before Wednesday morning so it had to be now. He didn't want to be the only one who couldn't go on the trip. "I've got a science trip on Wednesday, to London. I need you to sign the form."

"This Wednesday? That's a little short notice."

"Well, it's a Science Club trip; I only recently joined."

"Science Club?" Sam said, his eyebrows disappearing beneath his cap.

"Yeah, my friends are all going, so I thought it would be fun and um … educational."

"Right," said Sam, clearly unsure of George's motives. "This with your new friends?"

George bristled. "Well, yes, but …"

Sam sighed. "It's OK, George, I'll sign it. I'm happy you're getting involved in something. Just keep out of trouble, will you?"

George's nostrils flared, but he bit back his words and just yanked the form from his bag. Silently, he watched his dad sign it.

We're on!

Tuesday flew past, and George was happy to find out that everyone was on track to make the trip. Mr Jefferson was still absent which made the day much more bearable.

Wednesday morning came around, and George leapt out of bed, genuinely excited to be going on a school trip, and equally keen to finally find out what Mr Phillips and his friend were up to. Having overpacked his backpack with snacks, water, pads, pens and various items from around the house that may come in handy like binoculars, a first aid kit and his phone, he made his way to the bus stop slightly regretting the weight of his bag.

By the time he reached the modest main line station, it was busy with commuters. He squeezed his way down the steps and easily spotted Dr Root halfway down the platform.

George was the last to arrive and was quickly introduced to all those present, including Jess' dad, the impressive Professor Stone. He looked just as George had imagined: upright, smart and professional with an expression of deep concentration. He smiled at George and shook his hand politely, although he seemed distracted by his own thoughts – maybe because he was about to host hundreds of intellects at his famous college.

George couldn't imagine what it must be like to be so clever that people wanted to hear you speak. He could barely string a sentence together whenever he was asked to speak in front of the class; the thought of speaking to a whole crowd scared the life out of him.

The journey to London was always a rare adventure. The city felt like a different world compared to sleepy Chiddingham. As they hurtled through the stations between home and the Capital, everything mutated. Sprawling, open, wild countryside morphed into compact, confined, bordered gardens and courtyards. The stations grew busier and noisier, and squat cottages and outhouses slowly clustered and grew into sky scraping towers of incredible variety and design. George stared out of the window, trying to take in all its size and rawness.

"Hey, George," said Josh, "you look like you've never seen a city before."

His mind was dragged back into the carriage.

"Huh?" he said, realising that he hadn't really paid any attention to the others the whole journey.

"It's so dirty," said Francesca, screwing up her slender nose. "The air is practically toxic."

"Well actually, it is exactly that," said Jess. "Nearly 95% of London's population live in areas where PM2.5 exceeds–"

"Alright, Prof," said Josh. "You know we have no idea what you're babbling on about."

"Strange that – thought this was a science trip?" she said, getting back to the book she was reading.

The conversation paused as they glided over one of the many bridges that span the historic Thames. They squinted as the low sun bounced off the glimmering water that was bustling with water vessels of every sort. London's majestic landmarks looked magnificent to George. The next stop was theirs.

Dr Root counted them all as they piled off the train at Charing Cross and were carried along by the morning surge, down into the depths of the London Underground. Hot, dry and gritty; the air blasted their faces as the tube rattled its way into the worm-hole of a station. Squeezing onto the train was like playing sardines with complete strangers. George managed to get himself lodged between a rather bulbous gentleman with less than pleasant body odour and a straggly looking teenager who was quite audibly listening to heavy metal and head-banging to the rhythm. It was a very long eleven minutes. As they were finally ejected out of the station into the daylight, George refilled his lungs with slightly fresher air. He felt like he'd held his breath for the whole stifling journey.

The short walk to the Imperial College London took them past the front of the Natural History Museum. George had been there once before when his gran had taken him to see the dinosaurs. It was a beautiful and imposing building, stuffed full of mind-boggling bones and terrifying taxidermy. It filled George with wonder, fear and fascination, but he would have to wait until lunch to get any closer, and even then they had a job to do.

Moments later, they were approaching the gleaming glass atrium of the main entrance to the Imperial College London. It was already bustling with guests, but luckily,

Professor Stone's standing whisked them to the front of the snaking queue. He showed them where to sign in and then bid them farewell until they were due to watch one of his lectures later.

After being issued name badges, maps, timetables of lectures and having their bags searched, they finally made their way into the heart of the sprawling campus. The place was alive with activity and young eager faces, including those of their group. George immediately felt out of place. Looking around he saw that Jess, Will and several of the others looked like puppies in a pet store. They were excitedly absorbing the timetable of events and debating which displays and workshops to attend first. He, Josh and Francesca stood in idle silence.

"Do you think there's a snack bar?" Josh asked, already bored. He had brought nothing with him but his wallet and a miniature rugby ball that he'd fiddled with all the way up on the train.

"I certainly hope so," said Francesca, whose bag had been mainly filled with, what looked like, a change of clothes and hair accessories.

Dr Root pulled the group together and did one final count.

"Right, there are fifteen of you, so I suggest three groups of five. You have just over an hour and a half until we are due at Professor Stone's lecture. You are free to browse around the fair and visit the stands. Please stick together and no one is to leave the campus – obviously. We will then have a lunch break, and we will meet again for the afternoon's lectures at one forty. We will be leaving at two thirty."

It was a tight but convenient schedule. With the museum being next door, George figured it wouldn't be so hard to pop out for a few minutes over lunch to satisfy their curiosity. Several groups of students were already drifting towards nearby stands, and Jess was pulling at the chain to dive into her wish list.

"Right let's go," she said. "This way first."

"Can we find a snack place?" Josh asked, starting to edge away in the opposite direction.

"No, there's no time for that," she barked. "You can eat at lunchtime."

They trailed behind her and Will, as they swooped in and out of various impressive rooms hosting a myriad of weird and wonderful displays. One stall was filled with, what George could only describe as, giant mechanical straws all stuck together with gumballs.

"What's that supposed to be?" he whispered to Francesca, who just shrugged.

"It's a molecular structure modelling kit," Will whispered from behind, making George jump.

"Right – of course."

Before long, Jess had filled her previously empty bag with chemical reaction kits, crystal forming ingredients and a pile of leaflets; Will had spent most of the time engrossed in an Artificial Intelligence challenge, where he had managed to re-programme a robot to do his top three favourite taekwondo moves, and Francesca had found a display all about the chemistry of cosmetics. Meanwhile, Josh had made friends with two young ladies who were manning a stand promoting eco-friendly packaging and edible cutlery and was munching his way through several free samples.

George stood alone; his hands stuffed in his pockets. Unsure of how he should spend his free time, he drifted through the crowds, taking in the architecture, until he found himself back in the atrium. It was now packed with jostling visitors and the air was warm and clammy. He tried to push his way past several large groups that were gathered in the centre of the room. It was almost impossible to penetrate the wall of bodies. He was just ducking out of one of the heavy glass doors when a stray strap from his backpack caught on the door handle and sent him tumbling into a lady who was lurking by the entrance.

She was dressed head to toe in black with heavy make-up to match. She turned towards George with a look of annoyance on her face.

"I'm so sorry," he said, looking up at her.

"Oh … it's OK," she said, looking shocked. "It's fine; accidents happen." She was suddenly a little less bristly.

Her sharply cut, black bob closely framed her face and her fringe hung heavy over her darkly lined eyes, which jumped about, looking beyond him into the crowd. George apologised again and turned away.

"There you are." It was Jess and the others. "We need to go to my dad's talk."

Professor Stone was presenting in the main lecture hall and had saved them a row near the front. They filed in with plenty of other students. George had never been in such a room: a large, steeply tiered auditorium that must have made the lonely lecturer at the front feel like a bear in a pit, surrounded by a bating crowd. George felt dizzy as he turned to look up towards the furthest rows.

Soon, the room was stuffed full and buzzing with anticipation. A grand-looking lady in a scholars gown introduced Professor Stone and loudly informed those gathered that today's debate would be on 'The promise or peril of editing your DNA.' George wasn't even sure he understood the title so wasn't surprised when he couldn't make head nor tail of the debate.

Jess' dad was impressive, none-the-less. He presented his research with stately confidence and charisma. George could see where Jess got her self-assurance from. The presentation went on for at least forty minutes longer than George could concentrate, and it seemed that Josh and Francesca felt the same way. Francesca was doodling in her pad, and Josh had shrunk into his seat while he grabbed forty winks. All the edible freebies had obviously sent him into a post-snack snooze.

George fidgeted; unaware of his tapping foot until the woman in front turned and scowled at him. He glanced at his watch but time was crawling past. The closer lunchtime came, the more he just wanted to escape next door. He tried to busy himself by peering around the room. As he looked towards the very back, he spotted the lady from the entrance, and to his surprise, she was looking straight back at him. As soon as she saw him looking, she turned her attention back to her book, showing no interest in the debate.

A loud and rapturous applause suddenly broke out, and people were on their feet. Jess was bouncing up and down grinning with pride. She scowled at George who was the only one in the room still seated. Taking the hint, he jumped up and joined the ovation. When he turned back to look for the woman again, she had gone.

Chapter 10: Security Threat

Jess was still buzzing as they made their way out onto the green where most people were having their lunch. Dr Root was bending the ears of Professor Stone and the other panelists and had left her students to find something to eat. There was a grand selection of food stalls hemmed around the central lawn, mostly run by young enterprising students, raising money for one cause or another. Josh had rejuvenated after his power nap and was sniffing at the air like a dog on the trail of his next meal. George, however, was fired up and ready to get down to the real reason that they were there.

"We need to find a way of sneaking next door without being noticed," he said, as the group sauntered across the lawn.

"Surely we've got time to eat," said Josh, being led by his stomach towards a thatched hut that was pumping out soulful reggae music and emanating tantalizing odours of the barbecue kind. The others followed.

George rolled his shoulders. He knew they needed to eat but was too on edge to stomach anything too exciting. He wandered over to a small cart where two young men were proclaiming the benefits of chemical free food. The queue was short and the selection minimal, but George grabbed an organic hot dog. He regretted his choice immediately, as it tasted worse than the sausages at school, which were often filled with lumps of gristle. Joshua's burger, fries and 'sunshine' slushy looked far more appetising, but time was ticking and they needed to make their move.

"So, what's the plan?" asked Will, halfway through his chicken wrap; spicy sauce dripping through his fingers.

"Well, I guess we just sneak off from here without Dr Root seeing us and then we can go next door to the museum – it's free to get in," said George, having discarded the rest of his sausage.

"What do we do then?" asked Francesca. "Do we even know where they'll be?"

"At the entrance at one o'clock."

Although, George realised that they would be pretty lucky if they managed to spot them in such a vast place.

"We'd better get moving then," said Jess. "Oh, and I guess it's probably best if we don't make it too obvious that we're following them. I don't fancy getting recognised from the pub, and they are not the kind of people I'd choose to share afternoon tea with."

The others nodded in agreement, none more than George who had witnessed the fury of Mr Phillips first hand.

Getting away from the college was easy enough. Dr Root was still deep in conversation, and the other Science Club members were engrossed in their lunches. At one end of the green stood the monolithic Queen's Tower, casting a shadow big enough to swallow a bus. They ambled casually into the darkness, sidled around the edge of the tower and slipped out of a side gate into the fume-filled street. The afternoon sky was patchy, in places heavy with the promise of rain, and the cool wind was swirling London grime up around their ankles. They trotted around the corner and within minutes were standing on the steps of The Natural History Museum, staring up at its fantastic façade. It was one of the most breathtaking buildings George had even seen. It looked like a palace; a shrine. And it was no less awe-inspiring when you stepped inside its arched doorway to be greeted by the mammoth skeleton of the mighty Blue Whale diving down from the cascading staircase. It took George's breath away.

They joined the bag search queues with the rest of the eager visitors, typically managing to choose the slowest line. Josh quickly got fed up with waiting, so bullishly weaved his way forward and escaped into the depths of the busy entrance hall. George, who was far less assertive, stood politely waiting as the couple up ahead seemed to unload a bottomless bag with an unending number of pockets. He was fidgeting with impatience as one o'clock rapidly approached. He couldn't take it any longer and, with an accentuated huff, switched queues, hoping that this one might go faster. He peered around the guests in front, and to his horror the security guard overseeing searches up ahead was none other than Mr Phillips.

George ducked his head down behind the man ahead of him, not believing what he saw. Slowly, he poked his head back out to check that he wasn't going insane. Mr Phillips was wearing a peaked security hat, a dark shadow of stubble and thick glasses, which obscured his face, but there was no mistaking his distinctive eyebrow.

Careful to stay out of Mr Phillips eyeline, George tried to get the attention of the others. He considered switching back to where Will and Francesca stood, but Mr Phillips was now pacing up and down, skimming the head of each queue. He looked on edge and extra alert, like a sentry on duty, waiting for the enemy to make the wrong move. His eyes flicked back and forth, looking for something – or someone; surely, not them. He must be waiting for his counterpart, the guy with the hooked nose.

George couldn't decide whether to back down or take the risk and hope that Mr Phillips would miss him as he coursed back and forth. It was a huge gamble. As he neared the front, he hesitated. The Japanese couple behind him were impatient to enter and urged him forwards, just as Mr Phillips turned and came back his way. This was the moment. George dropped his chin and eyes down and turned into the desk sideways. He must have looked like a bowing crab. At that moment, two desks down, Jess had opened her bag revealing her chemicals and potions. The lady searching her bag looked up and called Mr Phillips over just as he was brushing past a genuflecting George.

George urgently ripped open the zip of his bag, nearly spilling all its contents over the desk and floor. The old gentleman at the desk seemed uninterested and quickly ushered him through. George raced away to hide behind a nearby stone pillar and breathe deeply. He glanced back to see Jess re-packing her bag and Will and Francesca coming towards him with a look that told him they'd spotted the familiar security guard too.

"What the hell," said Will, as he reached George's hiding place. "That was a close call."

"Do you think he recognised us?" asked Francesca.

"I don't think so. I don't suppose he took much notice of us in the pub," Will replied, looking back around the pillar to wave to Jess.

"Did you see–" Jess said, unable to finish her sentence.

"Yes!" they all chorused.

"Well, at least we've found him. No wonder they wanted to meet here. He obviously works here."

"Yeah, wouldn't have had him down as a security guard though," said Will, "more like a security threat."

"Er, where's Josh?" asked Jess, looking out at the huge crowd gathered by the Blue Whale exhibit.

"He skipped the queue," said George.

"Great! It's like babysitting a toddler," Jess groaned.

"Boo!" Josh jumped out from behind them. "Ha! You guys are so easy to spook."

No one looked impressed. Jess shook her head in exasperation before filling Josh in on their discovery.

"Well, that was easy," he said. "So now we can go, right?"

"No, you idiot," Jess said. "He's waiting for the other guy. We need to wait and see what they do when he arrives."

"Maybe they're going to steal something from the museum; they talked about artifacts," said Francesca.

"Maybe." But George wasn't so sure. He had a feeling that their intentions were more sinister than stealing skeletons.

They loitered a while longer by the pillar until it became obvious that they were attracting a little unwanted attention. A group of giggling schoolgirls had latched their eyes on Josh. He wasn't helping matters, of course, by grinning his cockiest smile in their direction.

"Will you cut it out," Francesca said, a little too curtly, jabbing him in the ribs. "We don't need to make a spectacle of ourselves. We're trying to be inconspicuous!"

She grabbed him by the shoulders and swivelled him around to face the opposite direction, looking back over her shoulder and glaring down her nose at the competition.

"Look!" exclaimed George. "It's him – the other guy."

He had just walked in; still wearing his long, crumpled overcoat, heavy boots and faded red cap. You could have mistaken him for a tramp if it wasn't for the assured, assertive aggression in his stride. He looked like a general in commoner's clothes.

Slowly, with his eyes shrouded by the peak of his cap, he turned his head, surveying the crowd. All George could make out was his hooked nose and a harsh, tense jawline that carried a weight of rage and wrath. Something about the way he moved made George slink back behind the pillar. He was more convinced than ever that this man was responsible for the body in the woods and capable of even more.

Mr Phillips spotted his cohort and made a beeline towards him, almost shoving the closest security guard head first into the waiting guests. He almost bowed as he greeted him, not like you would a colleague or an old friend but with a subservience, an aura of respect. He escorted him through the crowd, past bag search and off towards the stairs.

"Come on," yelled George. "We mustn't lose them."

He sped from their hiding place, weaving in and out of the clusters of tourists, desperate not to lose sight of the two men as they disappeared down a flight of stairs. The others followed close behind, catching up with George at the top of the steps.

"Where does this go?" asked Jess.

"There's an education centre, toilets, café …" Francesca said, reading from the plaque on the wall.

"Let's go down," said George.

"Just try to look … casual," Jess added.

They descended into the basement, just in time to see Mr Phillips passing into the corridor that led to the bathrooms.

"I don't really want to follow them into there," said Josh, curling up his nose.

"No, look," said George, as they peered out from the corner of the stairwell.

Mr Phillips was loitering by a cupboard door. He was waiting; watching as people came and went until there was a pause in the traffic. He pulled something from his pocket and unlatched the cupboard door. Taking one last look, he swung the door open and vanished inside, leaving the door ajar.

"Shall we go in?" said George, unsure of their next move. He didn't fancy being stuck in a cupboard with Mr Phillips.

"We could just perch by the door and see if we can hear anything," suggested Francesca.

"Maybe just one of us," said Jess.

"You volunteering?" asked Josh, smiling.

"No, you do it, Captain Marvellous," she smiled back.

"Always comes down to me to be the hero, eh?"

"Just get on with it."

Josh stuck his hands in his pockets and sauntered over just as the other man strode out of the bathrooms, almost colliding with him. Josh froze and chuckled awkwardly.

"Er – sorry," Josh said. "Just going to the loo – you know – are they nice?"

The man grunted at him like a disgruntled drunk, and not even raising his head, pushed past and headed towards the cupboard. He glanced back towards Josh who was forced to follow through and enter the toilets. George and the others slipped back behind the entrance to the corridor as the man checked that the area was empty and ducked through the door that Mr Phillips had left open.

Josh leapt back out of the toilets and ran to grab the others. "I think he must have followed the other guy."

"Well, he didn't come this way," said Will.

"What the hell are they doing in there?" said Jess.

The door was still slightly ajar. George edged forwards, half expecting them to exit at any moment. He peered through the gap into the darkness but couldn't hear any voices, just the low hum of some sort of machinery.

"Can I help you?" a high-pitched voice questioned from behind them. It was another security guard. "That is a service entrance and not for public access," she said, slamming the door shut.

"Oh, right. We just thought it was – you know – another exhibit," said George.

"Or a disabled toilet," Josh added, trying to flash his most disarming smile.

"Which one of you is disabled?" she asked, frowning.

"Um, none of us but …"

"Which school party are you with?" she asked, trying to read the badges on their blazers.

"Putney High!" Josh blurted out, trying to distract her and cover his badge at the same time.

Jess pinched the bridge of her nose.

"I'm pretty sure that's a girls' school," the security guard said, frowning. "Where's the rest of your group?"

"In the Investigation Centre – over there," Francesca said. "We're just off in that direction. So sorry to have wasted your time."

They all scuttled off after Francesca, leaving the woman standing with her hands on her hips, watching them until she was convinced that they were where they were supposed to be.

"Great," said George, sliding down the wall and squatting on his heels. "What do we do now?"

"Not much we can do," said Will. "Even if we wanted to follow them, the door had no handle, just a type of keyhole."

George was still peering through the glass doors, not taking his eyes off the service entrance.

"Where do you think it leads?" he said, to no one in particular.

"I think we need to give it up, George," said Jess. "We've done all we can. It's nearly one thirty. We need to get back."

George didn't want to give up. He was determined to prove everyone, including his dad, wrong. He was sure these guys were up to no good and couldn't suppress the feeling that he could do something to stop them. He had never felt such compulsion before. Regardless of what the others thought, he was going to get through that door.

"You guys can go back; I'm staying here until they either come back out or I can get in."

"George, come on, mate, there's not much we can do about it, unless you want to go and ask that lovely security woman if she'll let us in," said Will.

"Maybe we should tell her someone has gone in there, unauthorised," suggested Francesca. "She could stop them from doing whatever it is they're doing."

"Or maybe she'd end up in a bag too," snapped George.

"Rather her than me," said Josh.

The debate continued. George slumped down onto the floor and glanced back out to the corridor, just in time to see the woman from the science fair stealing her way through the service door. George was back on his feet and running. He managed to lunge out and jam his outstretched hand into the gap just as the door was about to seal shut. The pain seared through his fingers as he tried to yank the door back open with his other hand. Will was there in seconds.

"Man, you're crazy," he said.

"What were you thinking?" said Francesca, as the others caught up. "You could have broken your fingers."

They were throbbing. He rammed them into his mouth, as if that would help.

"She went in there," he mumbled.

"Who?" asked Jess.

"The woman from the fair."

Before the others had time to question him further, Josh bundled them through the door. They stumbled into the void and collapsed in a pile on the cold stone floor. The door clicked shut and they were sealed in complete darkness.

Chapter 11: French Connections

"For God's sake!" yelled Jess, from somewhere at the bottom of the pile.

"She was coming – the security woman," Josh said, rolling himself off the top of the heap. "I just saved your butts."

"Yeah, great one," said Will, feeling his way to the door. "The good news is we escaped her wrath; the bad news is there's no handle on this side either."

"Shh, quiet," George whispered. "What can you hear?"

"Don't know, but I can't see a damn thing," said Josh.

George listened. Pipes were creaking and the humming sound buzzed in his ears. The air was stale and dry with a faint smell of gas. George reached behind him and slid off his backpack. He rummaged inside, found his phone and flicked on the light.

"Whoa! Not in my eyes, man!" said Will, as he was blasted full in the face by the white blaze.

"Sorry," whispered George.

They surveyed their surroundings. They were in a long corridor of a room, lined with pipework, cables, levers and various boxes full of switches and flashing lights. It was some sort of plant room, maybe controlling the heating or air conditioning. Without warning, a small alarm sounded and something churned into action blowing a gust of warm air down the tunnel. Something up ahead clanked and rattled.

"Um … I don't like this," Francesca said. "We should get someone's attention and get out of here."

"Let's just see where it leads," said George. "The woman from the science fair is down here too. Maybe she can help us get out."

"What woman?" asked Jess.

"I bumped into her outside the entrance. I spoke to her. She seemed – OK – strange but OK."

"Right," said Will. "So now we're chasing two crazy men and one strange woman. Perfect."

"Let's just go to the end, down there," George said, pointing the light ahead of them.

"OK, just to the end," said Jess.

They pulled themselves together and carefully picked their way through the crisscross of pipes and wires. At the end of the room was another door, this time with a handle. It opened up onto a long straight passageway, just wide enough to travel in single file. They all filed in. It was cramped and breathlessly warm.

George was up front with the light. He turned to see Josh appear last.

"Don't let the …"

It was too late, the door slammed shut.

"Josh!" the others hissed.

"What? It's got a handle. Don't panic, I'm not that stupid."

He yanked at the handle. It rattled and screeched as he pumped it up and down with no success.

"Jeez! What's with the doors around here?"

Will squeezed over to help, but the handle was useless.

"Whoever built this rat hole never expected anyone to get out," he said.

"Great, so now we really are screwed." Jess said. "We're supposed to be back at the college now. Dr Root is going to blow her stack."

"This has to lead somewhere; we'll just follow it. Those guys must have gone somewhere from here." George tried to reassure the others.

"Great! I can't wait to join their little party," Will snarled.

George could sense that Francesca's breathing, behind him, was becoming sharp and erratic. The confinement of the passageway, the darkness, the sensation of being trapped was all too much for her.

"We need to move – find some air," he said, taking her reassuringly by the hand.

He'd never held a girl's hand before, but it felt like the right thing to do. Her breathing slowed and she moved forward.

They pressed on with George, and the only light, up front. He was straining his ears, trying to catch any sign of trouble ahead, but all he could hear was the shuffling and scraping of tentative footsteps behind him in the diminishing light. The passageway seemed to narrow before it finally turned a sharp corner and ended with a heavy metal door: riveted, dusty and peeling.

"Please tell me that opens," said Francesca, with a tremor in her voice. "I don't want to die in this hole."

George pushed. It budged but was heavy and the peeling shards of metal cut into his hands.

"Lend me a hand, guys. It's heavy."

Will and Josh shuffled forwards, trying not to step on the girls' toes.

"Excuse me, Miss," Josh whispered to Francesca, as he squeezed past.

George was sure he could sense Jess' eyes rolling.

The three of them lent all their weight on the door until it reluctantly shuddered open a few inches at a time, revealing a staircase leading – down. They stood in silence, but even their breathing echoed up from the depths below, along with a drifting cool breeze.

"Fantastic," said Will, "would have been too convenient for it to go up, I guess."

George shone his light down. It wasn't as deep as it felt.

"It's not that far down. It must come back up at some point."

"Oh yes, because that's the saying; 'what goes down, must come back up'," said Jess, obviously starting to lose her cool. "We need to go back. This is getting ridiculous."

"We can't go back; there are two lots of locked doors behind us," said Will.

"And soon to be three if we carry on like this," said Jess.

"We don't have many options," said George. "Maybe a couple of us could go down and see where it goes. The rest can go back and see if we can get anyone's attention by banging on the doors back there."

"I think we should stick together," said Francesca.

"I agree with George," said Jess.

"Hang on," said Will. "We've only got one light, unless anyone else brought a torch or a phone."

"That decides it then, we stick together," said Francesca, grabbing hold of Josh's arm.

They slowly descended, the air getting cooler as they went. The steps beneath their feet were ornate, worn metal. Their footsteps chimed and echoed back up at them from below. The metal handrail was covered in dust and rust, and the air smelt stagnant. As George stepped off the last step, his shoes slapped against water.

"Urgh, guys – watch out – there's water down here."

He shone the light ahead to reveal a short circular tunnel, six foot high with water and grime oozing down its sides. The smell of stagnation was strong in his nostrils and the sound of dripping water punctuated the otherwise still, chilly air.

The others reached the bottom and joined him, skipping around the puddles as best they could.

"This looks like a sewer," said Josh.

"Oh my gosh, please tell me we're not wading through excrement," Francesca squeaked, trying to inspect the sodden debris at her feet.

"It's just water," said Jess, "but it does seem like it's a drain of some sort."

"There must be some sort of service or maintenance exit somewhere," said George, hopeful that he'd not lead them into a complete dead end. He was sure that the others must have gone this way, so it must lead somewhere. Suddenly, they were thrown into darkness as George's light went out without warning. Francesca screamed.

"What happened?" said Jess.

"It's OK," said George. "It's just my phone. It's gone into battery save mode."

"Wait," said Will, "look up ahead, there's light."

He was right. A faint light was highlighting a bend in the drain.

"Let's go," said Jess, "before that light goes out too."

They sloshed their way towards the light, rapidly giving up on trying to avoid the inky pools of water, which grew wider, deeper and darker the further they went towards the bend. George's leather shoes weren't holding back the damp, and soon his socks were soaked through.

As they turned the corner, they almost tripped over an abandoned duffle bag that was lying open in front of a large hole in the tunnel wall. The stonework had been hacked away, rubble spilling out on either side. Water pooled around the entrance, and a paraffin lamp stood softly hissing; balanced precariously on a pile of stone.

Jess was the first to climb over the strewn rock and peer through the opening. "Guys, it's a room; there are some stairs – up," she said, looking back at them with a relieved grin.

"Well, what are we waiting for?" said Will, grabbing the paraffin lamp and clambering through the debris.

Jess was right. The other side of the hole was a clean, rectangular, concrete room, no bigger than a garage – four plain, whitewashed walls, no signs, no adornments. It looked like the inside of a prison cell. A small, single light cord hung from the ceiling but there was no bulb. In the far corner of the room stood a spiral staircase, leading up to a hole in the ceiling with a metal plate at its head.

"What sort of room is this?" asked Francesca, shrinking into Josh's side. "I don't like the feel of it."

"Looks like the kind of place you might hide something … or someone," said Will, shivering.

"What do we think is up there?" asked Josh, glaring up at the small plate.

"It looks like there's something written on it," said Jess, as she approached the bottom step. "Pass me the lamp."

She climbed up the narrow, curling steps. "It says something in French: Liberté, égalité, fraternité."

"That's the French national motto. You know, on their old coins and stuff like that," said Will.

"OK, genius, what does that mean?" said Josh.

"Er … freedom, equality and brotherhood."

"Right - of course, I knew that, but I mean what does it say about what's behind the hatch?"

"Only one way to find out," said Jess, pushing on the metal plate and inching up to peek through the gap. "It looks like an office!"

"Is anyone in there?" asked George, now at the bottom of the steps, eager to see.

"Don't think so." She pushed the hatch wide open and popped her head up. "Coast is clear."

They all clambered up, helping each other squeeze through the skinny hole, emerging in the centre of a windowless office. They stood, dumbfounded. A sole desk stood against one wall, stacked high with papers. The opposite wall was covered with a mosaic of newspaper cuttings, maps, photographs and hand-written notes. Rolled-up parchments, stacks of books and a jumble of clothes and bags were piled in one corner while the other corner was occupied by a thin, single mattress; laid out on the hardwood floor, neatly made, corners tucked in. Bookcases lined either end. There didn't appear to be any doors out.

Josh was the last to enter the room. He slammed the hatch shut revealing an identical metal plate on the other side: a perfect embossed circle in the exact centre of the room. It could easily be covered by a rug or piece of furniture. George was sure that the room below was not meant to be found.

Will was shuffling through the paperwork on the desk as George made his way over to the opposite wall. There was so much to take in, but his eyes fell immediately on a newspaper article from the Chiddingham News. Bewildered, he ripped it from its hanging place. The headline read: 'Local MP Forces Closure of Troubled Tunnels.' There was a grainy black and white photo of several dignitaries outside the Pendleton town hall, and there, standing proudly in the foreground, was a face he recognised.

He stood and blinked. No doubt about it; right in the centre of the picture was a younger, and more spritely-looking, Mrs Hodge. He ran his tongue over his teeth and tried to swallow, but before any exclamation could leave his lips, Will was shoving a handful of papers under his nose.

"Look at these!" he shouted. "This is who we've been chasing down these damn tunnels!"

The others gathered around. George grabbed the first sheet. The soulless face of a criminal stared up at him. The hooked nose; the unshaven, sallow jowl; the dark, menacing eyes; and without the hat, you could see his shaved head, half blackened with the tattoo of a falcon in flight.

Victor Sokolov. MI5 Most Wanted.

"This is him – the guy from the pub," said George, holding the picture up for the others to witness. "He's a wanted criminal. I knew it!"

"Er, what's he wanted for exactly?" asked Josh.

"It says he is a Russian defector. Wanted in Russia for espionage, assassination and weapon theft. Wanted in Europe for espionage, robbery, weapon trafficking… you name it, he's done it," said Will, reading over George's shoulder.

"Sounds about as lovely as he looks," said Jess. "What about the other guy, Mr Phillips?"

"No mention of him," said Will, flicking through the MI5 classified papers. "But look at the rest of this stack; a whole list of pretty foul individuals."

They looked through each sheet, one by one.

Alex Allaman – Swiss, security systems hacker.

From his picture, he looked like a Swiss gentlemen of wealthy standing. Precisely groomed, dark hair and pencil thin moustache. Neat. Well dressed. Upper class. The kind of person you'd expect to offer you a seat on the train or open the door for a lady. Not your typical thug, but according to the paperwork, he was a master at breaking and entering – a top class burglar who had broken into government homes, national banks and several high-profile casinos.

Sabrina Fraulove – German, assassin.

A blond, busty beast of a woman. She towered over most men at 6ft 4 tall and looked like a weight lifter. At closer inspection, her photo revealed significant facial hair and several missing teeth. She was down for various counts of murder and kidnapping across five European countries. Since fleeing Germany, she had kept low until she cropped up again as part of Victor's gang, reportedly killing several security guards at a Monte Carlo casino heist with her bare hands.

Austin Van der Berg – Dutch, computer hacker.

He looked younger than the other two. His tied back, dreadlocked hair, wispy goatee and pierced bottom lip

made him look like your typical cocky lay-about.
However, he obviously kept himself busy, as his list of
crimes included several cases of major international
corporate fraud and hacking into government databases.
He'd lined his pockets with millions of euros of stolen
online funds as part of a hacker gang in his early twenties.
He may not have shown any signs of violence, but he was
a real threat to national security.

Angelika Volkov – AKA 'The Wolf' – Russian,
assassin and spy.

Dark, delicate, dangerous. The kind of woman who
would slip into the room, slit your throat and leave
without you even noticing her breath on your neck. Her
defining characteristic was the tattoo of the number 17
on her left thigh – the number of assassinations she had
completed by her 21st birthday. She had trained in
Russian Special Forces but defected, making her an
enemy of her country. Victor aided her escape to the UK
where she offered up Russian military secrets for safe
passage. Impatient and reckless, she soon evaded MI5
surveillance with Victor, becoming his second in
command. She killed with no remorse – single bullet to
the head, from any distance.

Jose Gonzalez – Mexican by birth, US Citizen,
Weapons scientist.

Short, plump, over indulged. You could effortlessly
picture him with a glowing cigar in one hand and a
smoldering handgun in the other. His shoulder length
curly hair and bushy moustache made him look shady and

arrogant. He had started life as a weapon scientist for the US Government but soon took his skills into the private sector – lured by drug lords and weapon traffickers. He was responsible for the murder of several British and American counter drug officials. Wanted in the USA and South America, he fled to Europe where he met Victor at a shady arms deal in Turkey. They had instantly bonded over their love of high tech weaponry.

They all had something in common. They were all enemies of their home states and Victor had recruited them based on their impressive joint skill set. Victor himself had a personal vendetta against the UK Government after MI5 tried to sell him back to the Russians. He could never return to Russia. There was a bounty on his head.

Each page had the words 'IN CUSTODY' stamped in bold red ink across their intimidating faces, except Victor's, which read 'MI5: MOST WANTED'.

How has he avoided capture?

"If these guys are in prison," said Will. "Why are this Victor dude and Mr Phillips so interested in them?"

"Maybe that's it," Francesca said, clapping her hands together. "Maybe *they* are the artifacts they need to retrieve. Maybe they are going to break them out."

"Yeah, maybe this Victor guy is trying to get his gang back together," said Josh. "That's what I'd do if someone busted up my team and locked them away."

"Makes sense, I guess," said George. "But break them out from where?"

"Er Guys," Jess had wandered back over to the desk. "There's a bunch of photos taken of our school here – look."

She held up a photo taken from the grounds, looking back at the schoolhouse.

"What the hell has our school got to do with any of this?"

"I don't know," said George. "But I reckon it's got something to do with the tunnel we found. Look at this news article. That's Mrs Hodge. She lives in my village, and I've got a nasty feeling she's got caught up in this too."

"She's a bad guy?" Josh asked, confused.

"No, I think that maybe she had some information about the tunnels – maybe they questioned her. Last week I went to deliver a paper to her house and it was empty. No one was there. I thought it was pretty weird at the time as she was always in – she's old; never goes out."

"Oh man, you don't think that was her in the woods?" said Will, looking a little pale.

George didn't want to think about it. "I don't know. None of it makes sense. But whatever they're plotting, they're going to a lot of effort to hide away down here."

George was tired and hungry and couldn't make any of it fit together inside his head. He couldn't think clearly.

"There must be something here that gives us some clue as to what they're planning. We need to keep looking."

The lamplight flickered and shadows danced across the walls as they moved about, continuing to rifle through the room's secrets. George found an old tube map, dated from 1929; books and papers hand written in French; news articles about the crimes the gang had committed and old photos of World War II bunkers. Some of the hand-written notes were on headed paper, stamped with the seal of the French Consulate. There had to be a connection. He stuffed the MI5 papers and the article about Mrs Hodge into his backpack. He was adamant he wasn't leaving without evidence this time around.

As the others were busy filtering through paperwork, Francesca made her way over to the makeshift bed. Either its owner was extremely house proud or never slept, as the bed sheets were completely crease-free and the mattress showed no imprint of slumbering limbs. Carefully, she untucked and turned back the sheets. There, buried at the foot of the bed, was a tattered brown envelope. She slipped her finger into the opening, eased out the sealing flap and upturned the contents onto the bed. Several passports, a lighter, French branded cigarettes and a handful of Euros, Pounds and Dollars. She opened the first passport. It was French and the picture was Mr Phillips for sure, but the name read Philippe Bernard. She grabbed the envelope and its contents and continued searching the bed.

They were so engrossed in their treasure hunt that none of them noticed the paraffin lamp running low on fuel. It fizzed and spluttered and seconds later died out. They were thrown, once more, into complete darkness.

"Jeez man," someone cursed.

Chapter 12: Old Brompton Road

"George!"

"Yes."

"You got any juice left in that phone?" It was Will.

Sliding it out of his back pocket, George looked at the dimly lit screen. "It's low, really low."

"Don't turn the light on, it will drain the battery immediately," said Jess, a faceless voice to his left. "We need to call my dad. Tell him where we are and that we're safe. They'll be sending out a search party by now."

"But where are we? How can we tell them, if we have no idea where we are?" Francesca chimed in from the other side of the room.

"We'll have to give them directions from where we left the museum, by the toilets."

"Guys, I think maybe we're inside the French Consulate," said George. "The headed paper I found is addressed Cromwell Place."

"That's directly opposite the museum, we've travelled under the Cromwell Road," said Jess. "Perfect, let's call him and tell him. It will take no time for him to get to us."

"There's only one problem," said George. "I still have no signal. We need to get above ground."

With that, loud footsteps sounded from above and voices; French voices. Silence descended in the office as everyone froze. They waited, but the voices just grew louder, right above their heads.

"Who's that?" whispered Josh.

"It might be Consulate Staff," Jess whispered back.

"Or Mr Phillips," said Francesca. "I found his passport. It looks like his real name is Philippe Bernard."

"What the hell! Do we get their attention or not?" Josh said.

"Either way, I think we should get out of here," said Jess. "We need to get to somewhere with a signal and get help. These people are far too dangerous to mess with."

"How do we get out?" said George. "We need to find an exit – there must be one."

They slowly crept around the edges of the room, fumbling around in the dark. Someone kicked over a pile of papers that fluttered across the floor.

"Shh," hushed Jess.

"There's no door," breathed George.

"I'm not going back down that hole," Francesca squeaked.

"Ow!" Josh and Will had collided, sending something rolling across the floor and bouncing off the opposite wall with a deep thud.

The voices upstairs stopped and they all held their breath.

"We've been rumbled," whispered Josh.

George decided to light up his phone, just to find an exit. He turned to reach into his back pocket, but his sweaty hands fumbled and his phone slipped from his grip. He lurched forwards to grab it, smashing into the bookcase to his right. Expecting an avalanche of books to engulf him, he tensed, but to his surprise not a single book wavered.

"What was that?" Will said.

"It's me," said George. "This bookcase – I think…"

He skimmed his hands over the shelves and could feel the soft, rounded edges of each book's spine. He tugged at one or two but none of them budged. He pushed, pulled and yanked, convinced that something would give, and sure enough, there was a sudden movement, just an inch.

"It's moving. Help me – it could be a way out."

Several pairs of feet made their way towards him. Jostling and stumbling, they all leant on the bookcase and slowly it depressed into a recess and slid open, revealing a concrete corridor that was lit by a low green hue of a light.

"Genius, George," said Will, slapping him on the shoulder.

George dipped down and grabbed his phone from the floor as they all silently seeped out into the corridor, relieved to be back in the light. The smooth, grey, concrete wall stretched out to their left and right. At one end there was a heavy door, guarded by a metal gate, and at the other end, a wooden loft hatch but no ladder. Looking from one end to the other, George realised their choices were minimal. On one hand, the hatch led up but maybe into the path of Victor and Philippe, on the other hand, another mysterious door. He wasn't sure he favoured either option.

Jess was the first to move further into the open space. She nodded towards the hatch, but Francesca shook her head and pointed to the threat above. The voices had stilled, but that didn't mean they'd gone. Will pointed to the gated door.

"We should check this out," he said, careful to keep his voice down.

"We need to go up," whispered Jess.

"How are we going to get up there?"

"We can drag the chair or desk over. I'm sure we could reach from there."

Francesca was shaking her head again. "I don't want to stick my head up there, just to have it chopped off by those ghastly men."

They were at a crossroads, again.

"We should at least check out the door," George said. "It might be an exit. If not, we can wait until we're sure no one is up there and try the hatch."

"Great idea," said Josh. "I was about to say the same thing."

"Yeah, right," said Will, as he passed Josh on his way to the gate.

At closer inspection, the iron gate concertinaed and collapsed with minimal effort. There was no padlock and the metal was slippery with oil. Someone had been keeping it maintained. That didn't fill George with comfort. He was about to raise his concerns but was cut off by the pounding noise of feet overhead. Just one set this time, loud and echoey, followed by the opening and slamming of a door. Dust showered down from the wooden hatch at the other end of the corridor, catching in the glow of the light.

They were all staring up when the metal gate began to rattle, and the air was filled with a distant rumbling that resonated from behind the door.

"Maybe we should go back down the hole," Francesca muttered under her breath.

The rumbling dissipated and stillness returned. Will placed his hand on the door handle, pushed hard, expecting resistance. The door flew open, he lost his balance and pitched forward. Josh grabbed him just in time before he toppled out into the blackness. Regaining his balance, he pinned his arms between the doorframe and gently leant out.

"It's a track; six foot down I reckon. Train tracks."

"What like a tube line?" Josh said, peering over his shoulder.

Will suddenly leapt down.

"Will!" screeched Francesca.

"Shh!" said Jess. "Keep your voice down."

"I'm OK," Will called up from below. "It's not far down."

"You might get run down by a train. Please be careful," Francesca pleaded, clasping her head in her hands.

"I don't think we can expect a train any time soon," he said, his face re-appearing just below the doorstep. "One end of the tunnel is collapsed in."

With that, Josh leap-frogged over Will's head.

"That would explain the noise we heard," said Jess, turning back to George and Francesca. "It must have been a train – maybe on an adjacent line. Come on. We can follow the track – it must lead to a station."

Before George could digest it all, Jess has vanished from his side, plummeting into the darkness. He turned to Francesca.

"Would you like to go first?" he offered, standing aside.

"Um, OK, thanks," she replied, gracefully perching on the edge of the threshold and lowering herself down.

George was last. He took a last glance up at the hatch and wondered what Philippe and Victor were doing up there. Would he be able to stop them with the information he had? He felt a pinch of disappointment. He so desperately wanted to solve the riddle and prove to his dad, and the beefheads at school, that he wasn't a wimp or a fool. He felt like he'd come so close. Jess was right though. The stakes were too high now that they knew what kind of people they were dealing with. It was a job for the police, and surely they had enough evidence to make someone believe them. They could point them towards the Consulate, the hidden room; show them the MI5 paperwork they'd found and send out a search for Mrs Hodge. Surely that was enough to prove to everyone that they weren't frauds.

But as he lowered himself down onto the rails, doubt was creeping through him like a gnawing insect. What if they got back to school and were hauled in to see Mrs Hamilton, accused of truancy, reprimanded for disobeying school rules, found guilty of breaking and entering, stealing secret documents and causing mass hysteria? What if Mrs Hodge had just been sunning herself in Spain and Philippe and Victor really worked for the museum and his imagination had led him and his friends on a wild goose chase? His forehead sweated, ears pulsed and heart raced with the sensation of sheer shame and frustration.

"Hey, George, mate!"

"George, you OK?"

He was bent down with his head buried between his knees.

"Did you hurt yourself jumping down?" Will asked.

George looked up and saw the faces of his friends looking down at him, their eyes filled with concern. They were in this together, and for the first time he realised that that meant more than anything. He was no longer the lone fool that everyone laughed at; the shy, wimp of a boy who everyone teased; the quiet, loner who everyone else ignored. He had friends; friends who cared.

"I'm fine," he said. "In fact, I'm great. Let's get out of here."

He jerked up, filled his lungs with the warm dusty air and strode ahead, taking the lead.

Within a few feet, the feeble light that had escaped from the doorway had been swallowed up by the enveloping darkness.

"We're going to need that light," said Josh. "We could trip on these tracks…"

"Or any of the rubble and rubbish down here," said Will.

The line looked like it had been unused for almost a century and undisturbed for just as long.

"Even if I just light up the screen," said George, "we'll barely have enough power to get to the end of this line."

"Lighter!" yelled Francesca.

"What?"

"I found a lighter back in the office. It's in my bag somewhere," she said, her face buried in her backpack.

"Great, but no offence, a lighter isn't gonna' get us much further," said Will, half smiling.

"There's plenty of stuff down here we can burn," said Josh, kicking through the debris at his feet. "Look, here's a hunk of wood – it's pretty dry – should go up like a bonfire."

"Worth a try, I guess," said George, filtering through the rubbish around him.

Between them, they found a few sticks and an old green overall. They ripped up the fabric and made three impromptu torches. Francesca handed over the lighter and the torches lit first time, sending plumes of smoke drifting up towards the tunnel's ceiling. There was just enough light to make their way carefully along the splintered track.

They followed the line around several bends, up and down a subtle incline and, just when they thought it would never arrive at a destination, they rounded a corner, to be finally faced with a platform.

"We did it!" whooped Josh, springing up onto the platform, almost singeing his hair with his now glowing baton.

The others pulled and pushed each other up until they were all standing beside him like late night commuters. The platform was empty, and in places, inches thick with greasy, black dust.

"Look at the state of this place," Francesca said, tiptoeing through the grime.

"I don't know … looks like most other London Underground stations, I reckon," Will chuckled. "Just needs a few rats and it's spot on."

"Rats!" Francesca yelped.

"No, there are no rats," Jess quickly reassured her, glaring at Will, who shrugged in apology.

"This place must have been shut a good few years ago," Josh said, wandering down the platform and running his finger over the sooty tiles. "What line do you think it is?"

"Could be Piccadilly line," said Jess. "But what station is it?"

"Let's find our way up and out, we can worry about the rest later," said Will.

They followed the platform, towards the first hole in the wall that they could see. In places, ornate brown and green tiles could be spotted hiding beneath the layers of dust and grime, and as they reached the small archway, a mosaic of tiles spelled out the words 'To the stairs'.

"Perfect!" exclaimed Francesca.

It all looked quite promising, if a little dated, but their spirits soared as they exited the passage to see a wide bank of steps leading up.

"Race you to the top," Josh hooted, snatching a head start.

George caught his foot on the first step and nearly tumbled but managed to keep upright as he tailed after Will and Jess. It was almost impossible to see where the steps ended. The light from the torches was fading and barely penetrated the heavy air. Another set of tiles at a break in the flight, announced 'Ticket Office This Way', so George put his head down and powered up the second flight, his thighs burning with the exertion. He was about to give in and slow down when he suddenly crashed into Will's backside.

"What the … why'd you stop?" He leant around Will, who was now scowling at George, and quickly realised that they'd hit a dead end. His heart sank. There in front of them was a solid brick wall. The ticket office was no longer.

"What … why … I don't understand," he spluttered.

"That just about sums up our day!" fumed Will, throwing out a hefty kick at the brick barricade. "Why would they do that?"

"It's an abandoned station," said Jess, turning around and slumping down against the bricks. "They obviously don't want people poking around down here. God knows how long ago they bricked it up."

"Well that's just perfect. Are we ever gonna' see the bloomin' daylight again?" Will was losing it. He kicked out at the wall again, this time crunching his toe in the effort. He screamed at the wall as if it was its fault and hurled his torch in frustration, sending embers flying in all directions.

"Watch it!" shouted Josh, jumping back from the fireworks.

"I think we should try to calm down," Francesca said, from behind them. "There's surely another way out. I saw other footprints down there in the dirt, so someone has been down here recently. There must be a way in and out."

"What other footprints?" asked Jess.

"Back there, just about where you guys started whooping and hollering."

"Great – just great. So now we're trapped and possibly not alone."

"Come on, it can't be that bad. Let's go down and follow them. They could lead us out," said Josh, starting to slouch back down the stairs.

They had no alternative so followed in silence. George was starting to fear that they were well and truly lost. His phone was still out of signal, and the wooden stump in his hand was close to spluttering out. He didn't have the heart to remind the others that it wouldn't be long before they could be confined to darkness, indefinitely. They had to find a way out soon.

They alighted the staircase a lot less enthusiastically than they had ascended. Francesca grabbed George by the arm, taking him by surprise. She yanked his hand around to the left, shining the firelight onto the floor ahead of them.

"There," she said, "footprints."

They followed the invisible stranger's lead and passed into a tight central concourse. A sign on the wall read, 'Brompton Road, est. 1906', but George was distracted by what lay beyond. Pinned to the wall was an old map. It showed most of the southeast of England and had been marked up with scrawling crosses and circles. The surrounding tiles had been written on with red ink, most of which was faded and impossible to read. George lifted his torch to get a better look. Some of the scribblings were legible. Air raids, defences, Nazis. Further along the wall were lists of names and numbers. The map was dated 1940.

"World War II" he said under his breath.

"A little more light over here, mate," said Will from a few feet away.

"Sorry," George said.

"Look at this," said Will, pointing past a tangle of pipework and down a small set of curving stairs. At the bottom, George could just make out a collection of folding chairs, a blackboard and some old trunks, covered in tattered dustsheets and stained with rusty streaks. They descended the stairs and peered around the small room. Two old gas masks hung from a peg on the wall.

"This place may have been shut for a while, but it looks like it was well used at some point," said Will, tentatively plucking at the heavy sheets.

"Maybe it was an old war bunker, or even a military hideout," said George, feeling excited by the discovery. "Felix told me that loads of old tunnels and abandoned hideouts in the southeast were used during the war. This must be one of those."

"Ha! Look at this," called Josh, leaning against a heavily riveted and reinforced door. A grimy, stained piece of paper had been taped to the metal with red duct tape. It read, 'WARNING – Sheer drop behind this door – Do Not Enter.'

"That would put anyone off," he laughed. "Do you think it's true or maybe it's a trick and that's where they stashed all the doughnuts?"

"Don't be ridiculous," snapped Jess. "Don't you dare open that!"

"Alright, I was only trying to lighten the mood," he huffed.

The room was oval shaped and the staircase continued further down to another identical room. Around the edges of the room were several doors, air vents guarded by metal bars, pipework, large electrical junction boxes and fuse boards. Something brown and glutinous oozed from cracks in the brickwork.

They slowly made their way around the room. The next door modelled a more recent-looking bright yellow warning: 'DANGER OF DEATH: 630 volts and moving trains'. Josh was about to make another jovial comment when the ground started to shake and the air was filled with a familiar rumbling. A warm gust of air puffed through the cracks of the doorframe, making George's, already haywire hair, stand on end, and extinguishing the last of the flames that were clinging to his torch.

"That must be a live line!" shouted Jess over the magnifying noise. "That has to be a way out!"

"Yeah, great idea. Let's go through the door that says 'Danger of Death'!" Josh yelled back. "I prefer my chances with the doughnut cupboard!"

The noise faded as rapidly as it had arrived.

"I don't think this is at all a joking matter! We're lost, stuck down a hole and running out of options," Jess said, slamming her fist against the rusted metal.

With that, the whole room filled with the deafening roar of an explosion. The floor shook and they were thrown off their feet. George slammed into the wall and fell to the ground as a metal grate from high above them came clattering through the pipework and crashed down onto Will, forcing him to the floor like a collapsing house of cards. George cowered, burying his head beneath his arms.

The booming noise reverberated around the room as more debris fell from above. George grabbed at his ears; they felt like they were splitting right down to the drum. The noise was so immense that he couldn't hear his own voice as he screamed out in pain. Something had slammed into his back – hard and sharp.

George struggled to control his breathing as the room filled with choking, thick dust; filling his lungs and making him gag. The noises around him were muffled and distant and his eyes were streaming; he could barely see. His phone had landed face up and its screen gave off a weak, foggy light, so he crawled towards it, trying desperately to recover his bearings.

From somewhere to his right, someone was groaning.

"Will?" George tried to call out, his words clinging to his gritty throat. "Will, you OK?"

"Man – something hit me – my head," Will replied.

"I'm coming to you."

"Guys, is everyone OK?" It was Jess' voice from his left. "Everyone try to get to George's light. Josh? Francesca?"

"I'm here. I'm OK, I think," said Francesca, her voice shaky.

"Josh?"

"I'm here! I can't hear a damn thing!" Josh shouted, still partially deafened by the blast.

Slowly, they emerged from the dark like zombies, drawing themselves towards the light; faces, clothes and hair coated in a ghostly dust. Will seemed to be in the worst shape. His head was bleeding from a small gash just above his temple. He'd deflected the blow with his arm, but the metal plate had torn through his blazer.

"We need to stop that bleeding," said Francesca, wiping her eyes with her sleeve and trying to inspect the wound.

"It's not that bad – I swear," he said, feeling his sticky hair.

"Wait, I've got something." George suddenly remembered; he'd packed a first aid kit. It was basic but at least had some plasters. He turned to get his pack off and felt a shooting pain up his right side. "Argh!"

"What's wrong?" Jess asked, helping grab the pack from his shoulder.

"Something hit my back."

Jess pulled up his shirt. "You've got a nasty red mark but nothing worse. Your bag must have saved you from the impact."

She pulled out the first aid kit and his bottle of water. Francesca washed Will's gash, dried it and used the plasters as best she could. The blood was already congealing. They all took a swig from the bottle, and George splashed his face.

"So, what do we think that was all about then?" Josh said, prodding his ears in the hope of recovering his hearing.

"I don't want to know," said Francesca, her voice wavering again. "I just want to go home."

"That's exactly where you should be!"

They all turned to be blinded by a beam of torch light, shone directly down at them from the top of the steps; its owner masked by the glare.

From: J21
To: Chief
Cc: Group - BOP
Re: Bird of Prey {Encrypted}

Update 24.1

Urgent.

We lost track of the Bird of Prey somewhere between the French Capital and Dover.

We have reason to believe it crossed the channel a few days ago and is already on UK soil.

We have raised all alerts and set all agreed protocols into play.

We are making the assumption that it will try to rendezvous with its previous flock, so we have moved them to the agreed higher security enclosure and increased security at The Hub.

I will personally keep you informed of all updates.

End.

Chapter 13: The Vault

"You shouldn't be here," the voice continued, as the light moved steadily down towards them. "I don't know what you think you're doing, but this is no place for children. You are in real danger."

They sat mesmerised, huddled together on the floor, like a pack of trembling cubs, glaring up at the intruder entering their den.

Josh was the first to speak. "I think we worked that out by ourselves, thanks."

"Are you injured?" the voice went on, circling behind them.

They must have looked like soldiers after a battle: their blazers filthy; their faces camouflaged with soot. Will's head was smeared with blood and George's shoes had split open.

"We're fine; just a little shaken," said Jess, turning her head to follow the light. "Who are you?"

"That doesn't matter. You need to get out of here, now. Get back up to the concourse and try all the exits until you find one that leads up to street level. You're looking for a red door." With that the torch came looping through the air towards them. "Take this and get out."

Will managed to catch it before it crashed to the ground. He fumbled with it in his hands and eventually turned it onto the stranger, just as she was lifting herself up into the lattice of pipework. It was her, the lady from the college. Strong and nimble, she effortlessly pulled herself up through the pipes and into an opening high above their heads. Will followed her with the torch beam until she had vanished completely from sight.

"Wait!" George called after her. "We need your help!" But she was gone.

"Who the hell was that?" said Josh. "Spiderwoman?"

"I think it was that woman – the one from the fair. I told you she came in here," said George, straining his neck to see where she had gone.

"Well, whoever she was, she was right. We need to get out of here," said Jess, getting up, readjusting her bag and brushing herself down. "We need to check every door. She said there's a red one that leads out. Come on."

Josh and Jess helped Will to his feet. He reluctantly accepted their support, a little wobbly at first. George picked up his phone, stuffed the first aid kit and water back inside his bag and followed the others up the stairs.

Everything looked completely different with the aid of a high-powered torch. Archways, side passages and new doors appeared that hadn't been visible before. They systematically visited each feasible exit, most of which were sealed shut. It was impossible to tell the colour of most of the doors as they were all caked in a crusted, murky veneer. They had dipped in and out of several side passages and were starting to lose track of where they'd been.

"We've tried this one already," said Francesca, pulling at another rusted handle. "I'm sure of it."

"No, we haven't," said Jess. "I've been keeping track of where we are. This is definitely new."

"I'm sure we've been here."

"I'm sure we haven't!"

"What makes you the oracle?"

"I think my brain has a slightly higher capacity than yours…"

"Well then, think us up a damn way out of here!"

"Er, guys – this one is definitely new," interrupted George, who had moved on ahead. There were signs of red paint flecks amongst the grey and someone had painted the words 'Ammunition Store' in red across the front.

He tried the handle and it glided open with ease. He felt a flurry of anticipation in his chest. Clean, crisp air flowed from the opening. Something about this room felt different.

"Will, bring the torch over here," he called back towards the others.

Stepping over the raised threshold, he could feel something unfamiliar beneath his feet. The gritty, uneven concrete was replaced with smooth, polished, inky-black sleekness. As Will approached with the light and the view ahead of George exposed itself, he couldn't believe his eyes. There in front of him, was a room that looked like the entrance lobby to an ultra-modern hotel: gleaming from floor to ceiling in glossy, black tiles and panels of highly polished frosted glass.

The others gasped as they entered.

"What is this place?" Francesca breathed.

"I have no idea," George said. "But this must be the door she meant."

As they moved further in, they must have triggered a motion sensor. Low-level lights illuminated around their feet and a screen, previously hidden from view behind a sheet of glass, buzzed to life above a solid black marble desk. A message flickered onto the screen.

'Welcome to Unit 256, please present your weapons and ID.'

A small green cube popped up from within the marble desk, revealing some sort of scanning device. It swept a web of red light across their astonished faces.

"What the hell is that?" said Josh, frozen still, as if pinned by a sniper's target.

"I think it's scanning us," said Will. "I've seen similar technology that my dad uses for security systems. It's not quite as cool as that though."

The red light swept over them one more time then vanished, sending the green cube sinking back into its hole.

"Did we pass?" whispered Jess, not daring to move.

"Um, I guess we'll find out," said George.

They stood, waiting for the verdict, but nothing happened. The screen was empty except for a single flashing bar – awaiting a new message.

"How long do we wait?" Jess asked.

"Screw this," said Will, striding around to the other side of the long, imposing desk. "Whoa!"

"What?" The others quickly joined him.

The other side of the desk was lined with small flat screens, each had been smashed and the desk was littered with tiny fragments of glass. There were several buttons, a keypad, and lying on the floor, an upturned stool and an abandoned handgun.

"So, whoever was manning the reception has obviously gone on an emergency loo break," said Josh, picking up the gun and turning it over in his hands.

"Put that down!" yelled Jess. "You haven't got a clue how to use it; you could kill someone!"

"I'll have you know, I'm a pretty good shot. Been clay pigeon shooting with my dad plenty of times," he said, holding the gun up and eyeing up a shot.

"Don't be ridiculous, put it down!"

There was a muffled crackling from behind the glass.

"What was that?" said George, jerking his head around to see where the noise had come from.

"Sounds like a radio," said Francesca.

"It came from behind this door," said Will, turning towards the heavily frosted glass that stood sentry behind the desk. "Maybe one of these buttons opens the doors."

He started punching each button in turn. Nothing budged. The keypad had been half ripped off; wires exposed. He lifted it up to inspect it further. As he did, a buzzer sounded and the giant glass panels rumbled into action, sliding apart and opening the way into a room full of surveillance and computer screens. Lights sprang to life revealing another heavy desk and two thin corridors disappearing down either side of the bank of screens.

They rounded the desk, following the radio noise and almost tripped over the bodies of two men, collapsed on the floor, blood pooling from their heads. Will's hand managed to reach Francesca's mouth just as she began to scream, muffling the sound and drawing her back from the ugly scene.

"Shh," he hushed in her ear. "It's OK."

"Are they dead?" she whimpered.

"Er … I think so," said Josh, who was inspecting a little closer. "They look like security guys."

Francesca sobbed and clamped her hands over her own mouth. The crackling sound repeated.

"It's these two-way radios," said Josh. "Here, on the floor."

One had been flung aside and was by the first man's foot; the other was still wedged under the second man's hip. Josh carefully lifted him and freed the device.

"That's gross," said Jess. "How can you touch him?"

"We might need these, by the looks of things," said Josh, hooking them to his belt. "There's another torch here too."

"We just need to leave, actually." But as she said it, the glass doors rumbled closed.

Will and George raced around the desk but couldn't make it to the doors in time.

"OK. I'm – trying – not – to – panic," Francesca said, breathing deeply between each word. "We are stuck in a room with two dead bodies!" she erupted, the deep breathing obviously not helping.

"Look, the lady said the red door. This is the closest thing we've seen to a modern facility since we left the museum," said George, calmly.

"What if she killed them," said Francesca, pointing at the bodies but refusing to look at them. "What if she's lying to us?"

"I trust her," he said. "I don't know why, but I do. She didn't try to hurt us. I think she's on our side. I reckon there's an exit in here somewhere. I say we take the radios, split into two groups, take a corridor each and whoever finds an exit first, calls the other group."

"Maybe she's police," said Will, grabbing one of the radios from Josh. "I agree with George. I say we split up and find a way out."

"Great idea," said Jess. "I'm with Will."

"OK," said George, looking over at a quivering Francesca and Josh, who was still pretending to shoot invisible targets. "We'll … er … take the right corridor."

He was sure he'd feel safer with Will and Jess but wasn't sure that leaving Francesca and Josh alone was a good idea. At least Josh had a gun and, supposedly, knew how to use it.

"Keep in contact," instructed Jess. "But keep the noise down. We don't need to attract any unwanted attention."

"OK – good luck."

As they went their separate ways, George felt considerably more vulnerable in a group of three. He was starting to regret his decision. They passed a cupboard, not far down the corridor. It was hanging open, several guns missing from the mounted clasps.

"Shall we take another one?" whispered Josh, his eyes lighting up.

"Not unless Francesca knows how to use it because I certainly don't," replied George, looking doubtfully in Francesca's direction. She shook her head vehemently. "Let's just keep going. The sooner we get out of here the better."

They pressed on down the long, thin, gleaming corridor, the lights springing to life as they passed, but there wasn't a door, exit or even a nick in the perfectly smooth walls. After a while, the path ended with a single blackened glass door. Etched into the glass were the words; 'UNIT 256'.

"This is the only exit. Call the others. Tell them what we've found," said George to Josh, who stuffed the gun in his pocket and unhooked the radio from his belt.

"Guys," Josh whispered into the handset. "We've found a door at the end of the corridor. Over."

There was static – nothing else.

"Guys, you there. Over." Josh repeated.

Still no response.

"What do we do now?" Francesca asked, looking hopefully at George for an answer.

"Um, I guess we see what's behind the door and then try to get hold of them again," he said, a little unsure of what else they could do.

The door slid open easily and they snuck through, George first. The space opened up into a vast two-storey, vaulted crypt. The walls were ornately tiled and finely bevelled pillars stood sentry around a large central pit. It reminded George of the Roman Baths he'd studied in History. At the lower level, each side of the rectangle housed several darkened archways; so dark, it was impossible to tell what lay within them. The central pit was empty except for an impressive marble slab. George almost mistook it for an altar, but the core was missing and several screens and pieces of unidentifiable technology rested on its edges. It looked like some sort of control centre.

They edged further in and looked up. A fine mist hung in the air and there was a strong smell of burning. A balcony ran three quarters of the way around the upper perimeter; security cameras every two metres. George noticed several had been damaged, wires hanging down and glass smashed. That's when he saw, at the far end of the balcony, a gaping hole in the wall.

"Guys, I think this is where the explosion came from," he said, as quietly as he could. "The whole of that back wall is missing."

Josh opened his mouth to answer but was cut off by the loud crackling coming from his hand. It made them all jump.

"Shh, turn it down," said Francesca, backing away behind one of the pillars.

"It might be the others," said Josh.

Just then, voices echoed from one of the archways on the left and then more from the right. A beam of light appeared on both sides highlighting shattered glass, contorted steel bars and the outline of several figures climbing through the mess.

Francesca gasped and dragged Josh and George backwards into the shadows. "It's them," she squeaked.

As they appeared out of the darkness, you could make out the faces from the MI5 mug shots. Every one of them as gruesome-looking as described. Victor was striding ahead, glory and defiance in his stance. He cradled a large machine gun and several more handguns hung from his waist. He had discarded the cap, exposing his identifying tattoo.

Alex Allaman and Sabrina Fraulove emerged behind him. Sabrina roared like a bear, beating her chest as she spotted her advancing comrades from the opposite side of the room. The once obese Mexican, Jose Gonzalez, was the hardest to identify. Captivity had done him a favour and left him half the man he was before, although his thick moustache and lank, curly hair had survived. He entered the vaulted room and kicked out viciously at something on the floor, spitting in disgust. George could just make out the feet of another fallen guard.

How many have they killed?

A slip of a woman, Angelika Volkov, appeared, her oily black hair slicked back into a tight knot. She was accompanied by Philippe with Austin Van der Berg trailing behind them, dragging his feet. All the convicts wore petrol blue overalls and looked pallid and drawn. Angelika saw Victor and a sly grin spread across her icy face.

"You did it!" she screamed, punching her fist in the air.

She was about to exit from under the overhead balcony when the sudden crack of gunfire exploded around the room. Someone was raining bullets down on them from above. They ducked for cover and Victor responded; fire for fire.

George twisted to see who they were shooting at. He saw something black streak across the balcony. It was her, the woman from the fair. She returned fire as she darted from one refuge point to the next. She was making her way towards the gap in the wall. Was she trying to stop their escape?

Francesca had sunk to the floor and was covering her ears with her hands. The exchange of shots intensified. Bullets ricocheted off the walls and clattered down around them, skidding across the glassy marble floor.

"We need to get the hell out of here," said Josh, trying to pull Francesca to her feet.

"What about Will and Jess?" said George, backing towards the door through which they'd come. "What if that hole is the only way out?"

"Then we find the others, wait it out and leave when this nightmare is over. Come on Francesca, please get up!"

George had a sudden thought. He grabbed his phone – one bar. He had one bar of signal!

He dialled 999 and turned to make for the door, slipping on a stray bullet and losing his balance. His phone tumbled out of his grip. He lurched to his knees to grab it, only to find himself staring at his own reflection in the surface of the shiniest pair of shoes he'd ever seen. George's head drooped.

Of course.

Mr Jefferson stood towering over him, a twisted smile spreading across his face. He bent down and retrieved the phone, dangling it in front of George.

"I thought I said I never wanted to see this again, Jenkins!" he snarled.

"Mr Jefferson?" Josh had finally managed to lift Francesca from the ground and stood saucer-eyed. "Oh man - are we glad to see you. How did you find us? We need to get the—"

"Shut up, Palmer!' Mr Jefferson spat, as more shots echoed around the room. "I have no interest in listening to your insane drivel. Get down on the floor and join Jenkins, both of you!"

Josh's draw dropped.

"But …"

Mr Jefferson lifted a gun from inside his jacket, pressed it firmly into Joshua's forehead and forced him to his knees. Francesca collapsed back onto the cold floor, babbling uncontrollably.

The gunfire suddenly died, and Victor's voice could be heard barking in Russian. George watched over his shoulder as Angelika Volkov scaled up a ladder to the balcony and searched for the female assailant. George didn't speak Russian, but he could make out from Victor's body language that the report back from above was negative; she had vanished. Victor raged, firing a round of shots into the balcony, causing a shower of rubble to cascade down from above. He dispensed more orders and the others followed Angelika's lead up to the balcony and through the hole in the wall. Victor was the last to ascend the ladder. He turned in their direction as he reached the exit and looked straight into George's eyes. George felt his breath catch in his throat.

"Deal with them and then deal with all this," Victor said to Mr Jefferson. "Join us when you're done." With that he turned and left; his job done.

"Well, well," Mr Jefferson grinned, pointing the gun at George. George had never seen him smile, and it was probably a good thing too. One half of his face contorted, and the twitch in his bug-like eye intensified. It was as if the muscles on that side of his face just didn't work, leaving him with a lopsided grimace.

"What are you staring at?" he hissed, moving his face within inches of George's. George flinched. "Am I making you uncomfortable, Jenkins?" George shuffled backwards. "I've been looking forward to showing you what real discipline is. Mrs Hamilton isn't here this time to rub your back and sing you to sleep."

George turned his face away and could see Josh rising to his feet and raising his arms, shakily pointing his gun at Mr Jefferson.

"Move away from him or I'll..."

"You'll what? You'll shoot me?" Mr Jefferson straightened up, threw back his head and howled with laughter. "I think you'll find the security guard from whom you stole that tried the same thing – did you see how well he was sleeping, Joshua? Don't be foolish, boy. You couldn't shoot me, even at that range."

"I will!" Josh screamed, sweat beading on his forehead. "I've had enough of being stuck down this hole … and of you. Step away from my friend!"

"Oh, I say, what brave and loyal sentiments," Mr Jefferson said, his gun still firmly pointed at George. "But you've forgotten one thing…" Josh's hand was shaking; his finger tense around the trigger. "I've got friends too!"

In the blink of an eye, someone had rounded the pillar and swung something heavy down onto Josh's outstretched arm with a shattering crunch. The gun flew from his hand, and he collapsed to the floor, grasping at his arm; screaming through clenched teeth.

"No!" Francesca cried out, trying to get to her feet, as Philippe showed himself and raised his metal baton, threatening to bring it down a second time. "No, please!"

"Silence!" Philippe bellowed. "Enough!"

Mr Jefferson was still smiling his hideous smile.

"Enough nonsense," Philippe said, turning to Mr Jefferson. "We will lock them up. We must stick to the schedule. Rapidement!"

They exchanged tense words in French. George could tell that there was no friendship between the men, neither keen to take orders from the other. Finally, Philippe grabbed Joshua, his baton pressed across his neck and shoved him in the back, out into the open. Mr Jefferson ushered George and Francesca to their feet and followed close behind, his gun trained on the back of their heads.

George tried to steady his breathing and focus on his surroundings.

We need to get away.

They were moving past the control station and could now see several bodies, cast down and bleeding. Francesca screeched and lurched to the side, trying to avoid the stream of blood beneath her feet. Mr Jefferson shoved her in the back, making her stumble into George's path, almost sending them both sliding on the mess towards the victim's body.

"Keep going, Jenkins, or you can join them!" he laughed.

As they reached the far side of the room, Philippe stopped. There was a rustling noise coming from one of the archways to their left. Out of nowhere, something came hurtling towards them – small and round. It looked like a water bomb. Then another. George instinctively ducked and pulled Francesca down with him. The projectiles hit the floor, and they were rapidly engulfed in smoke. Confusion and chaos ensued.

Before they knew what had hit them, Will was flying through the air, both feet hurtling towards Mr Jefferson, knocking the gun from his hand and laying him out flat. George leapt to his feet, spotting Josh taking Philippe out at the knees.

Mr Jefferson tried to get up, but Will was on top of him in a flash, pounding punches into his gut, one after another. He twisted, knocking Will to the floor. He reached for his stray gun, but Francesca was up on her feet, kicking the gun aside. She slipped her backpack off her back, took a swing and walloped Mr Jefferson around the head. He fell to the floor clutching at his temple.

Meanwhile, Philippe had raised his baton to crack over Josh's head, but Jess had appeared out of the haze behind him, grabbing the baton before he could bring it down. George felt helpless. He couldn't decide who needed him the most. His eyes darted from one battle to the other. It was time he got involved.

Philippe was wrestling to get the baton back from Jess while Josh had him in a headlock from behind. George lunged towards Philippe, aiming for his legs, but Jess' hands slipped just as George arrived, and the baton flew out of her grasp and straight into George's face. *Crunch!*

He felt a crack across his cheek, searing pain, a rush of blood to his head. His eye felt like it was exploding out of its socket. He tasted blood. He stumbled backwards, tripping over Will and colliding with Francesca, sending them both crashing to the floor.

As George recovered from his daze, he lifted his head to see a blurry Mr Jefferson, gun in hand, standing over him.

"You have a flagrant disrespect for authority, Jenkins, and you are going to pay for your insolence."

He grabbed George by the hair, dragging him up to his feet. For a weedy-looking man, he was surprisingly strong. George grabbed at his hands and struggled to loosen his grip. Philippe was still struggling to control the other two.

In all the chaos, no one had noticed Sabrina Fraulove and Jose Gonzalez re-entering the vault.

"You can't even control ze' kiddies!" Sabrina bellowed, her huge chest heaving up and down as she spoke. She fired two shots into the air and they all froze.

"You are foolz. I know not why Victor has chozen such foolz!"

Jose was chuckling to himself; a gun on each hip.

"I wish we had been entertained like this for the last seven years. It would have made things a lot more bearable," he said, spitting out of the side of his mouth, narrowly missing Mr Jefferson's gleaming shoes. "Shall we make them dance?" he said, angling his aim towards their feet. "Those look like fantastic dancing shoes." He began laughing again, much to Mr Jefferson's agitation.

"We are done here. Lock ze' kiddies in ze' cell block. They can cry 'zemselves to sleep."

"Move out!" Jose ordered.

They were herded towards one of the gloomy archways, down a tunnel and into a tight, stark cell. Once all five of them were packed inside, Philippe slammed the door shut, shunting a heavy bolt and engaging some sort of electronic lock. He peeked through the tiny slot in the door.

"Sleep tight children. Bonne nuit!"

With that, they were gone.

Chapter 14: The Great Escape

The footsteps faded away leaving an eerie silence. Jess was on her feet, straining to see out through the few inches of window that were embedded in the narrow, padded door. The others had given up; slumped on the floor, beaten, heads hanging like wilted flowers. They had come so close to overpowering Philippe and Mr Jefferson.

George hid his face between his knees. "It was my fault," he groaned, his face still throbbing with pain, blood dripping down his once pristine white shirt.

"No, it was my fault," said Jess, turning her attention back inside the room. "If I hadn't lost grip of his baton, you would have taken him out and you wouldn't be sporting that…" She screwed up her face. George must have looked as bad as he felt.

"It was no one's fault," said Will, lifting his head. "Even if we had managed to get the better of them, the man-woman and Mexican dude would have taken us out anyway."

Silence filled the tiny room. They were out of ideas and resolve. They really were trapped with no way of escaping. The room was sterile, spotless, featureless. The only sound was the buzz of the overhead strip light, bright and lacking any warmth. It reminded George of an operating room. He was filled with the same sensation – awaiting your fate, waiting to be put to sleep, would you wake? What would they do to you while you slept? It gave him the chills.

Josh exploded to his feet and threw himself at the door shoulder first, crashing into it as if it was the advancing opposition, trying to tackle the ball from his grip. He rebounded off the padded leather, landing hard on the floor.

"This sucks!" he screamed, thumping the floor in frustration. "How the hell are we gonna' get out of this one? It took them years!" he yelled at the others, grasping at his injured arm.

"Take it easy, Joshua," Francesca said, leaning over to comfort him. "Your arm is already badly swollen; you don't need any more injuries."

"Look, sooner or later, someone is going to realise that this place has been broken into and prisoners have escaped. Someone will come," said Jess, perching on the wire-framed bed that was screwed to the floor.

"I guess," said Josh, collapsing back onto Francesca's outstretched legs.

"At least we have water," said George, raising his head and looking towards the corner of the room where a small water fountain and squat stainless-steel toilet stared back at them.

"Man, George, your face looks bad," said Will, taking a closer look. "That's gotta' hurt."

"Yeah – pretty much," he said, trying to smile but finding it too painful.

"Get that first aid kit out," said Jess. "We can make a cold compress. You're swelling up like a puffer fish."

They busied themselves tending to wounds and taking it in turns to drink from the fountain. But before long, boredom set in.

"Dr Root and my dad must be going crazy," Jess said, breaking the silence.

"I guess they've told our parents by now," Francesca sighed. "My mother is going to kill me."

"Surely she'll be worried about you. I'm sure once you explain…" said Jess, trying to reassure her.

"You don't know her," Francesca frowned. "She's never happy with me. I'm always doing something to disappoint her."

"Maybe that's how you feel, but I'm sure she's proud of you really."

"She never wanted me." Francesca uttered, her eyes glistening. No one responded. "When she met my dad in LA she was getting jobs with all the big brands. She fell pregnant with me and blames me for everything. She always says that, if I hadn't come along, she'd still be famous."

George felt for Francesca. He knew what it felt like to have a parent that seemed angry and distant.

"I'm sure she's worried to death about where you are," he said, clearing his throat. "My dad and I aren't that close, but my gran says he worries about me a lot; he's just not any good at showing it, apparently."

"Hey, you should try having three parents to cause you grief," Will said, trying to lift the mood. "My dad's new girlfriend is a head case. She's forever trying to tell me what to do. Wouldn't mind, but she should spend more time worrying about her own sons. They're a nightmare."

George half smiled. He'd give anything to have two parents, let alone three.

"Anyone else starving?" asked Josh, interrupting the conversation.

"Wait, I've got snacks," said George. "Not many though, I'm afraid."

He rifled in his pack and pulled out a packet of crisps, bag of cookies, a can of drink and a piece of Gran's fudge cake that now looked like a plastic wrapped mudball. They shared them out.

Silence descended again, but it wasn't long until Francesca interrupted their thoughts.

"Um … I need to use the Ladies Room," she said, turning a mild shade of pink.

"Be our guest," said Will, gesturing towards the metal bowl. "We won't watch – promise."

"Um … I'd rather have some privacy."

"Oh, OK," said Jess. "We'll all just step outside, shall we?"

Francesca frowned. "Girls are supposed to stick together in these kinds of matters."

Jess rolled her eyes and huffed. "OK, here, I'll hold this up," she said, stripping the sheet from the bed and creating a curtain.

"Fantastic!" Francesca beamed. "That's what real girlfriends do."

"I'm sure," Jess grimaced.

"Now turn around boys and close your eyes and ears."

"Oh, for God's sake, just get on with it, will you or I'll steal your place in the queue," said Will, swivelling around and clapping his hands over his ears.

Just as Francesca had finished, voices could be heard in the distance. They all leapt to their feet.

"Someone is here!" shouted Jess, peering through the slit. "Make as much noise as you can, we need to get their attention."

They all started shouting and banging on anything nearby.

"Help!"

"We're in here!"

The lights in the corridor lit up.

"I can see someone, a man, I think. He's coming this way," screeched Jess.

"Let me see," said George, taking her place at the door.

Someone was backing their way down the corridor, unrolling some sort of cabling. It was difficult to see much through the tiny opening. They were getting closer.

"I don't think he's heard us," said George. "These doors are padded. We need to be even louder."

"Francesca, what have you got in your bag?" Josh asked, grabbing it from its resting place. "You smacked Mr J over the head with something hard."

"Um, I think that would be my straighteners," she said. "Why?"

Josh pulled out the long metal wand and started whacking it against the bed frame. The clanging noise reverberated around the room. Still the figure outside didn't stray from his task.

"Those are a hundred-pound straighteners!" Francesca cried.

"They'll be no use to you shrivelled up and dead, which is what you'll be if we don't get the hell out of here. Keep making noise!" Jess yelled back.

George peered back through the gap. The man was right outside their door, bent over. He suddenly straightened up. It was Philippe. He stared at George through the window, held up a small black device and waved goodbye, smiling sickly as he backed away.

George felt his pathetic snack and prison water rush back up his oesophagus with a vile burning sensation. Slowly, he staggered away from the door.

"They … they're … gonna' b… blow it up," he stammered.

"What?"

"It was Philippe," he said turning to face the others, his face ashen. He felt like a solemn judge handing out a death sentence.

"They've rigged the place with explosives – they're going to blow it up."

Several faces around him went white.

"How can you be sure?" said Jess, grabbing him by the shoulders.

"Look for yourself," he said, his throat tightening.

Will was already at the door.

"George is right," he said. "We need to get out and – like – now."

"How on earth are we supposed to do that?" Francesca screamed, yanking on the door lock.

"Empty your bags!" George said, thinking out loud. "We must have something between us."

They all unzipped their packs and turfed the contents into a heap on the floor.

Jess and Will were on their knees, searching through the supplies.

"This could work," Jess said, grabbing several items.

"I think I know what you're thinking," said Will, climbing over the others to lend her a hand.

"We need to rip the leather off the door – near the lock. George, Josh, that's your job," ordered Jess.

Unsure of what she was planning they did as they were told. They yanked at the leather covering. It was stuck firm. Francesca pushed past George carrying a small pair of nail scissors. She started hacking at the edges of the material. Soon Josh could get his fingers buried deep in the severed gash and heaved, ripping it clean off, revealing the solid steel door beneath.

"That's perfect, now stand away," Jess ordered.

The others stood back and watched in wonder as Will and Jess worked their magic.

"I need the can – empty," Jess said, while splitting open sealed packets from her bag.

Will drained the rest of the drink from George's can and handed it over. Jess filled it with a variety of powders from her chemicals kit. She shook the can violently and hung a small piece of shiny tape out of the hole in the top.

"Start chewing gum," she instructed, as Will handed everyone a piece from his stash. They all chewed madly then spat them back out, handing them over to Will. Jess stuck the can to the door, right next to the lock. She tied it to the handle with wire and hairbands, anything to keep it in place. She placed some more of the powdery mixture into the lock.

"If this works, you mustn't look at the light – it will be really bright."

They huddled in the corner of the room. George was almost on top of the toilet. Jess held the lighter to the tape. Several seconds passed but nothing happened.

"Damn it!" she cursed, shaking the lighter violently.

"Keep going," said Will. "It needs to get really hot."

There was a hiss, followed by a crackle of sparks.

"It's lit," Jess said, hurrying back to shelter with the others.

With that, the whole can went up in flames. It fizzed and sprayed out a fountain of sparks. It looked like a bonfire sparkler. The light was brilliantly white, and George could feel the heat from the other side of the room. He shielded his eyes as it burst into a fiery, glutinous ball. Finally, a large molten globule fell to the floor, exposing a perfect crater in the steel. The room was filled with the stench of burnt metal. It reminded George of Dr Root.

Will ran over to the door. He couldn't get near the lock. The heat was still intense. He grabbed Francesca's straighteners, jammed them into the hole and levered them back and forth. The lock had melted clean through. The door swung open letting in a gust of clean air. George grabbed as much stuff as possible from the floor and rammed it into his pack.

"I don't know what you did, but it was awesome," said Josh, as he chased Jess and Will out into the corridor.

"I can explain later," she replied, as they charged down the passageway past wires and charges.

The place was set up to be completely demolished and they were about to be buried alive, unless they could get out before Philippe hit the detonator.

George was sweating by the time they emerged into the vault. Cables ran down every corridor.

"This could blow any second," shouted Will, as he ran to where the ladder had been. "Where's the ladder gone?"

"Look," Jess said, pointing up to the balcony. "It's been pulled up."

There it stood, staring down at them, teasing them with the possibility of escape.

"There must be another way up," said George, spinning around, searching the perimeter of the room.

But before he had time to finish his search, Francesca was pulling herself up a pipe that led to a small platform above their heads.

"Careful!" George shouted, as she crawled onto the ledge.

"It's OK," she called back.

The others stood and stared as she clambered along the ledge and onto a long, metal pipe that was suspended from the ceiling. Slowly she began to shuffle, one foot at a time, tiny steps, along the narrow pipe. It creaked and bowed in resistance.

"Francesca, it won't take the weight," called Jess. "Please, go back. We'll find another way."

"I'm almost there," she called down, her forehead creased in concentration. "It's just like being on a beam."

The others held their breath as they watched her edge towards the balcony. George glanced towards the escape route and back down the tunnel.

We don't have much time.

But by the time he looked back up, Francesca was leaping from the end of the pipe onto the balcony.

"Come on – I'll let the ladder down," she called.

George felt like cheering but wasted no time scampering up the ladder after the others and tearing out of the chasm in the stone wall and into a blur of an underpass. He didn't stop to take in the scenery. All he knew was that his legs had found a new energy, driven by fear and powered by the desire to get as far away from the threat of death as possible.

By the time they stopped, George was fighting against a stitch in the side of his gut that felt like a searing hot poker. Pain shot across his temple from his swollen eye and throbbing cheek. It felt good to stop running. He dragged air into his lungs, bent double. As he raised his head, everything was spinning. He could see colours, patterns, words – blurring into one. Slowly, his vision steadied. They were in a long underpass; the kind that takes you under a road or railway. It was littered with rubbish, abandoned trolleys, make-shift cardboard homes and decorated entirely with graffiti.

"It hasn't gone off," someone said from behind him.

"What?" said Will.

"The explosion, it hasn't gone off," said Francesca, looking back the way they'd come. "Why haven't they set it off?"

"I don't care," said Jess, looking in the opposite direction, grinning. "Look – I see daylight!"

Up ahead, the underpass ended. There was a shred of daylight. George had never been happier to see something he so often took for granted. They raced out of the underpass and broke free from the concrete constriction, out into a deserted junkyard. Chunks of hacked-up tarmac littered the ground like scattered pieces of a giant jigsaw; old train sleepers were stacked in precarious piles, enveloped by thick clumps of overgrown weeds; and lonely, drifting, plastic bags cartwheeled across the uneven ground like tumbleweeds. It was a sorry sight but looked like paradise after hours of being trapped under the streets of London.

They spread out, taking in the freedom and the air. One end of the yard lay in the shadow of an overhead viaduct. Hiding in its crumbling underbelly was an infestation of pigeon nests. The scrawny looking birds peered down at them, their heads twisting from side to side, surveying the human intruders.

"Well, it's not pretty, but we're above ground at least," said Josh.

"Man, we actually made it out alive," Will said, shaking his head, chuckling to himself. "I really thought we were gonners."

The others looked at each other. Smiles broke out all around and George relaxed for the first time since they'd left the college.

The pigeons' end of the yard was cordoned off with a high chain mail gate, topped with razor sharp barbed wire; a chunky padlock and chain slung about its middle. The other end looked a little more promising. It was open and seemed to lead towards the back of an old factory or storage block. There was no sign of life, except a small abandoned car.

"This way, I guess," said Jess. "We can't be far from a train station."

They weaved in and out of the clutter towards the factory. A roughly tarmacked road could be seen up ahead. They quickened their pace and were just passing the vacated vehicle when they heard the clank of metal, the clatter of a chain and the muffled voice of someone coming from the shadows behind them. It was Mr Jefferson. He had appeared as if from nowhere. George dived behind the car, followed rapidly by the others. He peered out from behind the rear tyre, trying to see where Mr Jefferson had gone but scrambled back in a heartbeat, as a small grey van swerved into view, driven by Philippe.

"They're coming this way," said George. "They're going to drive right past us."

"Quick! Into the car!" yelled Will.

With that, they scampered around to the far side of the car just as the van began bumping down the track, crashing through the piles of litter.

"Get inside," whispered Josh. "Get down on the floor."

The passenger door was already open. Will and Josh dived into the front seats, while George yanked open the back door and the others piled in. They were squashed in. Legs and arms crammed in at all angles. George's feet were wedged under the driver's seat.

The van passed them and stopped. A door flew open.

"Shut it properly!" yelled Philippe out of an open window. "We don't need anything falling out."

They all held their breath.

Footsteps crunched through the grit. Mr Jefferson was cursing, mumbling to himself. More footsteps. Another door slammed, and the van pulled off, screeching tyres, wheels spinning in the dirt.

"Stop kicking me," Jess said, under her breath.

Francesca was squirming. "There's something touching my leg!" she squeaked. "Oh, it's a rat – I'm sure it's a rat." Her squeak had turned into a squeal. "Get it off me!" She was now yelling, flailing around in the back of the car. George grabbed at her, trying to drag her back down, out of sight.

The van must have reached the road. It screeched to a halt. George peeked his head up over the back headrests.

"They've stopped. I can't see them, but they've stopped."

Francesca was now balanced on the back seat, her legs and arms pulled in tight like a curled-up woodlouse. Jess was squashed down behind the passenger seat. The car suddenly roared to life.

"What the–" Jess tried to say before they were thrown backwards as the car jerked into action and shot off towards the barbed wire gate.

George's already swollen face smacked against the headrest as they hit a large rut in the tarmac. He then tumbled sideways, rebounding off Francesca's huddled form and ending up head down in the foot well, his soggy feet protruding upwards towards the roof.

"Who the hell is driving?" cried Jess, who was still wedged in her hiding place.

"It's Josh!" yelled Will, who had managed to get himself in an upright position in the passenger seat.

"Will you slow down," garbled George, struggling to get his head out of the foot well.

The car skidded as Josh pressed the brake a little too hard. Will nearly ended up flying through the front windscreen. They came to a stop. Jess was wriggling out of her hole as George turned himself the right way up.

"You want to explain what happened there?" said Jess, glaring at Josh in the rearview mirror.

"I got us out of trouble – again," he said. "You're most welcome."

"Where exactly did you learn to hotwire a car?" Will asked, slightly impressed.

"My brother taught me."

"I didn't know you had a brother," said Will, puzzled.

"He's much older, doesn't live with us anymore," replied Josh.

"Where does he live – prison?" said Jess, managing to squeeze onto the seat beside George.

Josh frowned in the mirror.

"Do you think we got away without them seeing?" George asked, looking back to see if they'd been followed.

"Don't think we should stick around to find out," said Jess. "Now we have wheels, let's get the hell out of here."

Josh stamped on the clutch and ground the gear stick into first. They catapulted forwards several feet, stopped and jerked forwards again.

"What are you doing?" asked Jess.

"I said I could hotwire a car, not drive one," replied Josh, wrestling with the gear stick with both hands.

George looked around. They had made it through the wire gate but were still in the shadows of the viaduct. The front windscreen was filthy with dirt and bird droppings, but it looked like there was a track up ahead. He glanced back to check that they were still alone.

Finally, Josh found first and they hurtled off towards the track.

"Wait!" screamed Francesca. "There's something in the road!"

Josh slammed on the brakes and screeched to a halt, millimeters before hitting a large obstruction.

"What was that?" said Will, trying to peer through the smeared windscreen and over the bonnet.

"I think we hit it," said Francesca. "We should check."

"No, just back up and we'll go around it," said Jess, leaning past George, trying to see out of the side window.

"Um … I'm not sure I know how to go backwards," said Josh, yanking again at the gear stick, a shrill grinding noise coming from the underside of the car.

"Give me a go," said Will, trying to find the right gear.

"This is useless, just drive over it," said Jess.

"No," said Francesca. "What if it's an animal?"

"Man! I'll just get out and move it," said Will, opening the passenger door.

He slid out of his seat and made his way around to the front of the car. George could see him bending down, heaving at something heavy. He suddenly jumped back in shock.

"It's alive!" he shouted.

George leapt out of the car to join him. Lying under the front bumper was a long, bulging hessian bag, tied at one end with rope. Whatever was inside was roughly the size of a deer.

George prodded it with his exposed toe. It groaned.

"Er, guys, it's definitely alive."

By now, everyone had exited the car and come to see what the obstacle was.

"Should we open it?" said Francesca, looking anxious.

Jess bent down, pulled at the rope and peeled back the opening of the bag. A sickly, sweet smell drifted from within. White hair, a forehead, eyes – it was no animal – it was a small man.

He groaned again, turning over to face the light. His face was pale, his eyes rolling in his head as he tried to speak. Jess pulled a little more at the fabric covering his face. His mouth was gagged. She leant in further to pull at the curling corner of the silver duct tape and his eyes shot open.

He stared at them all as they glared back at him. He suddenly started thrashing about, desperately trying to free himself from the bag.

"It's the guy from the library," Francesca gasped. "Wilbur Cook."

George blinked. "What?" He looked a little different scrunched up in a bag, without his smart bow tie, but George could just make out the ends of his long white moustache poking out from behind the tape.

"Shh, it's OK," Francesca hushed, bending down to calm the little old man. "Lie still, we'll help you out."

His eyes locked on Francesca and he slowly stilled. She gently peeled the tape from his mouth as Jess and George helped him out of the bag. They sat him up. He was dazed and dishevelled. He had a nasty egg-shaped lump on the back of his head, and his hands and bare feet were bound. Josh went to work uncoiling the wire that was digging into his ankles, making them raw, as Jess helped unbind his wrists.

"Are you OK?" Francesca asked, crouched at his side.

"Oh, my head," he croaked, swaying about like he'd been at sea.

George had refilled his water bottle during his stint in the prison cell and passed it to Wilbur.

"Thank you," he said, guzzling as if it was the first drink he'd had in a week.

"What happened?" Will asked the Curator, once he'd finished drinking.

"They took me hostage," he slurred, his eyes still drifting in and out of focus.

"Held me … trapped me in my own dear museum … they wanted to know things … things I didn't know." He swayed violently to the left, crashing into Francesca. She propped him up again.

"Who did this?" asked George, already knowing what the answer might be.

"The man – the horrible French man. He was so angry – he was so …"

He drifted out of consciousness again.

"Wilbur?" George squatted in front of him. "What did they want to know?"

Wilbur gasped and snapped back into consciousness. "The school – the tunnels – buried…"

He was mumbling, not making any sense.

"Let's get him to the car," said George. "We can take him with us."

"He needs a doctor," said Francesca. "He's had a nasty blow to the head. He's barely conscious. We should take him to a hospital."

"We need to get to the police," said Jess. "We can tell them everything. They can call our parents and the school, and they can deal with Wilbur."

Will and George grabbed Wilbur and tried to encourage him to walk around to the side of the car. He collapsed, totally out cold. Josh came to help, but Wilbur's arms and legs flopped about like a drunken rag doll. It was almost impossible to move him, let alone squeeze him into the back seat of the car.

"He's not going to fit anyway," said Josh. "The car is tiny. It barely fits you three in the back."

"Let's put him in the boot," suggested Will.

"You can't do that," exclaimed Francesca. "He's already been through such a terrible ordeal."

"He's out for the count. He won't know any different."

The boys dragged him to the back end of the car and heaved him into the small boot. It was only just big enough for an average-sized suitcase. They squeezed his arms and legs in as best they could. He didn't even stir.

"He needs air," Francesca ordered. "You'll have to leave the boot open."

"OK, fine," said Josh. "I can't drive in reverse anyway, so it's not like I'll need to see out of the back window."

With that they all piled back into the car, its undercarriage now hanging incredibly close to the ground. Josh sparked the engine back to life, and they set off, the boot lid flapping up and down like crocodile jaws.

From: J21
To: Group – BOP
Cc: Chief
Re: Bird of Prey {Encrypted}

<u>Update 24.2</u>

Urgent.

We have a top priority alert: There has been a full-scale breach at UNIT 256.

All members to respond as per protocol 17.

Approach with severe caution.

Communications on Channel 4.1

End.

From: Chief
To: J21
Cc: Group – BOP
Re: Bird of Prey {Encrypted}

<u>Response to update 24.2</u>

Get this locked down.
We cannot allow any fallout.

We had only just relocated the flock to this location – we must have a leak – lock down all communications to need-to-know basis only, and send me a list of all personnel who knew the Unit location and contents.

Set project 'Bait' into action with immediate effect.

End.

Chapter 15: New Scotland Yard

The car groaned and creaked under the weight of all its cargo, and the boot lid was thumping up and down as they kangarooed down the bumpy track. They finally made it out onto a smoothly tarmacked road only to find themselves faced with a group of curious onlookers. Gathered on the corner of the small back street was a group of teenagers. They looked like they were up to no good themselves but stopped in their tracks as the car flapped its way towards them.

"Keep going," said Jess from the back seat. "We don't need any hangers-on."

Josh tried to steer confidently around the corner, but the pack of observers gaped at them as they passed. George could see one of the boys lift his phone out of his pocket and take a photo of the spectacle. He turned back and slid down in his seat. He didn't need his swollen face splattered all over the internet.

"We should have asked to borrow their phone," said Francesca, who had now relaxed a little, having accepted that the car wasn't writhing with vermin.

As they trundled along, George tried to make sense of everything that had happened. Dead bodies, MI5 wanted criminals, escaped convicts, hidden underground vaults, mysterious vigilantes, a sinister school teacher and now a kidnapped librarian. It had to all link together somehow.

They were just coming to a crossroads when the air was filled with the blaring sound of sirens.

"Police!" yelled Will. "Up ahead, look."

Two strobing squad cars were storming towards them. Josh slammed both his feet onto the brake pedal and leapt out of the car, waving his arms around manically.

One of the squad cars screeched to a halt in a cloud of dust, but the other one continued to steam straight past them, rocking their bean can of a car in its wake.

"Can I help you, son?" asked the tubby officer, who had stepped out from the passenger side of the car. He looked friendly enough to George. His partner stayed behind the wheel, talking into his radio.

"Yes – we want to report a – breakout – crime," Josh was stumbling over his words. He obviously didn't know where to start.

The others had piled out of the car to join him.

"Stand still where you are," ordered the second officer, who had now joined his colleague. He looked a lot less friendly and was easily a foot taller and much leaner. He whispered something into the first officer's ear.

"We've just come from the underpass, over there," Jess said, pointing back in the direction they'd come.

"There's been a breakout," said George. "They've got guns, explosives and–"

"They locked us in a cell," exclaimed Francesca.

The officers were still whispering to each other.

"Whose car is this?" the second officer asked, moving towards the vehicle, which now had all four doors and the boot flung open. It looked like an aircraft waiting to take off.

"Um … don't know. We found it," said Josh, shrugging.

"You found it," smirked the second officer. "Just thought you'd borrow it, did you?"

"No, you don't understand," said George. "We were being chased by these criminals. They had guns–"

"They were going to blow us up," added Francesca.

"Right, I see. So, you felt the need to steal this car – I understand," he said, writing something in his small notebook.

"No, that's not what happened," said Jess and Will together.

"Save it for the station. You're coming with us. You try any nonsense and we'll cuff you."

"But wait, we're not the criminals here," said George. "You're not listening. We just witnessed–"

"That's enough! You can make a formal statement at the Yard."

"But I've got these MI5 papers. I'll show you…" he said, swinging his backpack off his shoulder. But before he had time to finish his sentence, he was bundled to the floor by both officers.

"Get your hands away from the bag!" one of them screamed in his ear.

George lay flat on his back, pinned to the tarmac, staring up at the early evening sky. His arms were restrained and quickly cuffed. The others stood dazed. The second officer lifted George to his feet. He ordered the others to stand in a line with their hands above their heads.

The first officer had wandered around to the back of the car.

"Wilbur!" Francesca gasped.

But it was too late. The officer had peered into the boot and quite quickly realised that the car-jacking teenagers were, not only in possession of a stolen vehicle, but also carrying a, seemingly, dead body in the boot.

"He's not dead," Jess blurted out.

"Oh good," said the second officer, who still had a firm grip on George. "That will reduce your sentence, somewhat."

"No! We found him like that. We were taking him to a hospital."

The officer nodded sarcastically. "I see, of course, in the boot. Best place to stow an injured man."

"No, but—"

"I suggest you keep quiet, otherwise I will officially arrest the lot of you and read you your rights."

The first officer was gently trying to wake Wilbur up. George could hear him groaning.

"He's barely conscious," he yelled back to his colleague. "We need an urgent paramedic – I'll call it in."

The officers busied themselves taking notes, tending to Wilbur and intermittently speaking into their shoulder mounted radios while George and his friends were made to sit on the edge of the pavement in resistant silence.

An ambulance finally arrived, followed soon after by another squad car. The paramedics lifted Wilbur onto a stretcher. He flailed about, fighting the help, mumbling incoherently. One of the paramedics asked the officers if she could approach the teenagers. They agreed, and she came over to ask if they knew what had happened to the poor old librarian.

"His name is Wilbur Cook," said George, keen to help in any way he could. "We found him tied up in a bag, over there. He was gagged and really dazed."

She nodded. "You're looking in need of some medical attention yourselves," she said, looking at George's face.

"I'm fine," he said. "It looks worse than it is."

Just as they were loading Wilbur into the back of the ambulance, he strained his neck, turned his head towards George and croaked two words, "The school."

"What did he say?" asked Jess.

"I think he said something about the school," replied Will.

As the ambulance raced off, George and the others were bundled into two waiting squad cars and taken to the nearest police station.

George was wedged between Jess and Will. The handcuffs bit into his wrists. He tried to speak to the two officers up front, but they completely ignored him.

It was a short journey to New Scotland Yard and, although they were in deep trouble, George finally felt safe as they were marched through the back door and shoved into a waiting room. A rather inflated looking woman with an expressionless face signed them in, took their details, catalogued their confiscated belongings and relieved George of his handcuffs. The officers that had brought them in seemed to evaporate. They sat in silence in the cramped, icy room and waited for someone to return.

George was infuriated. At every turn they had been mistreated, misunderstood, ignored and patronised. He was boiling up inside. Why did being young make you a liar and ensure that every adult would disregard anything you said as mere attention seeking or bad behaviour. He was adamant that he would make someone listen to him.

After a short while, a young lady came in and offered them a drink. She was bombarded with questions but just shrugged, handed out flimsy plastic cups of water and left without saying a thing.

Finally, the two officers re-appeared with a broomstick of a woman who was carrying a clipboard. The officers introduced themselves as PC Rick Manning and PC Jim Ellis. PC Manning read through a list of legal blurb that meant nothing to George. The woman looked down her nose at them with an insincere and well-practiced smile. PC Ellis introduced her as Cassandra Clovelly, youth liaison officer. She looked like she had already decided they were guilty.

"We should be allowed to call our parents," Will said, before she had a chance to say anything.

"Don't you worry my dear – your parents will be notified," she said.

George could just picture his dad's reaction to a call from the police saying that he'd been found driving a stolen car with a body in the boot: disappointment and despair. It wasn't exactly the victorious homecoming he had pictured.

"We need to report a crime," said George. "And the longer we sit in here, the further away the real criminals are getting."

"Yes, yes dear," chirped Cassandra. "There's plenty of time to make a statement."

"You're not listening – none of you are listening!" shouted Will, getting to his feet, but before he had a chance to get any further, he was shoved back down into the hard, plastic chair by both officers.

"It's time for you to listen right now, son, unless you want to be put in a cell," PC Manning growled.

"I've spent more than enough time in a cell today," Will mumbled.

Just then, there was an urgent knock at the door, and a young policewoman popped her head through the doorway.

"There's been an explosion – two officers down. We need all available personnel as back up."

With that, her head disappeared, and PC Manning and PC Ellis dashed from the room, sending several chairs clattering to the floor in their haste. Cassandra gaped after them.

"The explosion," whispered Jess. "You don't suppose it's the vault, do you?"

"I'd put money on it," said Will.

"Um … right," said Cassandra, her attention still wandering out of the open door.

She stood, looked down at her clipboard and back out into the corridor. She went to leave but hesitated. It obviously wasn't a scenario she had experienced before and wasn't sure if she should stay or go.

"I will need to contact each of your parents," she finally said and scuttled out of the room, pulling the door to behind her.

Just as the door was slowly drifting closed, George could hear a man's deep voice. Someone had stopped Cassandra in her tracks. They exchanged muffled words and the clicking of her chunky heels disappeared down the corridor. Two minutes later a male officer stepped into the room. He wore full police uniform and helmet. As he lifted his head, they all recognised him at once. It was Philippe.

What!

George sprung to his feet, but Philippe raised his gun and placed a gloved finger to his lips.

"Keep nice and quiet now, and I won't have to dispose of you," he whispered, no longer attempting to hide his French accent. "We will be leaving now."

"I'm not going anywhere with you – you ghastly man!" squealed Francesca.

Philippe lunged out and snatched her by her long hair, dragging her from her chair. She squealed even louder. He pressed the gun to her temple as she scrabbled to keep on her feet. The others were up out of their seats.

"If you all do as you're told," he snapped, "I won't plaster her pretty little face all over the walls."

They all froze. They completely out-numbered him, but he had the upper hand. His gun was loaded with, what looked like, a silencer. He meant business.

George could sense Josh behind him; his breathing drawn and deep; his knuckles taut and white around the back of his chair. He lifted it, and went to hurl it at the Frenchman, but Philippe saw him coming and fired a single muffled shot. Jess screamed as the bullet grazed against Joshua's already swollen arm, sending a fine spray of blood flying from his shoulder, ripping a gash in his blazer and sending him staggering backwards into the wall.

Josh wailed.

"You monster!" screamed Jess, throwing herself at Philippe.

Will lunged in front of her and tackled her to the floor, just as Philippe adjusted his aim.

"It's merely a scratch," he hissed. "Next time I will aim to kill."

There was silence.

"Now, I assume I have your attention and your obedience."

They all nodded meekly. Josh was crumpled on the floor, grasping at his shoulder.

"Get up – all of you," Philippe barked. "Once I have checked that the path is clear, we will exit together in an orderly fashion. I won't hesitate to maim anyone who steps out of line. I am not particularly attached to any of you."

He opened the door a crack and peered out, still holding Francesca close to him, his gun pressed hard into her cheek. When the coast was clear, he nodded to the others and dragged Francesca out with him. Will and George helped Josh to his feet. He was wobbly and dazed. Philippe stood on guard as the others filed out. They made it out into the deserted corridor and were ushered a few meters forwards, towards a fire exit.

As they reached the exit, Philippe tapped on the door with his toe, not moving the gun from Francesca's face for a second. The door swung open, and Mr Jefferson stood at the back of the grey van, the back doors wide open.

"Nice and quiet now," Mr Jefferson said, herding them into the van.

They were bundled into the back and forced to the floor. Philippe slammed the doors shut and padlocked the latch with a heavy clunk. They were sealed in total darkness inside the metal cabin. George could hear Josh groaning to his left and Francesca quietly sobbing to his right.

"What do we do now?" asked Will. "Do you think they'll kill us?"

"No – they would have done that by now," said George, trying to stay calm.

"Well, they obviously intended for us to die in that vault, so what's the difference?" said Jess.

"They didn't kill Wilbur," said George, still trying to convince himself and the others that they weren't going to die.

"He didn't exactly look in great shape," said Jess.

"Neither do we," said Will.

The engine rumbled to life, and they were thrown across the cabin as the van lurched forwards.

George ached all over, his face was tight and stinging, his wrists sore, his back bruised. He tried to pull himself up, but the van was bouncing them around like lottery balls. They swerved violently, and Josh went crashing into the side of the van. He screamed out again in pain.

"Where the hell are they taking us?" shouted Jess, over the sound of the engine.

"No idea, but we must have to go out onto the streets of London," said George. "Once we hear other traffic, we should start banging on the van sides and yelling. Maybe someone will hear us."

But before they had a chance to put their plan into action, the cabin filled with a fine, sweet-smelling mist. George could feel his throat tighten. Something about the smell made him think of Wilbur. He felt dizzy and his vision started to blur.

"What's happening?" Francesca said.

"What are they doing to us?" said Jess.

"They're killing us!" croaked Will.

Will tried to stand up, stumbling in the effort. He pummelled his fists into the side of the van. The others tried to do the same. George could feel the strength leaking from his limbs. His head felt heavy. The noises around him were fading; sinking inside his head. He felt like his ears were filling with water. He tried to move to the back door; crawling on all fours. His stomach lurched as the van swerved. Everything around him began to spin. He desperately tried to cling on to his consciousness – fight the encroaching sleep, but slowly he drifted away into the darkness. He had one last fleeting thought – he was sitting on the seesaw, looking straight into his mum's dark eyes.

From: J21
To: Group – BOP
Cc: Chief
Re: Bird of Prey {Encrypted}

Update 24.3

UNIT 256 is fully compromised.

Our agents were not first on the scene.
A 999 call was made from within the complex – uniform first to arrive.

The unit had been rigged.
Several injuries.

We have locked down the site and are conducting a full sweep, but we are doubtful that we will find anyone alive. We must assume that all birds have flown.

Project 'Bait' initiated.

End.

Chapter 16: Night Terrors

I'm dead. I can't hear or see or speak. Only think – dream.

Lights flickered in front of George's eyelids. He was on a ferris wheel, going around and around. The sound of distant voices – far below.

I'm tired – so tired.

He could hear the fluttering of wings. His friends were trapped in a glass dome, beating their wings against the sides, over and over. He couldn't reach them, save them. They were slowly suffocating. The ferris wheel kept spinning, faster and faster.

I'm so weak – so tired.

He tried to brace his arms to lift the bar that held him down.

I must get off the wheel and save my friends.

He was screaming now, screaming their names.

Finally, the wheel ground to a stop. He was at the very top, peering out across the valley. He could see his school in the distance, engulfed in flames. Huge, black, billowing clouds of smoke flew into the air – shaped like dark, feathered falcons, they rose into the sky – breathing fire.

I must put out the flames. I must stop the falcons from taking flight.

His eyes slowly opened. The fire had gone. There was no smell of smoke. Only the sweet smell from the van lingered in his nostrils and left a sickening taste in his mouth. His body felt heavy and limp. Something coarse and scratchy lined his resting place. His eyelids ached to fall closed again. He desperately fought the lethargy.

I must not sleep anymore.

He tried to take long, deep breaths. Opening his eyes as wide as he could, he turned towards the source of light. A warm lantern hung from the rafters. It was gently swinging to and fro, pestered by a dozen moths.

Slowly, George dragged himself from his subconscious. His mind had woken before his body. He could barely move. Glancing from one side to the other, he could see that he was lying in a bed of straw. As his senses returned, he could hear distant voices, the rustling of straw from elsewhere and the dull rumble of an idling engine. His nostrils were clearing. He could smell the straw and something else – something rotting, putrid. He could feel his hands now and his feet. They were bound.

From somewhere behind him, someone groaned. He pulled up his knees and dug his heels into straw. Pushing as hard as he could, he struggled to turn himself over to see who was behind him. He flipped and rolled onto his side. Terror coursed through him like a shock wave, as he realised he'd come face to face with Mrs Hodge. Her swollen, puce face was inches from his nose. She looked like she'd ballooned. Something was foaming from her lips. The smell was engulfing. The acid burnt in his throat as it rose up from his gut. He tried to turn away but managed to push himself even closer. A shot of adrenalin burst from his heart, pumped through his veins and sent his legs flying out in sheer panic, pushing him away, again and again.

"Argh!"

He'd collided with someone else.

"Who's that?" he said, trying to turn and see who he'd flattened.

"It's me, Jess."

George flipped himself over. He was so relieved to see her.

"You're alive," he exclaimed.

"We're alive," she replied.

"Where are we?"

"A barn, I think," she whispered. "I heard voices. I don't think they are far away. We should try to keep quiet."

"Are the others here?"

"I hope so."

George tried again to push himself to a sitting position. It was so hard with his hands tied behind him and his feet bound.

"Turn around. We can help each other," said Jess. "We'll push at the same time."

"Ah man, I don't want to look over there," he said, gagging at the thought of Mrs Hodge's decomposing body.

"Close your eyes then," Jess ordered.

He did as he was told and, with some difficulty, they pushed each other up to sitting. George's head spun. He felt faint and dizzy. Jess was breathing hard behind him.

"You OK?" he asked, as he slowly regained his balance.

"Yeah – just a bit woozy. I can see Will – look."

George swivelled to see Will still asleep a few feet from them, buried deep in the straw.

Someone groaned again. It was Josh, curled up in a ball, pale and shivering.

"He looks in a bad way," said Jess. "He needs a doctor."

"We all do," said George, suddenly aware that the pain in his face was rapidly returning.

"Where's Francesca?"

"I'm here," a croaky voice said from the other side of a pile of boxes. "I don't think I can move."

George hadn't noticed the boxes before then. He took a moment to take in his surroundings. The spacious rectangular barn had large double doors at either end. One corner was cluttered with old farm machinery. Rusty and weathered, it looked like it hadn't been moved in a decade. Something had even nested in the handlebars of what looked like an upright mower. There were several cardboard boxes, stacked in the middle of the space, leaning against a pile of wooden crates. Cobwebs draped around the room like ghostly curtains and there were several broken panels of wood on either side of the far double doors that stood slightly ajar.

Distant voices drifted in on the cool, crisp night air. *What time is it?*

George twisted to glance at his watch. Its face was cracked, the digital display was fractured, making it impossible to read.

"How long were we out?" he whispered.

"I don't know," Jess replied. "I reckon it's nearly dawn."

The idling engine spluttered and died. A door slammed and someone shouted something foreign.

"It's definitely them," whispered Jess. "They've been loading up the van with stuff from these boxes."

"What's in the boxes?" George asked.

"Explosives," Francesca whispered, her head appearing from behind one of the crates.

She had managed to pull herself up. She shuffled backwards to get a better view of the others.

"There is a warning printed on this side of the crates," she went on. "It says 'tratar con cuidado'. That's 'handle with care' in Spanish. 'Explosivos'."

She didn't need to translate the rest for them. Most of the boxes held the same warning.

There was another slamming of doors. More voices – coming their way.

"Pretend to still be asleep," Jess said, as she dropped back down into the straw.

George quickly followed Jess' lead. He flopped into the straw, keeping his distance from the bloated body of Mrs Hodge. Pretending to be asleep was harder than he'd imagined. He struggled to keep his breathing even and his eyes from flickering as the barn door swung open and the cool air swept across his face.

"What are we supposed to do with these?" a man's voice asked.

George was desperate to open an eye to see who was talking but concentrated hard on staying still.

"We should dispose of them all. They are an unnecessary risk." It was a woman with a Russian accent – Angelika.

"They are only kids," the man said.

"Kids – ha! I had killed by the time I was their age. They aren't kids. They are just baggage."

"They won't get in the way. They can stay tied up here until we're finished at the school. Then it will all be over and we will be long gone. Someone else can deal with them and the old woman."

Someone moved further into the barn, shuffling through the straw, shifting boxes and disturbing clouds of dust. George could feel his nose itch. A strong smell of smoke floated in on the air – cigar smoke.

"We need to hurry up – come on, one more load." It was Jose. His deep South American drawl was interrupted by a long, hissing drag. He took his time blowing out the smoke, savouring the moment.

"We need to be ready for Victor's signal," said Angelika.

"We'll be ready, alright," said Jose.

He was standing just a few feet from George. His smoke filled George's nose and trickled into his lungs. George tried not to breathe. He so desperately wanted to scratch his nose and could feel the smoke catching at the back of his throat – he was sure he was going to either cough or sneeze or both.

With that, someone else let out an explosive sneeze, making Jose flinch.

"What was that?" he proclaimed.

"My God, Jose, it was someone sneezing – you gone soft in the clink? You're as jumpy as hell," the other man said, laughing.

"One of them is awake – that one," said Angelika, striding towards Josh, disturbing more dust and kicking straw into George's face.

He couldn't hold it any longer, he sneezed with such force that he almost head-butted the crate that lay open next to him.

"They're all waking up," Jose said, staring into George's now open eyes.

He couldn't pretend any more. He lay still, staring straight at Jose, who bent down and blew a lungful of smoke right into George's face, making his eyes sting.

George spluttered. Jose chuckled.

Angelika had reached Josh. "You awake little boy?" she whispered, jabbing her steel-capped toe into Josh's ribs.

"Argh – get the hell off me!" Josh yelled, twisting in his restraints to face his antagonist.

"I'll do what I like – you are garbage to me," she said, kicking him again, this time stabbing her toe into in his blood-soaked arm.

He thrashed out with both his feet, catching her squarely on the shins.

"You little piece of–"

"That's enough!" It was the other man, Alex Allaman. He was tall, composed and carried an air of sensibility. "Leave them. We don't have time for any games," he said, his slither of a moustache hardly moving as he spoke.

"We need to silence them," Angelika said, kicking straw into Josh's face.

"We will gag them before we leave. I'm sure they are clever enough to realise that it would do no good to make any noise before then." Alex said, looking at George and Josh in turn.

"I think we should silence them permanently," Angelika hissed, taking a long thin handgun from her belt and pushing it hard into Josh's wounded arm.

He screamed out through gritted teeth and lashed out again, this time just missing her knee. She lifted the gun and brought it down hard. Josh raised his legs to deflect the blow.

"Leave him alone!" George screamed, trying to push himself to his feet. But before he could get himself upright, Will had kicked out, sending two loaded boxes flying into Angelika's back. She stumbled and fell into Josh who quickly raised his legs again and managed to get them over Angelika's head. He had her in a head lock between his knees. Will was hurtling more boxes her way.

"Enough of this child's play!" Alex shouted again.

Jose was creased over, laughing so much he choked on his own fumes.

Alex clambered over to where Angelika and Josh were wrestling. She fired a shot, missing Jose by inches and putting an abrupt halt to his chortling. She was just trying to turn the gun on Josh when Alex grabbed her by the arm and pinned Josh to the ground with his boot.

"I suggest you stop right there, young man, or you will make an enemy for life, and trust me, she is the last person you want to have as your enemy."

Josh stilled. He was breathless and wincing in pain.

Alex hauled Angelika to her feet and dragged her away from Josh. She spat and swore something in Russian.

"I will kill you!" she screamed, as Alex dragged her from the barn. "I have killed more people than you have had birthday parties, you little baby. You won't see me coming. I will haunt you in your nightmares…"

Alex had pulled her outside and slammed the barn door. By now, all five of them were awake and sitting up. Francesca glared at Jose.

"You're all monsters," she said, under her breath.

Jose chuckled again. "Yes, little girl, you are quite right, but after tonight we will be free, rich and powerful monsters. So maybe you should just keep your pretty little mouth shut, and I won't set alight to the barn as I leave."

Alex re-entered.

"We are ready. Check their restraints and gag them," he ordered, pointing towards Jess and George. "I'll deal with the other three."

It was pointless struggling, although Will and Josh tried.

George looked into Jose's eyes as he slapped the tape over his mouth. There was no guilt, no remorse, no care. George couldn't believe such people existed. He scowled as Jose tightened the rope around his feet, but Jose barely registered his existence. It was all part of a job – he was clearly devoid of emotion.

Jose was the last to leave. He slammed the barn door closed and dropped the metal latch. The last they heard was the van trundling off into the night.

Silence filled the air. George was struggling to control his breathing. The dust and putrid smell that filled the barn was beginning to constrict his nostrils. Panic was creeping through him as he realised he could suffocate if he didn't find a way to remove the tape from his mouth. He slid his jaws back and forth, desperately trying to loosen the gag. His nose closed even tighter as his blood pressure rose and breathing quickened.

To his left, Jess was on her feet. She had pushed herself up against a crate and was shuffling in his direction. She reached him, turned and spread out her fingers behind her back. Looking over her shoulder she nodded at him.

"Hmmm hmm." She tried to say something.

She wiggled her fingers again. George got it. He lifted his head so that his mouth was at the level of her outstretched fingers and braced himself. She fumbled a few times, trying to grip the edges of the silver tape with her fingertips. Finally, she caught a corner and pulled. Her fingers slipped. She tried once more, and the tape ripped off in one swift tear.

George gulped in a lungful of air.

"I thought I was going to suffocate," he gasped. "Thank you."

"Hmm Hmmm!" Jess tried to say, turning towards him.

She was going slightly red.

"Oh, man – sorry," George said, realising that she was also desperate for air.

He pushed his way over to the nearest crate, dug in his heels and lifted himself unsteadily to his feet. Before long, Jess was gag free as were the others, who had followed her lead. Francesca had made her way towards Josh who was still curled up in pain.

"How the hell have we ended up in this mess?" said Will, leaning against the back wall of the barn.

"It's my fault," said George, propping himself against a tower of crates.

"It's no one's fault," said Francesca. "We're in this together."

"I thought we could stop them," George said, hanging his head.

"What are they up to?" said Francesca. "Do you think they're going to blow up the school?"

"I think so," replied Will.

"Why would they want to do that?"

"I don't know," said George. "But we need to stop them. We need to get out of here and somehow raise the alarm."

"We can't exactly get very far tied up like this," said Will. "Unless you think we can untie each other's knots – they seem pretty tight to me."

"I'm up for trying," said Jess. "I need to get away from the smell of that poor dead woman – I'll cut off my arm if I have to."

Jess and Will shuffled towards each other, nearly overbalancing in the effort to wade through the straw with their ankles tied together. George watched as Will awkwardly squatted down and tried to untie Jess' ankles from behind his back.

"It's impossible!" he shouted, after a few frustrating minutes.

George scanned his eyes around the old barn.

"There must be something in here that we can use," he said, waddling towards the abandoned machinery in the far corner.

There were various old mowers, rollers and spare wheels. He was hoping to find an old saw or axe, but nothing sprang out at him. Jess and Will joined the search, sticking to the edges of the barn to avoid Mrs Hodge.

"Hey, what about this?" cried Will. "It looks like an old blade from a lawnmower."

"That would be perfect," said George. "Can you get to it?"

Will dropped to his knees, bent to one side and used his elbow to push aside some stray straw. Standing up against the wall was a large, rusty blade. It didn't look particularly sharp, but it was the best they had.

"I can't do this alone," he said. "I need someone to hold it still."

Jess and George shuffled towards him. Between them they managed to wedge the blade into a crack in the wood, a foot from the ground. Jess held it steady with her feet at its base. Will sat and lifted his heels towards the blade. Pumping his legs back and forth, he began to saw at the rope. It was slow progress. The blade wobbled and fell several times. George stepped in and tried to steady it with his feet from the other side. Eventually, the rope began to fray.

"It's working!" cried Jess. "Keep going."

"I'm trying," said Will, sweat beading on his forehead.

He took a deep breath and then pushed hard against the blade. The rope broke, his feet slipped and his ankle slid up the length of the blade.

"Goddamn it!" he cried out.

"Are you OK?" gasped Jess.

"It took forever to cut the rope, but it sliced straight through my bloomin' sock."

"Did it cut you?"

"It's just a scratch, I think."

"At least we know it works," said George, smiling.

"OK, George, you have a go," said Will, not smiling back.

"Try your hands," said Jess. "If we can get our hands free, we can untie the others."

It was hard work. George tried to run his hands up and down the swaying blade behind his back. His movements were small and jerky. He slipped several times, catching the rusty metal on his fingers.

"This isn't working!" he shouted in frustration.

"Let me try," said Jess.

She slammed her heel down onto the base of the blade to hold it steady and ground her wrists up and down the blade. She had fierce determination in her eyes.

"You've got it," cried George. "It's breaking through."

Moments later the rope fell away to the floor and her hands were free.

"Yes!" cheered Will. "Now untie us."

Jess helped untie George and Will, and they all made their way back over to where Francesca lay with Josh, who was still shivering.

"He's not good," said Francesca, as they untied her.

Jess felt his forehead. "He's freezing."

She gently pulled aside his blazer collar, trying to see the damage to his shoulder.

"He's lost a lot of blood. We need to bandage that arm up. Stop any more bleeding."

"We'll have to get his blazer off," said George.

They gently helped Josh to sit up, untied his wrists and feet and removed his torn blazer. His shirtsleeve was crimson. The bullet hadn't lodged, but it had made a mess on its way through.

"Give me your tie, George," said Francesca, not taking her eyes off Josh.

She tied it tight around his upper arm as he groaned in pain.

"It will help, I promise," she whispered. "We're going to get you to a doctor."

"We need to get moving," said Jess.

"Agreed," said George. "And, if we've got any chance of interrupting their plans at the school, we will need to find help – and soon."

George and Will slowly helped Josh to his feet. George propped Josh's good arm over his shoulder. He wobbled.

"Easy, mate," said Will. "You good?"

Josh nodded. He was taller than George and well built. George ached under the weight of him. They slowly made their way towards the far end of the barn. Jess and Will pushed hard on the doors. The wood rattled but didn't budge. George glanced back at the other doors – they were tied shut with a heavy chain and lock.

"Trapped again," Francesca sighed.

"Our best hope is to break through these broken panels," said Will, digging his toe into one of the cracks. "If we can kick a few more in, we could climb through."

"Sounds as good a plan as any," said George, distracted by Jess who had disappeared back into the corner of the barn.

Will took a run at a flimsy looking panel with a hole in it. The whole wall of the barn shook, but the small hole remained about as wide as a fist.

"Wait," said Jess. "Use this."

She had returned with the mower blade. She pulled off a shoe, whipped off a sock and wrapped it around one end.

"Not a bad axe," she grinned.

Will stood back as she wheeled the makeshift tool around her head and slammed it down into the pitted wood. Two, three, four times it came crashing down. The wood creaked and splintered under her attack. George stood in awe as she gradually ate away at the opening.

After the seventh or eighth blow, she looked like her arms might fall off.

"Anyone else want a go?" she panted.

Will stepped forward. He attacked the hole with the same fury and soon pieces of the wall were flying out in all directions. One hefty blow split half the panel in two. He dropped the blade and yanked at the shattered pieces of wood, ripping them aside. Jess stepped in to help. Before long, the hole was big enough to get their shoulders through. They continued to pull at loose pieces of timber below the hole. Francesca joined in beside Jess, now that the hole was bigger, and they made even faster progress.

They were so close. Will grabbed hold of one final plank that obstructed their exit and pushed down hard. The long, thin shard of timber snapped, sending an arrow of wood straight through the centre of his palm. He screamed out, grabbing his speared hand.

"Arrghhh!"

He flew at the wall, kicking out and cursing at the top of his lungs.

"Will! Will!" shouted Jess, as he flew again at the wall. "Please stop! – STOP!"

He crumpled to the floor, tears in his eyes, exhaustion screaming from every muscle.

"I've had enough!" he bellowed.

"I know," said Jess, dropping to his side. "We all have."

Francesca bent down and took his hand in hers.

"That's a pretty nasty splinter," she said with a sympathetic smile.

A three-inch pencil of wood had entered his palm by his thumb and protruded out just below his little finger.

"You need to take that out," said Jess.

"Um … I'm not sure that's a great idea," said Francesca. "It's not your average splinter. Whichever way we pull it out it's going to leave debris behind."

"You should always pull it out the way it went in," said George. "That's what I was told."

"No one is pulling anything out of anywhere," said Will. "It can bloomin' well stay in there until we get out of this nightmare."

No one argued. Will grabbed his own tie and wrapped it around his hand. He stood, brushed himself down and pushed his way through the hole in the wall. The others followed, Josh and George last.

George paused, straddled halfway through the hole. He glanced back at Mrs Hodge's lifeless body. She looked cold, lying in the straw, one shoe missing and her arms and legs bare. He felt sorry for her. She had done nothing wrong. She didn't deserve to be left alone in the forgotten, dusty barn. He wished there was more he could do.

I'll make sure they don't get away with it, he promised her.

With that, he turned away, more determined than ever to stop Victor and his crew. If nothing else, he would have to stop them from killing again, and that meant stopping them from getting anywhere near his school.

From: Chief
To: J21
Cc: Group - BOP
Re: Bird of Prey {Encrypted}

Update 24.4 - Project Bait

The day we have been waiting for has come.
After seven years, the bird has returned to our soil.

We may have lost the flock, but the bait is set.
We are confident that they will try to access the target
site.

We will trap the birds once they are all inside.
Take no risks. Make no mistakes.
This may be our only chance to catch the bird, once and
for all.

All officers to converge on target site as per drill.

Good luck.

End.

From: J21
To: Group - BOP
Cc: Chief
Re: Bird of Prey {Encrypted}

Response to Update 24.4

I advise caution until we know if and where we have a leak.

It would be foolish to pull all officers from their posts. We cannot be sure that the bird will take the bait. We will leave ourselves open.

End.

From: Chief
To: J21
Cc: Group - BOP
Re: Bird of Prey {Encrypted}

<u>Response to Update 24.4</u>

I appreciate your input Officer J21, but we will need all manpower at the target site if we are to succeed. Continue as instructed.

End.

Chapter 17: An Uphill Climb

The crisp dawn air made George shiver. He could see his own breath, and that of the others, as they stood and took in their surroundings.

"Where do you think we are?" said Francesca, rubbing her hands together to fight off the cold.

George slowly turned around. The barn was behind them. It looked even more neglected from the outside. To the left of the barn sat the burnt out chassis of a tractor. Its giant tyres had fallen away and were now bursting with a variety of weeds and young saplings; oversized plant pots in a forgotten garden. A muddy path led off to the right and ended with a sagging, wooden gate and an undulating fence that had been crushed under the weight of fallen branches.

Beyond the barn stood thick, tangled woodland. The weak, dawn light and wispy, early morning mist curled through the shadowy undergrowth. The hairs on the back of George's neck stood on end. As he turned with his back to the barn, he could see a wide, rutted dirt track that split the woodland in two. The trees were more thinly spread and the air seemed lighter.

"I guess they went that way," he said, pointing to the track.

"Maybe we should go the other way, then," said Francesca, glancing over her shoulder. "We don't need to run into them again."

"Er, I think it's better that we follow the track," said George. "It's more likely to lead to a road or a village."

"But what if it just leads us to them?"

"They were headed for our school, remember? It has to be this way," George said.

"Yeah, they didn't say they were coming back here," said Will. "They said they'd be 'long gone'."

Josh had propped himself up against a tree trunk, his blazer slung over his shoulders. He seemed to be coping a little better, although the cold air was making him shiver violently.

"We need a ride," he said, through chattering teeth.

"I agree," said Jess.

Francesca looked at Josh and back at the others.

"OK," she nodded, walking over to him, pulling his blazer tighter and wrapping her arm around his waist. "We need to get Josh to a hospital."

"And me," grinned Will, holding up his injured hand.

"Yes, Will, of course you too," Francesca smiled.

With that agreed, they started dragging themselves slowly down the track, Francesca helping Josh as best she could.

As Josh staggered past Will, he lay his hand on Will's shoulder.

"You're a big wuss," he said, grinning. "My gunshot wound trumps your splinter."

"I think you're probably right there, mate," Will smiled back.

They followed the track as it wound past overgrown fields, abandoned out-buildings, stagnant algae-encrusted ponds and back into thick woodland. They were gradually climbing as the sun rose higher and the temperature crept up. Josh and Francesca were falling behind.

"Let me help him for a bit," George offered, hanging back.

"Thank you," she sighed.

George could feel his bones shudder with exhaustion. His stomach growled, his tongue felt like sandpaper. It had been hours since they had eaten or drunk any water. Josh was dragging his feet, leaning heavily to one side. It was slow going.

"Hey, guys!" Jess called from up ahead. "There's a proper fence here – it looks new. Maybe there'll be someone around."

With that, something leapt out of the darkness and threw itself at the fence. Jess staggered back in fright.

"What the hell was that?" Will said, approaching the fence.

A large Alsatian was pacing back and forth, baring its teeth.

"Hey, pooch, where's your owner?" he whispered, edging closer; trying to see beyond the trees.

The dog went crazy, barking and clawing at the wire fence.

"Let's move on," said Jess. "I don't think it wants to play fetch."

"Not unless it's with your shin bone," said Josh, who had finally caught up with them, bolstered by George.

"Do you think there's a house in there?" said Francesca.

She got a little too close to the fence again and the dog went wild; this time he was joined by two others. They growled at her as she slowly backed away.

"If there is, they don't want visitors," said Will.

They pushed on. The track wound its way around several boundaries and back into thick woodland. George's feet were burning. His shoes were barely held together, and his still damp socks were rubbing up blisters that stung with every step. Josh was getting heavier as he lent more and more of his weight on George's shoulder. He was shaking again.

"I think we need to take a break," George called to the others. "Josh is exhausted."

Josh's knees gave way and he slumped down onto the path.

"Just rest for a moment," said Francesca, crouching down beside him.

Will and Jess joined them and they all sat on the damp ground.

"He's getting worse," George whispered to the others. "I'm not sure how much further he can go."

Josh mumbled something and winced as he tried to roll onto his good side. He looked even paler than before, his skin almost translucent. George took off his own blazer and laid it over him. He groaned something in return, closing his eyes.

"OK, let's rest for a few minutes," said Will. "Jess and I could maybe go ahead and see if we can bring back help."

"Just a few minutes," agreed Jess.

The sun finally edged over the tree line. George could feel the faint, welcome warmth on his skin. He could hear birds calling, a light breeze disturbing the trees and – a car. An engine. And it wasn't that far away. Jess must have heard it too. She sat up.

"Do you hear that?" she said.

"It's a car," said George.

"Yes," she paused. "It must be a road." With that she sprang up. "Come on. It can't be far."

Josh groaned again.

"Come on – we'll help you," said Francesca, helping him to his feet. "We can get you that ride."

George stood and helped prop him up.

"Are we sure it's a road?" he called to Jess, who had powered on around a corner ahead.

"Yes," she called back. "The track ends up here. There's a gate."

They tried to speed up to join her, but Josh couldn't move any faster. He could barely put one foot in front of another.

"You go ahead," George said to Francesca. "I'll stay with Josh."

"No," she said, holding Josh tighter. "I'll stay with him, you go. We'll be right behind you."

As they rounded the corner, George could see the wide, metal, farm gate slung open and a road beyond. His spirits lifted. He couldn't help running to catch up with Will and Jess who were nearly at the gate.

"We should hail a car down," said Will, speeding up. "Maybe they'll have a phone we can use, too."

They emerged from the woods, only a short distance to the gate. George could see the smooth black tarmac, the white road markings and hear the grinding whine of an engine. He raced ahead just as a double-decker bus steamed past the gate, pushing its way up the hill.

"Wait!" he screamed, sprinting the last twenty yards to the roadside. "WAIT!"

Jess and Will were on his tail, shouting, waving their arms. They hurtled out into the road, but all they could see was the back end of the bus winding its way through the tunnel of trees.

"That was Mr Steckler!" George said, panting. "It was the school bus."

"We've been in the school woods this whole damn time," said Will.

"I know this bend," said George. "The school is at the top of this hill."

"Come on then," said Jess. "What are we waiting for?"

"You guys go ahead," said George. "We'll follow with Josh. Send back help."

The hill felt a lot steeper to George now that he was hiking up it rather than being chauffeured by Mr Steckler. Their progress was slow. Not another single car passed them, but then the road didn't lead to much else other than Oakfield Manor. A gusty wind had picked up, blowing in their faces and sapping their energy. Will and Jess were already a few hundred yards ahead of them when Josh stumbled and tripped, pulling George and Francesca to their knees. He collapsed to the ground, barely conscious.

"George, I don't know how much longer he can cope," said Francesca. "He's lost so much blood. He's too weak."

With that, a loud horn blasted from behind them and tyres screeched to a halt. George looked up. A small, blue smart car had almost crashed right into them. The door flew open and Dr Root threw herself out in such a panic that she almost clattered to the ground. She staggered towards them and threw her arms around George.

"Oh my goodness – Oh, I am so happy to see you – where on earth have you been?" she babbled. "Oh, we have been beside ourselves – how on earth did you get all the way back here? We thought you were lost in London and then the police – and then you were gone. Oh my goodness me!"

Her words spilled out at such speed, that they didn't know which question to answer first. Before they had time to speak her eyes locked on Josh.

"He looks dreadful. What happened to him?" she said, bending down and taking his head in her hands.

"He was shot," said George.

Her head jerked up to meet George's gaze.

"Shot?"

"Yes – it's a very long story, but he needs an ambulance."

Will and Jess had sprinted back down the hill.

Dr Root looked pale and dazed. "My God," she said, looking around at the young faces peering down at her. "What happened to you all?"

"We need to get to the school," said George. "We think someone is trying to blow it up."

Dr Root visibly froze. "What?"

Her jaw hung open, her eyes distant. George could see that she had probably not slept since discovering that her students had gone missing and that his words were taking a while to sink in. He needed to take control, to be the adult and to take the lead.

"Dr Root, I need you to take Josh up to the school and call an ambulance. You also need to tell Mrs Hamilton to evacuate the school. We think the people that shot Josh are planning to blow up the school. Can you do that for us?"

She nodded. "Right. Yes – Josh – ambulance – evacuate school," she said, rather dreamily.

George was worried that she wasn't quite taking it all in.

"You need to go now," he said, lifting her to her feet.

"Yes, of course."

They loaded Josh into her tiny car and watched her as she disappeared up the hill.

"I have no idea if she believed us or understood a thing you said, mate," said Will. "I think we need to get up there as quickly as we can."

"Agreed," said George. "Let's run."

From: J21
To: Group - BOP
Cc: Chief
Re: Bird of Prey {Encrypted}

<u>Update 24.5</u>

Urgent – the bird has <u>not</u> taken the bait.

We have traced the 999 call from inside UNIT 256 to a mobile that is now on route to The Hub. We must assume that the Bird knows the true location of The Hub.

Re-direct all officers to The Hub and wait for my signal. I am on my way there now – all officers needed as back up.

Repeat – the bird has <u>NOT</u> taken the bait.

End.

Chapter 18: Inferno

The four of them broke into a jog. George's body could no longer feel any pain. His legs felt like someone else's, his feet had gone numb and his head felt like it was floating above his body.

As they pounded up the hill, he whispered to himself. "I must stop him – I must stop the falcon from taking flight."

By the time he lifted his head to see where they were, the familiar school gates were in view. George had the most surreal feeling as he entered the school grounds. It felt so safe and so reassuring to be back at school. He wanted to stop running and just rest, but he couldn't stop. His school was in grave danger. More than ever, he had to make himself heard.

As they pulled open the front doors, Mrs Hamilton, the school nurse and Dr Root were in the foyer leaning over Josh. He was unconscious on the floor. Mrs Hamilton looked up, her face full of fear.

"Francesca, William …" she breathed. "Thank God you're all safe."

She stood, but before she could say anymore, George pushed forwards.

"Mrs Hamilton," George said, standing tall. "I know no one believed us when we said that we'd found a body in the woods, but you have to believe us now. The people that took us hostage and shot Josh, are here in Pendleton, and we believe they came last night to blow up the school."

Mrs Hamilton looked from George to Josh and back to George.

"George, I know you've been through an absolutely horrid ordeal. I do believe that, and I can see that Joshua here is in urgent need of care. We have called an ambulance and the police are on their way. But why would anyone want to blow up this school?"

"Please, Mrs Hamilton," Jess said, stepping in to support George. "He's telling the truth."

"It's true," said Francesca. "We heard them talk about the school when they had us tied up in the barn."

"Tied up – in a barn?" Mrs Hamilton looked like she might pass out herself. "But no one can get into the school overnight."

"Mr Jefferson could," said George.

"Well, yes, possibly, but what's he– "

"He's one of them," cried Will. "He locked us in a van and knocked us out!"

"He did what?"

They were getting nowhere. Mrs Hamilton was becoming less composed by the second. George had to get out of this conversation and soon. With that, the front doors flew open and Mrs Stone raced in.

"Jessica!" she screamed, nearly knocking Jess over with her embrace. "Your father has spent all night searching the streets of London … my God, what happened to you all? What happened to Joshua?"

Another round of frantic exchanges filled the foyer. George stood staring at the scene. Jess and Will were answering Mrs Stone's questions and Mrs Hamilton had turned her attention back to Joshua. George couldn't wait, he slipped past them all and dived into the belly of the school.

The first lessons of the day were in session and every classroom that George passed was brimming with students.

Why does Victor want to kill all these kids?

He dashed through the lower corridors, looking for any sign of explosives.

Where has he hidden them?

The modest, familiar schoolhouse now felt like a sprawling maze – it was like searching for a needle in a haystack.

As George came up opposite the year nine locker room, he almost tripped over Baxter who was scampering down the corridor, followed by Mr Hill. George quickly ducked into the locker room and hid behind the door. He didn't want to waste any more time explaining himself to the caretaker. Baxter was barking and jumping up in his usual frenzy. George slunk down behind a bank of lockers.

"Be quiet, dog!" Mr Hill said. "What's got into you?"

He dragged the dog away and out of the nearest exit. George stuck his head out of the door.

I'm running out of time.

He slipped back out of the locker room and raced down the next corridor, past the Science Lab.

"Wait!" he shouted.

He skidded to a halt and turned to face Dr Root's lab. The entrance was taped over with duct tape. That wasn't unusual. Dr Root was known to have the odd accident in the pursuit of bringing science to life, but the large silvery X that barred the door was made from the very same tape that had been suffocating George only a few hours previously.

"Dr Root was in London all day and night," he said out loud.

He looked up and down the deserted corridor. "Surely not…"

Unable to stop his hands from trembling, he took a deep breath, pulled the tape aside and cautiously pushed the door open. Standing on the threshold, barely daring to step inside, he scanned the room. The usual smell of burning was absent. George could smell the fresh autumn air instead. He took one tentative step inside. The blinds were pulled down half way, obscuring the light and throwing half the lab into shade. He urged himself further in, passing down behind the first row of benches. Nothing looked unusual or out of place. A strong gust of wind whistled through the thinly paned windows, sending the blinds billowing out like sails. A broken window. The wind came again. Chalk dust swirled through the air, catching in the light and George's eyes landed on something poking out from behind Dr Root's heavy, wooden desk.

He froze. The blinds flapped about madly, sending a shadow bouncing across the desktop. In the far corner of the room, something red flickered in the dancing light. George's heart was pounding faster and faster. He wanted to turn and run. He screwed up his eyes, filled his lungs and stepped around the bench. Opening one eye he saw it, standing right where Dr Root would conduct her class – a bundle of three large black cylinders, wired and flashing.

He could feel the blood pumping around every vein in his body. He couldn't take his eyes off it. It seemed to stare back at him, ticking with every blink. He dared not move, paralysed with the fear that even his breath might disturb its stability.

The school bell screamed in George's ears. He leapt backwards. The scraping of chairs above. The clatter of feet. He snapped out of his trance and looked up.

What's above here? – Maths!

The classroom above was full of year nines.

This was it – this was his moment. He had to get every last person out. He tore out of the lab, up the stairs and nearly crashed straight into Felix.

"George! What – where…." Felix stood gaping at George. "What happened to your face?"

"We need to get the hell out of here, Felix," George said, grabbing him by the arm. "I need to get everyone out."

He looked around. The corridor was slowly filling up as all students from all years sauntered out of one lesson and into another.

"Everyone needs to get out!" George started yelling. "Get out now!"

Several people stopped and stared, a few were laughing. He looked at their faces. He knew them all. Passed them every day, jostling in the corridors, laughing out on the lawns. How could he possibly save them all if none of them would listen.

"George, mate," Felix grabbed him. "What's got into you? Where the hell have you been?"

"There's a bomb – downstairs – in the lab." George twisted to face Felix. "You have to believe me."

Felix hesitated. "Mate, I…"

"Please, Felix." George looked straight into Felix's eyes.

"The fire alarm," Felix said, pointing back towards the maths room.

George had never noticed it before, a tiny red box, protruding from the wall. "Of course."

He pushed past several students, balled up his fist, punched the flimsy perspex and yanked the handle. The siren wailed, cutting all conversations dead; students froze, confused. They'd never had a real alarm, only the termly drills.

"Get out!" George yelled. He climbed up onto the windowsill. "GET OUT!"

The panic in his voice seemed to have the desired effect. Students started making their way to the fire exits, filing out of the classrooms and down the external stairs. George watched as they streamed out, anxious to see every last person leave.

He grabbed Felix. "Let's go."

But before they had made it to the top of the stairs, they were thrown across the corridor, slamming into the wall. The explosion rattled every doorframe, shattered every window. George's ears rang. He could feel his face sting as glass shot through the air, slicing his skin. The crack of the explosion was immediately replaced with the sound of screaming and choking. A thick, black smoke filled the corridor. George covered his mouth with his shirtsleeve. His eyes streamed. People pushed past him, running for the fire exit.

"Felix?" he choked.

He pushed himself up, his back against the wall. He was opposite the maths room. Flames were crawling up the walls. Half of the floor had been ripped away. He could make out the silhouette of something slumped by the doorway. Someone was in the maths room, out cold.

He staggered towards the door. The heat overcame him, pushed him back. His face felt like it was melting, his eyes burning. He dropped to the floor, crawled over to the doorway and grabbed a foot. He pulled. Whoever it was, they were heavy. He pinned his feet to the doorframe and heaved. Slowly the body moved, he dragged it over the threshold just as the ceiling crashed down into the maths room crushing the remaining desks and chairs.

"George!" Felix was behind him. "Come on – get out!"

"There's someone here – help me," he screamed.

Felix crouched down, shielding his face from the heat. Wiping his eyes, he leant over the body. "It's Liam."

"We need to drag him out." The smoke was circling around them, closing in like a ghostly predator. "Stay close to the floor."

Inch by inch, they dragged him the length of the corridor, towards the fire exit. The flames were eating their way down the corridor, engulfing everything in their path. The searing heat crept up George's legs, he could feel it trying to pull him back, trying to make him give up and run. With one final surge they burst through the door. The fresh air danced with the smoke as it billowed out of the doorway. George gasped in a lungful. He felt it burn as it raced down his windpipe and caught in his chest. He was on all fours, peering down the fire escape – two flights of metal stairs. His head spun. He coughed until he had no air left in his lungs. Mucus and bile. He vomited.

Falling back against the metal railing, he could hear sirens, shouting, voices. Someone was coming up the steps. A masked figure, a gloved hand. He was grabbed and hoisted down the stairs. Next thing he knew, he was on his back, cool air on his face, soft grass beneath his neck and an oxygen mask clamped over his mouth. As he opened his eyes, Jess and Will were peering down at him.

"You OK there, crazy man?" said Will.

"Did they all get out?" he croaked, pulling off the mask.

"Difficult to tell, mate," said Will, peering over his shoulder. "You, Felix and Liam were the last out, but the firefighters have been in and can't find anyone else."

"Where's Felix?"

"I'm here," said a hoarse voice from behind him. Felix was collapsed under a tree. His face was black, his hands smeared with blood.

"What happened to Liam?"

"He's over there," said Will, pointing towards a stretcher. "He's giving some poor paramedic a mouthful of grief."

George pulled himself up. His throat felt like he'd swallowed razor blades. The scene was chaotic. Ambulances, fire trucks, and police cars filled the driveway. The schoolhouse stood half intact, half engulfed in smoke and flames. The flashing lights, strobing through the haze. The air filled with a mixture of smoke and fine spray from the hoses. The grounds were swarming with bodies, some on their feet, dashing from one task to another, some collapsed on the ground. Students in tears. Teachers trying to control the chaos, counting heads.

"I couldn't stop it," George muttered. "I couldn't stop him."

"Who?" asked Felix. "Who did this?"

"Victor," George spat, staring up at the towering spirals of smoke.

"George, look around you," Jess said, resting a hand on his arm. "All these kids got out. You did that."

"Yeah," said Will. "That's all that matters."

"I didn't want him to win," he said, turning away from the sight of it. It made him sick. He looked down towards the drive. He could see Mrs Hamilton consoling Francesca as an ambulance sped away through the gates.

"Oh God, what about Josh, what happened to him?" George was up.

"George – relax," said Will, jumping to his feet and taking George by the shoulders. "He's OK. The ambulance had already arrived by the time the fire alarm went off. They already had him loaded up in the back. He was stable. He's going to be fine."

George looked back to the school entrance. Two paramedics were winding their way towards them.

"Just relax, OK," said Jess. "You need to get your face sorted out. You look like you've been through ten rounds with Liam."

"We'll go get you guys some water," said Will, as the paramedics dropped their bags at George's feet.

George sat and watched the flames slowly die back as he and Felix were fussed over by the medics. He felt exhausted. He just wanted to be left alone. They cleaned up his face, took his vitals and bandaged Felix's bleeding hands. Happy that they weren't in critical condition the medics moved on, leaving Felix and George together under the tree.

"Why would anyone want to blow up a school and kill a bunch of kids?" Felix took the words right out of George's mouth.

"Honestly, I have no idea." George sighed. They sat for a while in silence.

"I'm sorry I didn't believe you, George," Felix said, staring at his bandaged hands.

"About what, Felix?"

"All of it, I guess."

"It's OK, mate. I don't think I would have believed me either."

"There really was a body?"

"Yeah," George looked up at Felix, "old Mrs Hodge. I think they kidnapped her, questioned her. Did you know she was the local MP that closed the tunnels up?"

"My God." Felix stared into the woods. "What did they achieve?" George sat. His brain churned. Something wasn't right. "You know – I went home and asked my dad about the tunnels– "

"The tunnels! That's it." George leapt to his feet. "That's it, Felix. They didn't achieve a thing. It's been about the tunnels this whole time. This was all just a decoy!"

George was running. His feet skimmed the grass as he raced down the slope towards the school drive – towards the chaos. He needed to find someone to tell – someone who would listen. He headed for the main drive where several police cars stood, lights still flashing.

"George!" someone called. It was Mrs Hamilton. She was headed straight for him. "George, slow down. Where are you going?" She threw herself at him, engulfing him in a hug. "George, you were right. I'm so sorry we didn't listen." She pulled away. "Oh my goodness, look at you. You need to sit down."

"I'm fine. I need to find a police officer. I know who did this and I need to tell them…"

Someone had him by the arm. He flashed an ID in Mrs Hamilton's direction. "Excuse me, Mrs Hamilton. I'd like to speak to George, if that's OK? It won't take long. We need to ask him some questions."

"Right, of course," said Mrs Hamilton, smiling at the gentleman. "You come down to see me when you're done, George. There are a lot of people who want to thank you for what you did."

George looked up at the man who had him by the bicep. He wasn't in uniform. He wore a charcoal, ribbed turtle-neck, tight fitting black trousers, plain black pumps and a cap. You could make out every muscle. He looked like a swimmer; broad shoulders, slim waist. He steered George towards an unmarked car.

"Who are you?" asked George, staring into his well shaven, chiselled face.

A faint memory was slowly waking in the back of George's brain, trying to claw itself to the forefront.

"Do I know you?" he asked.

"No" the man said, trying to smile. "We've never met."

But George was sure he knew this man, maybe they hadn't met, but he definitely recognised him from somewhere.

"Who are you?" George repeated.

"I'm Officer Crane," the man said, opening the car door, looking around over his shoulder. "We need to talk."

Gran's words were echoing in George's ears.

You're dad doesn't trust the police after all the nonsense with your mum.

George yanked his arm away. The man lurched forward, trying to grab him again. George ducked and managed to evade his grasp. The man stared down at him.

"Don't be a fool, George. I'm here to help you."

"No," shouted George. "I don't need your help."

A female officer in uniform appeared from behind a nearby police car.

"Everything OK here?" she asked.

The man turned to answer her and George took his chance and ran. He raced past the ambulances and fire trucks, dodged between groups of onlookers and didn't stop until he reached the edge of the woods. Once under the cover of the trees, he slipped behind a large oak and turned to check that the man hadn't followed him. He could see him, weaving in and out of the chaos, searching. For now, he was in the clear.

George stood, catching his breath and peered into the woods. This is where it had all begun. He could see himself, face down in the dirt, Liam's foot in his back, Jess and Will on the path ahead. He closed his eyes. He could see the ridge, the escarpment, the fallen tree, Mrs Hodge's body and the tunnel. His heart pounded.

"I should go back for help," he said, glancing back past the pavilion and towards the schoolhouse. He could just make out Will and Jess, wandering across the lawn. He thought of Josh groaning in pain, of Francesca quivering in the dark, of Will thrashing out in anger. He had dragged his friends through so much.

He looked again at the path to the dell. He felt like a different person from the one that Liam had shoved down into the dirt over a week ago.

It will have to be me this time – just me.

With one last look over his shoulder, he turned and strode down the path, past the campfire, through the woods and up to the ridge.

Chapter 19: The Grubhole

Something felt different. The view down the escarpment was lighter, airier. Soft, pale sunlight hung amongst the branches – sleepy and tranquil. The wind had calmed. A tendril of air caressed the back of George's neck and curled up around his ears, making his hair tickle his forehead. His breathing was even and shallow. The buzz and clatter of the chaos surrounding the schoolhouse had faded away. He felt cocooned in the blanket of the woods. The trees hushed, the leaves elegantly parachuted down around him and birds sang overhead.

George's eyes glazed over as he stood staring at the journey down. He had no plan, no clue of what lay waiting for him on the valley floor. Stalling, he tried to think of a reason why he should go back, give in, leave it to someone else. He thought of his dad and Gran.

They must be worried sick.

He paced back and forth past the old tree stump, stopping once or twice to peer down at the valley below. With every passing moment Victor was escaping, getting away with all he'd done. Mrs Hodge, the security guards at the vault and god knows who else. They all had family, sons, daughters maybe. He thought of Philippe and Mr J, their nasty, spiteful faces. Of Angelika lashing out at Josh and Jose laughing at his pain. George's teeth ground, his fists were closed tight. He wanted to see Victor brought down, stopped, caught. And he wanted to be the one to do it. For himself, for his friends, for Mrs Hodge and those poor dead men and, most of all, to show his dad that he wasn't a foolish child.

He took a deep breath, his nostrils flared, his chest filled, his hazy glare cleared and he charged down the descent.

It seemed to take no time at all to reach the stream. George stopped a few feet from the fallen tree. Hidden by the undergrowth, he searched the surrounding area for any sign of Victor and his crew. All he could hear was the water passing beneath the bridge and the whisper of the breeze in the trees. He climbed onto the trunk, shuffled along its length and slowly slid off at the other end. Still no sign of anyone else. The holly bush stood guarding the path to the tunnel. Nothing much seemed to have changed. Maybe he was wrong after all. Maybe there was no one here. Pain ran up his side and his headache had returned. His neck was stiff and tense. He rubbed his temples then stretched his arms ahead of him and cracked his neck.

Steadily and carefully, he pushed the holly branches aside and slipped into the clearing facing the tunnel.

Someone has definitely been here.

The ivy had been hacked away, revealing a neat arch of stonework framing the tunnel entrance. George edged closer. There was a smell lingering in the air. Soil, smoke, damp wood. Leaves covered the floor but had been swept aside in places. He dragged his foot through the leaf litter. There, half buried in the pile of leaves, was a cigar butt. It smoldered as he kicked it.

"Jose," he said, nudging the cigar again with his toe.

His words floated down the tunnel and disappeared into the darkness. He scanned the woodland behind him before tentatively stepping forward.

They must be down there.

His breathing was no longer slow and steady. He could feel his pulse throbbing in his temples. He rubbed them again, this time closing his eyes, listening to his own breath, coming and going, in and out. There was a sudden crunch behind him. He turned to see someone stumbling through the barricade of holly. Their face was obscured by a large sheet of crumpled paper. George braced himself. The anonymous figure tripped on the ferns at their feet and almost collided with George as they lurched forwards. The paper fell from their hands and a familiar face looked up at him.

"Felix! What are you doing?"

Felix grinned. "Ha! Found you. I knew you'd come here."

"How did you know where I was?"

"Well, if you hadn't have scarpered midway through our conversation…" Felix scowled.

"Sorry."

"I was just saying that I asked my dad about the tunnels and he had this map in his study. He'd copied it from the library." Felix snatched up the paper from the floor.

George stepped beside him and inspected the finely detailed map. It covered a significant area of the Kent countryside and detailed all the known tunnels.

"Wow," said George. "That's amazing."

"I know," grinned Felix, proudly.

"So, where are we?"

"Here," said Felix, pointing to a small red line that ended with an X. "This is one of the entrances that was sealed shut."

"It doesn't look very sealed," said George, stepping forwards and sticking his head into the darkness.

"Apparently, many of them were sealed with concrete and steel."

George looked back at the map. The tunnel led in a straight line before splitting several times. One branch made its way towards the old station in Pendleton, one or two continued south.

"Why are some parts dashed lines?" he asked.

"They've either caved in or not been investigated so the exact direction is unknown."

"Right."

One large section between them and Pendleton was dashed.

"What do you plan to do, George?" asked Felix, looking concerned. "You can't stop this man on your own."

"I know. I just need to see where he's gone. See what he's doing." George had an idea. "Come with me," he said. "Once we've got eyes on them, you can come back for help. Get Mr Hill or Mrs Hamilton. Get them to send the police down here. I can keep an eye on Victor while you go back for help."

Felix frowned. He wasn't the bravest person George knew. He sighed and scratched his head.

"I must be mad. OK, I'll come with you but no being a hero again, George – promise?"

"Promise."

"We'll need this." Felix pulled a torch from his back pocket – the one he kept in his locker.

"Genius, Felix. I hadn't planned this that well. Not sure what I'd do without you."

Felix smiled. George grinned in return and patted Felix on the shoulder. It felt good to have his friend back.

With that, they sank down into the dark tunnel, down the worn steps and into the woods' hidden underworld.

The framing stonework of the tunnel entrance was neat and elegant in comparison to what lay before them at the bottom of the decline. The rock had been ground away, maybe by hand, some time ago. It was uneven, lopsided and nowhere near as straight as the map suggested. It looked as if a giant grub had wriggled its way through the rock, gnawing and scraping at the sides, forcing its way onwards, leaving a trail of coarse debris in its wake.

George and Felix stood staring at the stark view ahead of them. The air was cool and still, and all they could hear was the faint murmur of the forest's voice, whispering down the stairwell. George's nose twitched. He could still smell smoke, but he wasn't sure it was from Jose's cigar. He searched in the rubble at his feet. There was no sign of more discarded cigar ends. He motioned Felix forwards. They stalked along the tunnel, glued to each other at the shoulder, Felix's torch lighting a small circle of light onto the path.

"What's that?" Felix whispered, shining the light on a dark mound up ahead.

George edged closer. He had a nasty feeling he already knew what it was. There, lying in a crumpled heap, was a torn black bag, a lonely shoe and a shattered pair of glasses. He swallowed hard.

"It's nothing," he said to Felix, pushing the torch away from the site. "It's just rubbish."

George could feel the heat rising up his neck. He didn't need reminding of why he hated Victor so much. He urged Felix to speed up.

Soon the grub-hole arched around to the left and became tighter. So tight that George had to duck to pass through it into a small chamber that was filled with a dozen old, rusted barrels. They were covered in dust and buckled and crumbling in places.

"What are these doing here?" George said out loud.

"Must be war relics," Felix said, crouching down and wiping the dust from the side of one of the barrels.

As he did, there was a squealing sound and something scampered from behind the rusted pile. Felix yelped and toppled backwards.

"It was a rat – you numpty," George laughed.

But his laughter was cut short by the sound of something falling further up the tunnel. They both froze. Felix was on the floor still. He went to lift the torch, but George lunged out and pushed it down into the dirt. He held a finger to his lips.

They waited, listening for any disturbance. The sound came again. It sounded like the dribble of cascading rubble. George lifted Felix to his feet. He took the torch and held it to his side, lighting only the ground at their feet. As they approached the sound, they could see ahead of them that the tunnel was filled with dust, and large chunks of rock lay on the ground. The smell that George had first picked up at the entrance was now so strong it stung his nostrils. He lifted the torch to see a gaping, twisted mess of contorted steel and shattered concrete.

"That's the seal," Felix said, running towards it. "They've blasted right through it."

"They must have used explosives to get through that," said George, inspecting the hole in the two-foot thick plug of cement and steel. "No wonder they needed a distraction up at the school."

"But the whole tunnel could have caved in," Felix said, glancing at the rock above their heads.

The steel grate had been bent and cut aside. George squatted down and picked up a stray arrow of steel that lay at his feet. It was sharply cut at both ends.

"Or a power saw, maybe?" he mumbled to himself.

"Whatever is hidden down here, they want it pretty bad," Felix said, sticking his head through the hole. "There's a fork in the tunnel up ahead. There's a light."

"Can you see anything else?" George asked. But before Felix had time to respond, voices were echoing down one of the forks.

He jerked his head back through the hole and sank onto his backside. George flicked off the torch and hit the floor. If they lay flat, they were hidden behind the debris and the remaining bulk of the seal. George's head spun. Should he run or hide? Were they coming this way? He could feel the cool spike of steel in his hand. He grasped it tighter, ready to pounce if anyone came through the hole.

The voices grew louder.

"Austin and I have deactivated all the alarms. No one will know we have been here until they get the little surprise we will leave them." It was Alex Allaman.

Someone chuckled. "I wish I could see their faces when the whole place crashes down around them." Angelika said.

"Yes," Alex agreed. "But I'm more than happy to be very far away by then. Are the escape routes clear?"

"Yes, Sabrina has cleared The Hub entrance. There were only two guards on duty. They seem to have been so busy trying to set their trap that they have left this place wide open."

"They really didn't see it coming?"

"No. Sabrina said they looked like they'd been slapped in the face when she appeared from *behind* the security door." Angelika laughed again.

"What about the other exits?"

"The tunnels south are clear. Philippe and Jefferson may be idiots but they had everything ready and in place. We can escape south, and Jose has set the charges. If anyone tries to follow us, the whole place will blow and they'll be buried alive."

"Sounds watertight," Alex said. "Let's just hope Austin and Victor can do their part of the job."

"Victor wants these last two boxes," Angelika said. "Then we're done."

With that, they lifted two boxes laden with explosives and disappeared. George waited until their voices had faded away. He raised his head out of its hiding place and peered through the hole. Two large caverns in the rock stared back at him like giant hollow eyes.

"He's down there somewhere," he whispered to himself.

"OK. I've heard enough, George," Felix said, getting to his feet. "I think it's time we go back for help. These guys are serious."

"I know. Trust me. I've been face to face with them."

Felix shuddered. "Please, George. Let's go."

"You go, Felix. Take the torch. Go and find Mrs Hamilton. Tell her to send every officer she can find."

"But..."

"Please, Felix," George pleaded. "I can't let him get away. I made a promise."

"A promise to who?"

"It doesn't matter. Just do this for me, please?"

"OK. But don't move from here."

"I can't go very far without a torch, can I?"

"I'll be as quick as I can." Felix turned to leave. "Here, take this." He handed George the map. "Just in case you need to escape – quickly."

"Thanks, Felix. I owe you one."

As Felix disappeared from view, the light faded and George was left sitting in the gloom. He listened until the crunch of Felix's footsteps had silenced. It was eerily quiet. He was desperate to know what lay beyond the gentle glow escaping from the fork in the passage.

Where have Alex and Angelika gone? Where is Victor?

He glanced at his watch. Its dimly lit, cracked face glared back up at him – useless. With no sense of time, he fidgeted, waiting for what seemed like an age. The ground was hard and lumpy. Small, sharp stones dug into his skin. He looked again towards the light. There was no sign of activity.

Has Victor gone already?

He looked at his watch again, then ripped it off and threw it down the tunnel in frustration.

I need to find him.

He heaved himself from the ground, his limbs sore and stiff, climbed through the hole and slid along the wall towards the light. The passage was littered with empty boxes, just like the ones from the barn. Several lamps had been left along the path. Before long, the passage split again, more boxes and crates. He looked at the map. If he kept to the left he would be heading in the direction of the old, abandoned station and the dashed part of the map. The path to the right was partly blocked by fallen rock. He inched further into the depths of the ancient warren, careful to note his position on the map. He placed each footstep with the greatest of caution, desperately trying to silence the crunch of his approach.

Stopping behind another pile of rusted drums, he listened. There was something drifting on the air – a faint noise – a dull, echoing murmur. He crouched down behind the barrels and steadied his breathing. He tried to train his ears on the noise up ahead but instead heard the rhythmic march of someone coming up behind him. His heart rate spiked, his breathing out of control. It was one set of steps, not several. It couldn't be Felix, coming back with help. It had to be someone else. George scrabbled to his feet and started running, the sound of his heavy gait rebounding off the solid, stone walls. He was heading towards the light, towards Victor. He tussled with the map, searching for another fork – another exit – a place to hide.

Up ahead. A T-junction.

Lifting his gaze, he sped forward and turned the corner, only to slam straight into Mr Jefferson.

It was like hitting a lamppost. George struggled to stay on his feet, the loose gravel beneath him slid from under his soles. He tumbled sideways just as Mr Jefferson leant out and grabbed him by the collar. George twisted, lashing out with his arms. He threw the map into Mr Jefferson's face, who lost his grip. George turned and ran, but the crack of Mr Jefferson's gun and the whistle of the bullet, made him stop dead in his tracks.

"Not so fast, Jenkins," Mr Jefferson said. "I think you'd be wise to stop right there."

George lifted his hands above his head and slowly turned to face his teacher. He could feel hatred course through him like an unseen energy, fuelling him. He wanted to explode, hurl himself at Mr Jefferson and unleash every ounce of his energy in a fit of anger.

Mr Jefferson laughed. "You really hate me, don't you, Jenkins? I can see it in your eyes." He was stalking towards George with his gun raised. "Well, I've got a little secret for you ... the feeling is mutual!" he spat, circling around George, just out of arm's reach.

George twisted his head to keep him in his sight.

"Do you know why I hate you so much, George Jenkins?" Mr Jefferson continued, smiling his hideous smile. "You see this face?" He pulled at his collar, revealing his scar. "You see this, George? I blame you for this."

"What's that got to do with me?" George snapped.

Mr Jefferson laughed out loud.

"Well, you see, George," he said, his smile vanishing, his eyelid still shuddering. "The person who shot me in the neck and destroyed the nerves in my face – I can't punish them, but I can quite happily punish you instead."

He lunged out and grabbed George by the neck. "Maybe I should start with *your* face," he growled.

George squirmed in his grip. "Get off me!"

"What are you doing?" a voice bellowed from behind.

Mr Jefferson released his grip and shoved George to the floor. George turned to see Philippe striding down the tunnel towards them.

"You just don't give up, do you?" Philippe said, staring down at George. "I thought you would have had enough by now."

Philippe glared at Mr Jefferson. "This is no time for personal vendettas."

"I've earned my chance for retribution," Mr Jefferson snapped back.

"We must stick to the plan," Philippe said. "We all need to stay focused."

"I'm perfectly focused."

"If what I heard is right, it was you losing your focus seven years ago that got you shot in the neck. Now take him to Victor. He may have a use for him yet."

Mr Jefferson bristled.

Chapter 20: Unburied Truths

George tried to concentrate on where they were heading – tried to think up a way to escape, but he couldn't quiet his mind. It buzzed with questions. After everything he'd seen and all he'd been through, he wanted answers. He needed it to make sense – to piece together in his head. He lifted his eyes from the floor and stared at the back of Mr Jefferson's head.

"Who shot you?" he blurted out.

"Silence!" bellowed Philippe from behind him, shoving him in the back. "Save your questions for Victor. He'll deal with you now."

George scowled.

They marched down identical passages and turned identical corners, a monotonous, featureless journey, until they finally stepped out into a spacious, domed cavern. Roughly chiselled walls, the same pale stone, a rubble carpet and, suspended in the centre of the vacuum, a large, shining metal box, large enough to hold a grown man. It floated like a cocooned victim in the centre of a web, anchored to the floor and ceiling by thick steel cables. George couldn't help gaping at it. Lights bounced off its mirrored surface, making him squint.

"Argghh!" someone screamed. "This isn't working. It's not what we expected."

George peered beyond the box. Someone was balanced on a platform, half obscured by the hanging spectacle. George could just make out a scruffy pair of untied trainers and an ankle tattooed with binary code. It had to be Austin Van der Berg.

"It's impossible!" he yelled, throwing something down. It clattered down the metal steps and landed next to an open case of tools.

"I pay you to achieve the impossible," someone said, descending the steps. George recognised the voice immediately. "Try again and this time don't fail. I haven't come this far to fail."

Heavy boots crunched to the ground and Victor turned to look at him.

"Ah, we have a visitor," he smiled, clapping his hands together.

George stood, wedged between Philippe and Mr Jefferson. He could feel his shoulders tense and his skin prickle as Victor slowly weaved between the cables and came to stand face to face with him. George could see every crease in his hardened skin, every scar on his clasped hands and the charcoal tips of the falcon's wings skimming the top of his ears.

"I've been expecting you, Master Jenkins," he said. "I'm so glad you could join us."

He paused, waiting for a response. His mouth turned up at the edges as if to show genuine pleasure, but his eyes stayed narrowed and full of contempt.

"No pleasantries, George? No 'how nice to meet you, Mr Sokolov'?" He paused again. "Oh, how very disappointing," he sighed.

Mr Jefferson sniggered. George shifted his weight. He wanted to stretch – breathe deep but felt pinned by Victor's gaze.

"I'm not really surprised you are so timid, George," he continued, now strolling back and forth, his hands behind his back; his belt of ammunition exposed at his waist. "I had heard you were a wimp of a boy."

George could feel his own teeth grinding.

"You can't believe how surprised I was when Philippe and Jefferson told me how much trouble they'd had shaking you from our tail. You are very persistent," he said, still smiling to himself. "Although, I must admit, I was overjoyed to see you in that dire, little pub. Of course, it took all my restraint not to dispose of you right there," he said, spinning on his heels and staring once again straight into George's eyes. "But that would have ruined all the fun," he chuckled. "Wouldn't it? Did you have *fun* chasing me across London, George?"

George tried his hardest to hold Victor's gaze. He didn't want to give him the satisfaction of a response, but Philippe rammed his baton into George's side and it took the wind right out of him.

"Have some manners!" Philippe hissed in his ear.

George clenched his jaw even tighter and resisted the urge to grab at his throbbing side. He could feel anger festering in his gut.

"Answer!" He jabbed him again.

This time, a sharp pain shot through George's ribs. He closed his eyes and sucked in air, trying to muffle any cry. Shaking off the pain he stood upright and bit his lip hard.

Victor stepped closer. George stared at the rubble at his feet. He'd had enough of looking into his dark, soulless eyes. Anger and hatred were creeping up inside him, like boiling tar, it burned at his insides. Every muscle in his body coiled tight. His fists trembled, his jaw set rigid.

"You are a very stubborn young man," Victor whispered, "just like your mother was."

George's head snapped up. His eyes locked onto Victor's.

"What did you say?"

"Ah, I thought that might grab your attention," he laughed. "Maybe you take after her after all. She was always so smart and curious – a little too curious for her own good, it turned out. Shame really. I could have made good use of her."

George had heard enough. He released all his energy into one sharp swipe. Lunging at Victor, his right fist uncoiled like a loaded spring, powered by all his hatred and fear, his exhaustion and disgust. His knuckles cracked. Pain reverberated up his forearm and into his shoulder. Victor stumbled backwards. George flew at him again, screaming, unloading every ounce of energy he had, but it was over as soon as it started. He was dragged backwards, hurled to the floor and pinned face down.

"So very determined," Victor said, spitting blood from his split lip. "However much we've tried to swat you away like a nasty little fly, you keep coming back for more."

George tried to roll onto his side, but Mr Jefferson had him weighed down, both knees in his back, his gun to his neck.

"Victor, you need to see this." Austin van der Berg had descended from the platform, his dreadlocked hair pulled tight into a bun. Victor went to join him.

"Well, focus! It can't be that hard!" Victor shouted. "They are idiots. Such idiots that they thought it would be hidden from me here. It can't be that hard to crack – where is Alex?"

"Here!"

Alex had just reappeared with Jose and Sabrina in tow.

"Come here. You need to help him," Victor said. "We're running out of time."

George shifted under Mr Jefferson's weight. He wanted to see what else lay around him. Philippe had disappeared from his side. George could now see him talking to Jose and Sabrina on the far side of the cave. Victor, Alex and Austin were by the platform. That only left Angelika. There were at least three other exits he could see.

"Don't get any funny ideas," Mr Jefferson said. "There's no way out."

George knew he had no chance of escaping them all, but if he could throw off Mr Jefferson while the others were distracted then maybe he could dart down the tunnel behind him. He knew there were several forks in that tunnel, and he guessed he could out run Mr Jefferson if he had to.

"It was my mother," George said, "my mother shot you."

Mr Jefferson flinched. "Shut up!"

"That's why you hate me. My mother screwed up your face."

"I said, shut up!"

George knew he was playing with fire, but he had one chance to get out of here alive.

"You got shot by a girl."

With that, Mr Jefferson grabbed George by the arm, turned him over and raised his gun. As quick as lightning, George slammed his heels into Mr Jefferson's kneecaps, sending him flying backwards. His gun clattered off the stone wall. George scrambled to his feet and lunged for the exit. He started to run, crouched low to the ground. The tunnel was a blur. The bright lights from the cavern had left him half blind in the dimly lit passageway. He hurtled head long into the blotched darkness, commotion and footsteps behind him. Pushing harder, bouncing off the walls, colliding into a tower of oil drums – he came crashing to the ground. As he lifted himself up he was stopped in his tracks by the searing light of a torch, full in his face.

"You little rat! Where could you be scampering off to?" It was Angelika.

She smacked him hard around the head with her torch and all the lights went out.

He woke to a throbbing head and a warm trickle of blood that was snaking its way down past his eyebrow, over his temple and pooling in his ear. She must have caught him right on the forehead. As he opened his eyes, Victor stood over him.

"Not many people would live to breathe another lungful after what you just pulled, but the funny thing is, you could be of use to me yet," he said.

George dug his heels into the dirt and pushed himself upright. A single drop of blood clung to his eyebrow. He wiped it away with his hand, feeling the sting as his fingers brushed the lump on his head.

"Pick him up," Victor ordered, striding towards the box. "And this time don't let go of him," he snapped at Mr Jefferson.

Mr Jefferson clasped his bony fingers around George's neck and dragged him to his feet. "Next time you try a stunt like that, I'll kill you myself," he said, squeezing so hard that George could feel his airway collapsing.

"Bring him to me," Victor barked.

George could barely breathe as Mr Jefferson heaved him across the floor by his neck. He felt faint and his lungs burnt. He struggled to stay on his feet.

"Tie him to the cables," Victor said, "He can be our insurance policy."

Mr Jefferson released George and he slumped to the ground, grasping at his throat with his blood stained hands. He gasped in a lungful of air and could feel his windpipe sting.

"If anyone enters this cave before I've got what I want from this safe, then your life will guarantee me a trouble free escape. See, I told you I could make use of you."

"I won't let you get out alive!" George spluttered.

Victor howled with laughter. George was on all fours, his head still dizzy, his eyes closed. Victor placed his heavy boot carefully over George's outstretched fingers.

"However much fun it has been playing hide and seek with you, this is where it comes to an end," he said, pressing down hard, crushing George's fingers.

"Argh!" George let out a scream. The pain had caught him off guard.

Victor pressed harder.

"See, as I said to your mother before I left her to burn, 'all good things must come to a satisfying end' and there is nothing more satisfying to me than getting revenge. And your mother…"

"Victor!" someone yelled from behind the safe. "Leave my son alone!"

George's eyes flew open, his head twisted. "Dad?"

Sam strode around the safe – a gun in his hand, raised and steady.

"Let him go – this has nothing to do with him!"

George's head swam.

Victor chuckled. "Ah, Officer J21 – for once in your pathetic career you are in the right place at the right time."

George looked searchingly at his dad, but Sam's eyes were firmly fixed on Victor. In fact, George had never seen his dad's eyes so alive, they were filled with fire – electricity.

"It's over, Victor. Let him go – he's just a child," Sam said.

"Yes, *your* child. A sweet satisfying revenge, don't you think? Look around you, Sam – every face you see has a reason to make you suffer – a reason to see you in pain and what greater pain than to watch your only offspring die."

Sam scanned the room. Mr Jefferson and Victor were ahead of him; Alex and Austin to his right, at the safe door; and Jose, Angelika and Sabrina to his left. He could see them all. There were several guns trained on him. They were all in his eyesight.

"He's innocent," Sam growled.

Victor leant down and lifted George to his feet. Sam's eyeline didn't shift, his gun didn't waver, he didn't look at George once.

"Dad, they–"

"Shut up!" Victor snapped, clasping his hand over George's mouth. "I'll tell you what, Sam – I'll give you one mercy – you can choose *how* he dies – slow or fast – it's your call, Officer."

Victor took a knife from his belt and pressed it to George's neck. George could feel the cold, sharp, prick of the blade on his skin.

"One quick slice or a long drawn out bleed? Your choice, Sam."

"Victor – I'm warning you – you harm my son and I'll self-destruct that safe – you'll never get your hands on its contents."

"Oh, Sam – firstly you're surrounded – and secondly I don't believe for a second that you've installed a self-destruct otherwise you would have used it the minute you figured out that we'd made it in here."

"It doesn't have to end like this, Victor."

"No, you're right – there is *one* other option," he said, lowering his knife. "How about you give me the code to this safe and I'll save your precious son's life?"

Sam's eyes dropped to George, and he finally looked at him. George could see his hard expression soften, the creases in his brow relax and a flicker of the pain and sorrow he so often saw in his dad's eyes flash across his gaze. The moment passed, Sam's face set rigid again and his eyes were back on Victor.

"I don't have the access codes," Sam said. "I'll give you one last chance to let him go."

"Don't think I don't know what you're doing," retorted Victor. "Stalling for time. I suppose the rest of the joke of MI5 are on their way here now. They've finally twigged that I didn't fall for your ridiculous trap. Did you really think I'd be so stupid? You know, Sam, my birds are nesting right under your nose, and if you know where to pressure them, they screech like unfed fledglings. It wasn't hard."

George flinched. Something moved in the shadows. He squirmed in Victor's grip; desperately trying to warn his dad. Sam's eyes dropped to him and he turned, but it was too late. Philippe appeared from the tunnel behind and was on Sam – a vicious blow to the head and he crumpled to the floor. Sabrina and Jose were at Philippe's side before Sam had a chance to retaliate. His gun kicked aside, he was pulled to his knees and dragged towards Victor's feet.

"The code, Sam – for your son's life," Victor repeated.

Sam tried to stand. Sabrina shoved him back down into the floor, her giant hands gripping his shoulders.

"You have ten seconds to decide. I will cut another inch of George's flesh with every second." With that Victor pierced George's skin, just under the left ear. George screamed through Victor's hand. A warm dribble of blood flowed from his neck. He could feel his knees going weak; tears blurring his vision.

"No! Stop!" Sam screamed.

"The code!" Victor growled back.

Sam looked from the box and back to Victor.

"Sam, you surely don't want to be responsible for the loss of another family member," Victor said.

Sam scowled.

"He does know what happened to his mother, doesn't he?" Victor continued.

"He's suffered enough," Sam said, his voice tight.

Victor laughed. "Oh, what sweet sorrow – he doesn't know, does he?"

"You killed her!" Sam spat, straining at Sabrina's grip. "You killed everything that was good about her!"

"Tut, tut, Samuel – you mustn't tell lies. He deserves the truth." Victor lowered his head to George's ear. "It is your father's fault you have no mother, George."

George searched his father's eyes, but he could only see anger.

"He sent her to hand me back to the Russians when it should have been him. After all I did for your parents. Your mother climbed the ladder – medals, commendations, and how did they repay me? By selling me out. And your poor mother paid the ultimate price, just like you are now. And once again it's your father's fault."

Victor drew the knife again. George's vision blurred.

"That's enough!" Sam screamed. "I'll give you the codes. Just let him go!"

"Excellent! See, Sam – all you have to do is press in all the right places." He shoved George towards Mr Jefferson. "Hold him!"

He turned back to Philippe. "Get him up," he shouted. "To the platform, now."

"Release him first," said Sam, looking back over his shoulder as he was dragged by Philippe and Sabrina to the platform.

"No, no. That's not how this works," Victor said, following closely behind. "I trusted you once, Sam, but this time I call the shots."

Sam mounted the steps, his eyes fixed on George. Alex and Austin held him by the shoulders as he punched in the code. A panel slid open and a green cube appeared, just like the one George had seen in the vault. The same web of light scanned Sam's face.

"Welcome Agent J21," an electronic voice announced. "Authorisation protocol in progress. Please wait."

"Well?" shouted Victor from the bottom of the steps. "You better not be double crossing me again, Sam. Don't forget I still have your son's life in my hands."

The cavern fell silent as all eyes rested on Sam and the box. The air itself seemed to still, before George's ears were filled with the shrill bleat of several long siren blasts. Victor flinched. The others took up their weapons and scanned the exits.

"He's triggered ze' alarm!" Sabrina screamed over the wail of the sirens.

But before they had time to react, the sirens were replaced with a loud grinding noise. The walls of the cavern shook, and rock dust showered down around them as the cables began to quiver and the box began to slowly lower to the ground.

"Finally!" Victor hollered. "Get him down from there." Philippe pulled Sam back down the steps. "Austin, Alex – get ready. It won't be long until we have more company." He turned towards the others. "Prepare to exit!"

The box hit the ground sending a tremor through the loose gravel at its base. A long, drawn-out hissing sound filled the air, and the four walls fell away revealing a solid glass box. Sitting inside was a solitary black tin, the size of a shoebox, with handles at either end.

Victor turned to Sam. "What now? You need to finish the job."

"Patience." Sam frowned.

"Seven years!" Victor screamed. "Seven years since you took it from me and destroyed everything I had built, and you ask me to be patient!"

He was striding towards Sam and George when the grinding noise returned and the cables lifted the body of the glass box two feet back into the air, leaving the metal tin stranded in the centre of the cave like forgotten luggage.

George stared at it. It looked so innocuous. How could anything that small and plain be worth so much planning, effort and devastation?

"Take it – but be careful!" shouted Victor. Jose and Sabrina bent down, took a handle each, slid it out from under the glass box and lifted it, careful to keep it level.

Angelika passed them a large case, and they lowered the tin inside.

"Now go," he said to Angelika. "You know the plan."

Victor turned to look at Sam. "And so my plans are almost at an end," he said. "Now I just have the final pleasure of watching you both die."

"You said you'd let him go," Sam said.

"Yes, Officer J21, and you said I'd be safe under British government protection – I guess we all lie sometimes."

There was a noise deep in the rocks behind them. Victor twisted. "Back up must be on its way. We must leave now. Is everything set?"

"Yes," Alex said.

Sabrina and Jose had already disappeared with the case down one of the tunnels, Angelika down another and Alex and Austin had gathered their equipment and were heading in another direction. They were splitting up.

"This is where you earn your money," Victor said to Philippe and Mr Jefferson. "Stall the back up and then take care of them." He turned to Sam. "I would love nothing more than to stay and watch you both die, but my transport is waiting, and you will serve as the perfect hindrance."

With that, he swept from the cave. As their footsteps faded away, George could hear someone else's approaching from the entrance he had come in by.

"Don't try anything or we'll kill you straight away," Philippe said, his gun to Sam's throat, his free arm locked around Sam's arms, pinning them behind Sam's back.

"We should kill them now," said Mr Jefferson. "How are we going to get out?"

"No – we must give Victor time to escape. We will use them as a defence."

Mr Jefferson had George around the neck, his gun between his shoulder blades. "I am going to enjoy killing you," he whispered in George's ear. "I only wish your mother was here to see me get my revenge."

George's hands were by his side. Something was scratching at his leg, something hard and sharp.

The metal bar!

He slowly moved his fingers across his thigh and into his pocket. Before anyone else could enter the cave, he swung both hands forward and stabbed them back with all his strength.

"This is for my mother!" he screamed, driving the piercing, steel bar deep into Mr Jefferson's thigh. He screeched in pain and dropped to the floor, grasping at his bleeding leg.

Philippe turned, lifting his gun, but Sam twisted from his grip and shoulder barged him to the ground, bringing him down hard. Philippe rolled onto his back, lifted his arms and aimed his gun. A single crack of a bullet echoed around the cave.

Sam gasped and spun to look at George. There he stood, his feet steady, his arms raised, a smoking gun in his hands. Sam's jaw dropped. He glanced back at Philippe. He was flat on the floor, blood oozing from his shoulder.

"Dad, I…" George said, every inch of his body shaking.

"George!" Sam cried. "Duck!"

George hit the floor just as more shots rang around the cave. Sam dived behind the suspended glass box. Mr

Jefferson had retrieved Sam's gun and was limping towards the exit, firing shots blindly over his shoulder.

George flattened himself into the dirt. Philippe's gun was inches from Sam's feet. He stretched out and dragged it in with his boot. Lifting the gun, he fired two shots back towards Mr Jefferson, then click – the chamber was empty. Mr Jefferson was firing madly at Sam, but his bullets only buried themselves into the glass sides of the box. It was up to George. He rolled onto his back and lifted his arms to take aim, his hands shaking. He felt sick. He closed his eyes. All he could see was the image of Philippe on the ground and his stomach turned. He dropped the gun, and it clattered to the floor, just as Felix appeared from the tunnel alongside the man in the turtle-neck sweater. The man fired three rapid shots and rock dust flew into the air as Mr Jefferson disappeared the way Sam had entered.

The gunfire stopped. Sam rushed over to George. "Are you OK?"

He sat up and stared at Philippe's bleeding body. "Dad, I … I didn't mean to…"

"It's OK, George," Sam said, kneeling in front of him. "Your instincts took over."

"But I…"

"It was him or us," Sam said. "He'll live to tell the tale."

"George!" Felix and the man in the turtle-neck ran over to join them.

"Freddie!" shouted Sam. "I needed you a little earlier."

George gaped from his dad to the man.

"I was trying to find your son, like you asked me," Freddie said, frowning at George.

"Oh, I – sorry," George stammered.

"It's OK," he said. "Your friend here managed to find me, and we got here as soon as we could."

"George, are you sure you're OK?" Sam asked, wiping the blood from George's neck.

"I think so," he replied, looking up at his dad.

Philippe groaned behind them. He was trying to drag himself up.

"See to him," Sam said to Freddie, pointing at Philippe. "I'm going to see where the others have gone."

Sam dashed towards the tunnel.

"Wait, Dad! Stop!"

But it was too late. The whole cavern was filled with the blast – dust and rubble flew from the tunnel, the ceiling cracked and Sam was thrown backwards.

"DAD!"

Chapter 21: The Flight of the Falcon

The dust began to settle, and all George could see through the pale haze was the dark outline of his father's body lying on the cave floor. He crawled towards him, his head still ringing from the blast and his eyes stinging, full of grit. He dragged himself over the fallen rocks, the debris sharp under his knees, scraping at his palms. The cave groaned all around him like a wounded beast. He reached Sam and grabbed him, heaving him on to his back. His head flopped to the side, his limbs limp.

"Dad!'" he screamed, choking. "Dad, come on! Get up!"

"George!" It was Felix. He appeared from the clouds of dust with Freddie at his side. He was limping.

"George, are you hurt?" Freddie asked, dropping to the floor beside him.

"No – but Dad…"

"Let me see him," Freddie said, taking Sam by the wrist. "He's OK, George. He's got a strong pulse. He's just been knocked out by the blast."

Sam groaned.

"Dad?" George's tears streamed hot down his face.

Sam opened his eyes. "George," he croaked. "You OK, Son?"

"I'm good, I…"

An almighty crack thundered overhead.

"We need to get out, Sam, and now. Can you stand?" Freddie asked.

"I'm good," he said, pulling himself gingerly to his feet.

George took him by the arm. "Let me help you."

"We need to get the Frenchman out," Sam said. "He's our only lead."

"I'll drag him if I have to," Freddie said, grabbing Philippe under the arms and heaving him from the cave.

They stumbled out, back through the tunnel through which Sam had entered. Before long, they passed through several iron gates and turned into a small tiled corridor that led into the ticket office of the Pendleton train station. They stopped, coughing, clearing their lungs. Felix propped himself against the old ticket barrier.

"I thought this old place was a rotten hull," he exclaimed.

It was gleaming. The old ticket desks had been replaced with glass fronted security posts and several CCTV feeds from outside the station were mounted on the wall.

"What is this place?" asked George, looking at his dad for answers.

"Um, well it *was* a hidden security hub," he said. "We converted it at the same time that we took over jurisdiction of the tunnels."

"We?" George asked, pushing his dad for more of an answer.

"I guess I've got a bit of explaining to do. But first, let's get out of here. Freddie, we need to call it in. We've got two guards down here. They must have been taken out from behind the security line. We've got one injured assailant, another one on the run and the remainder of the flock heading south in the tunnels."

Freddie nodded and grabbed a wall-mounted phone. "The line's dead."

"I figured as much," Sam said. "Alex must have deactivated the lot. I warned the Chief, but he wouldn't listen." Sam's nostrils flared. He rubbed the back of his neck. "Let's get out into the open and use the Sat Comm."

They made their way out, through several heavy barriers and into the overgrown grounds of the station. Freddie dumped Philippe by the entrance and walked out into the grounds to make the call. Something rustled in the undergrowth.

"Who's there?" Freddie barked, raising his gun.

"It's just me, you damn whipper-snapper!" Mr Steckler appeared from the bushes with a hefty spade slung over his shoulder. George's eyes nearly popped out of their sockets. At his feet was a bound and deflated Mr Jefferson.

"Found this lanky trouble-maker dragging himself through the jungle like a crazed gazelle," Mr Steckler said, grinning his toothless grin.

"You've still got it, Harry." Sam beamed at him.

"Never lost it," Mr Steckler winked. "May be retired but still enjoy a bit of scallywag hunting."

George and Felix stood gaping at him. "Er – Mr Steckler?" George said.

"Ah, yes, George. Please meet Harry, an old colleague of mine," Sam said.

George looked from Sam, to Mr Steckler, to the crumpled Mr Jefferson and back to Mr Steckler.

Mr Steckler chuckled and twisted the spade in his hand. George's eyes shifted to the spade.

"Not easy catching criminals with one finger missing, eh, George?" he winked.

"No, I guess not," George gaped back.

"Did I tell you how I lost it?"

"Several times," George said, smiling politely.

"Ah, but I mean the *real* story."

Sam grimaced. "He doesn't need to hear that," he said.

"He deserves to know the truth," Mr Steckler said. "Your dad shot it off." He giggled.

"What?" George looked horrified.

"It wasn't that straight forward," Sam protested.

Mr Steckler was chortling to himself.

Mr Jefferson groaned.

"Save the story for another time, Harry. We need to get these guys into custody before uniform are all over them."

With that, they heaved Mr Jefferson and Philippe to their feet and made their way out of the station grounds. They were met at the roadside by two unmarked cars and a large black van. George and Felix sat on the kerb watching as Sam delegated tasks, made calls and barked orders. George had never seen his dad like this before, it was like peering in on a dream. He seemed to come alive, fill with energy. George's head was bursting with questions.

"Mate, your dad's awesome," Felix whispered, staring in awe.

"Er – yeah – weird, huh?" George didn't know what to say.

Several officers made their way back into the station and spread out to scan the surrounding woodland. A helicopter buzzed overhead. Mr Jefferson and Philippe were loaded into an unmarked ambulance, and soon Sam was left with Felix and George and his old, beaten up van.

"Come on, let's get you two cleaned up and back to the school," he said.

They wandered towards the van.

"Let me grab my med kit," Sam said, swinging open the back doors of the van and revealing a grotto of technology and weaponry.

George blinked several times in disbelief.

"Wow! That's epic," Felix exclaimed.

"Yes, it's not a bad office," Sam grinned. He turned to look at George. "Not what you expected, I guess."

"Um – no, not really," George breathed.

Sam grabbed some medical supplies and started to patch up their injuries as best he could.

"I know this is a lot to take in," he said, as he cleaned up George's neck and handed Felix some water. "And I know you've had twenty-four hours from hell, but I need to ask you something quite important." He looked up into George's eyes. "You will need to keep all the details of what you've seen today to yourselves. I know it's a big ask, but a lot of what you've seen is top secret and not to be released into the public domain. Can you do that for me?"

Felix nodded. "Totally," he grinned.

"It's OK, I get it, Dad," George said.

"And you can't tell anyone about my job. You need to promise."

They both nodded.

"You and your friends will need to come in and be given a full debrief. You'll need to tell us everything you saw and heard and did. Not until you're ready of course."

Sam stood back and looked at George. "Hmm, not sure what Gran will make of my handiwork, but at least you're not bleeding anymore."

He turned to pack his things away.

"Dad, what about Victor? He's getting away and–"

"Don't worry, George, we've got people on it," Sam said, without lifting his gaze.

"But, Dad, he can't get away. He's murdered and stolen and–"

"I know, George – it's OK. We're on it," Sam said, slamming the doors of the van and ushering the boys towards the front cab.

"Dad – you can't let him get away with it," George said, stepping into his dad's path, frustration bubbling inside him. "He killed Mrs Hodge. Oh God – Dad – Mrs Hodge, her body is–"

"I know George, I'm sorry. She was reported missing by her niece last night."

"But she's in the barn, it's not far from here, I can show you."

"Just relax," Sam said, taking George by the shoulders. "There's a team on its way to find her. We'll bring her home to her family."

"Why did they kill her?" Felix asked, climbing into the cab of the van.

"She knew things. She was involved in the deal we did with the local government around taking over control of the tunnels and the old station. That's all you need to know."

"She didn't deserve to die though," George said, flopping down into the front seat and pulling the door closed.

"No," said Sam. "Reckon she put up a good fight though. She was an incredible woman."

Sam started the engine and backed out into the lane. They crawled up the hill into the light mist that clung to the surrounding trees. George stared out of the window.

He couldn't help wondering where Victor was now. It made him ache inside.

He turned to look at his dad. Felix sat between them, his eyes alive with intrigue, showering Sam with questions.

"So, how many bad guys have you taken down? Do you have those cool listening devices? Have you got an awesome car with loads of gadgets?"

Sam just smiled. "No, Felix, it's not like that."

George had many questions of his own but ones that were between him and his dad – they'd have to wait.

They trundled through the front gates of the school. The grounds were still filled with emergency vehicles and uniformed police and fire fighters. George looked up at the schoolhouse. The flames had died, but smoke still drifted from the carcass of the east wing. He let out a long sigh.

"It could have been a lot worse," Sam said, looking over at him.

They pulled up and Freddie was coming their way. They climbed out of the van.

"Everything's secure here, boss," Freddie said. "We've got the French guy and Jefferson locked down. The French guy is on his way to theatre. Turns out he's Philippe Bernard, ex-French Security Service, was previously attaché to the French Consulate."

"Hmm – makes sense. He was hidden right under our noses. What's his link with the bird?" Sam asked.

Freddie glanced over at the boys and lowered his voice. "We're waiting to find out. We'll have to question him when he's out of surgery."

"And Jefferson? Is he talking?"

"No, boss. He's asking for a lawyer, of course."
Freddie rolled his eyes. "He insists he's been framed. But I checked him over…"

"And?"

"Turns out his real name is Jerrod MacGuire, he's ex-Prison Service, changed his name by deed-poll about six years ago."

"I know that name – I'm pretty sure he was the guard on duty the day Victor broke out of custody." Sam frowned. "Wait 'til I've finished with him. He's been lying and scheming since the day he retired. I reckon he's got a lot more of a story to tell than he makes out."

"Felix's parents are down by the incident tent. They're desperate to see him," Freddie said, looking over at Felix. "Does he need debriefing?"

Sam turned to the boys. "Felix, you OK to see your folks?"

"Yeah, of course," Felix said.

"You remember what I said? It's best if you tell them that you and George went into the woods after the explosion because you thought you saw someone running away. You tried to follow them but got lost in the woods. Tell them that your injuries were from the blast at the school."

"Sure," Felix said, smiling. "Top secret."

Sam nodded. "Freddie will go with you and answer any questions they have."

Felix and Freddie disappeared leaving Sam and George alone.

"I've just got to sort a few things out, George, then we'll go home," Sam said. "You OK here for a minute? No running off to save the world."

"I think I'm done for today," George said, half smiling.

Sam strode down to the incident tent. George perched on the bumper of the van and stared at his sore hands, his broken shoes and tentatively prodded his swollen face.

"Hey, where the hell did you go?" It was Will, Jess and Francesca.

"How come you guys are still here?" he grinned, happy to see them.

"My mum and dad are speaking to the police about what happened in London," Jess said. "Mum can't leave until all pupils are picked up."

George looked towards the schoolhouse. Several students were still sat waiting for parents to arrive.

"My mum's away," Will said. "My dad is on his way, but he was on a job. He did say he'd send his girlfriend, but I'd rather be picked up by Mr Jefferson again!"

The others chuckled.

"What happened, George?" Francesca said, her eyes skimming over his head and neck. "Where did you go?"

He wanted to tell them everything, but knew he couldn't. "I went to follow Victor," he said.

"Where was he?" Jess asked.

George ran his hands through his hair. "Let's just say, we're not the only ones who were interested in what was hidden in that tunnel."

"And?" Will probed. "What was down there that he so desperately needed?"

"I don't know," George said.

It wasn't a complete lie. He still didn't know what was in the box. "The place was rigged. It blew before we could stop him."

"We?" Jess said.

"Um – me and Felix."

George couldn't mention his dad. It would be too hard to explain without giving everything away.

"So he got away?" Will said, disappointed.

"Yes – but Philippe and Mr Jefferson are in custody," George said.

"That's the best thing I've heard all day." Jess said, smiling.

"Guys, I'm so sorry I got you into all this. We should never have gone back down into the woods."

"No, you're wrong," Francesca declared. "Victor would still have gone ahead with his plan whether we'd have followed them or not. And we'd have been in school with everyone else when that explosion went off."

"Yeah, she's right," Will added. "And because of what we did and where we went, we got to the school in time and *you* got everyone out."

George smiled. "I guess, but we'd all be a lot less messed up."

"Nothing wrong with a few battle scars," Will said, holding up his bandaged hand with pride.

"Any news on Josh?" George asked.

"I made my dad call his dad," Francesca said. "He's doing fine."

"Flirting with all the nurses, knowing Josh," Jess said, laughing.

Francesca scowled.

"Francesca, it's time to get out of this nightmare of a place!" Her mother was teetering up the drive followed by her husband, who was dutifully carrying the dog.

Francesca sighed. "Great, I might take you up on that offer of a ride home with Mr Jefferson."

"Come on, say goodbye," Mrs Bonacci-Brown said, ushering Francesca away. "I don't think we'll be coming back here anytime soon. Time to find you *another* new school."

"What? No!" Francesca said, stamping her foot. "I love my school and my friends. I will be going nowhere."

Francesca's mother looked like she'd swallowed a lemon. "I don't think you have any say in it, young lady. Based on your behaviour today, you have proven that you are incapable of making sensible decisions for yourself."

"Francesca is one of the most level-headed, caring and savvy girls I know," Jess piped up. "I think maybe you underestimate her."

Mrs Bonacci-Brown was speechless. Francesca beamed and threw herself at Jess, squeezing the wind right out of her.

"I think you've got a great ability to choose good friends," Francesca's father said, stepping out from behind his wife. "You can't get very far in life without good friends."

Francesca ran and gave him a hug. His wife huffed, grabbed the dog and teetered back off down the drive.

"Come on, I think we better keep your mother happy, let's get you home," he said.

"OK, Dad," Francesca said, turning back to her friends. "Thank you," she smiled. "You're the best. Be safe."

It wasn't long before Will and Jess had been whisked away by their parents too. George was left on his own watching the school grounds empty out until only his dad, a few staff and a collection of officials remained.

Sam finally made his way back to the van. "Time to go," he said, standing next to George and looking towards the schoolhouse. "Will be a few days until you're all back at school, I think."

They clambered into the van and slowly bumped down the drive and out onto the winding lanes. The cab was silent. George stared out of the window. Sam cleared his throat.

"I'm very sorry you got caught up in all this, Son. I don't know how I managed to screw up so badly," Sam said, his eyes on the road. "I should have seen this coming."

"Dad, it's my fault. I went after him, I–"

"No, I should have predicted that he'd try to get to you. I didn't listen to you and for that I'm truly sorry."

"I'm sorry I let him get away with – whatever was in that box," George said, glancing over at his dad. "I should have told the police and not gone into the tunnel alone. If I hadn't walked right into Victor's grasp, you wouldn't have had to give him the code to the safe."

"Well, that may be what Victor planned all along, but nevertheless, he would have stopped at nothing to get his hands on it."

"What was it, Dad, in that box?" George asked, unsure of whether Sam would answer.

Sam sighed. "A weapon, George. A very dangerous weapon." He suddenly pulled the van up to the kerb, yanked the handbrake and turned to look at George.

"I owe you an explanation – it's well overdue."

George sat in silence.

"Over seven years ago, Victor stole a highly advanced weapon from the Russians. They'd been working on it for years. We knew of its existence and the threat it posed. Victor had stolen a prototype and was being hunted down by Russian Special Forces. We offered him asylum in the UK in return for information. He claimed he had abandoned the weapon while on the run."

Sam shifted in his seat.

"Your mother and I worked with him to gather intelligence, but he double-crossed us. He had assembled a group of criminals together right under our noses, he even conned us into bringing Angelika into the UK. He intended to replicate and sell the weapon to every major criminal network across Europe for billions of dollars."

"He still had it – the weapon?" George asked.

"Yes, and as soon as he had everything in place, he disappeared. Your mother saw it coming, of course. She never trusted him. She put two of her finest new recruits on his tail. They were both found dead, and your mother never forgave herself. She became obsessed with hunting him down."

Sam let out a long deep sigh.

"He and his gang ran riot through Europe until we caught him out and took him, his crew and the weapon into custody. He lost all his deals, all his credibility and all his funding. His network fell apart."

"So you had him. How did he get away?" George asked.

"He was held in a top security lock up in Scotland until the day we were to trade him with the Russians. That was seven years ago today." Sam stared out the window. His eyes glistening.

"When Mum died," George said, under his breath.

"Yes, when your mother died. I'm sorry, George. I hated lying to you, but you really couldn't know the whole truth – not until now."

"You told me she died in a fire in Edinburgh," George said, a lump in his throat.

"It was the truth, George, as much of the truth as I could afford," Sam said, his voice wavering. "I should have gone. Your mother was insistent that she did the escort. But she was obsessed by then. All she ever wanted was to make him pay for the loss of her young officers. She took several uniforms with her for the prison transport and it was supposed to be a low-key handover in a warehouse in Scotland. It all went wrong. Someone on the inside tipped off Victor's remaining allies. They were ambushed."

"Mr Jefferson!" George exclaimed.

"It seems so. He was the prisoner chaperone on the day. He was never really interrogated. He claimed to have been shot in the ambush and was signed off for physical and mental trauma."

"It was Mum that shot him, he told me," George said, sitting upright in his seat.

Sam frowned and ran his fingers through his beard.

"But what about the police escort?" George asked.

"They failed," Sam said, his eyes darkening. "They ran and left her on her own. She should have run too, but she chose her chance at revenge over her life – over her life with us."

Sam stared through the front window, his eyes glazed over.

"Do you hate her, Dad?" George asked. "You never talk about her or, you know…"

Sam sighed. "It's complicated, George."

He couldn't look at George – the pain and anger rippled through him. George wasn't sure he'd ever truly understand why Sam felt that way.

"So for seven years he's just waited?" George asked.

"Yes, hiding, moving, plotting. All he's ever wanted is to get his hands on that weapon and make himself extremely wealthy. His only way of getting his credibility back."

"What's so special about the weapon?"

"George, it's not that I don't trust you, but I'm breaking every protocol telling you this much as it is."

"I get it," George said, his chin dropping to his chest. Sam fiddled with his beard again.

"Look, all I can say is that we've had it for seven years and our most highly trained weapons scientists haven't been able to crack it. It's a cloakable, chemical weapon with devastating effects. In the wrong hands it could be catastrophic."

"So why aren't you racing after them?" George said, looking out over the dreary rolling hills. "They can't have got that far."

"I know where they're going, George," Sam said, peering out in the same direction.

"What?"

"Your dad may be stubborn at times, but I always plan ahead."

"Well?"

"Victor may have the weapon, but he has taken a few other little surprises with him. I'll be keeping a very close eye on him and, hopefully, he'll lead us directly to his buyers." Sam turned to George and smiled.

"So you wanted him to take it?" George said, puzzled.

"Not exactly, but I was outnumbered, and my only option was to convince him that I was desperate for him *not* to take it so that, if he managed to escape, he wouldn't guess that he's being tracked. At least, not until our tail is in place."

"Right," George said. "So…"

"Enough questions for now, George. Let's get you home."

Sam turned the key and the engine rattled to life. They wound their way down the hill towards sleepy Chiddingham. George watched the familiar streets drift past. His eyes were heavy, his body broken. He longed for his bed. As they trundled through the centre of the village, George peered out of the window: a young woman in sweat pants pushing a buggy, a toddler whizzing along on a scooter, an old gentleman walking his dog. He puzzled over how ordinary life could just continue after all that had happened. His thoughts were interrupted as an old red post van raced past, almost pushing them off the road.

"What's the damn rush?" Sam cursed, swerving to miss the wayward driver.

George chuckled. It was his same old dad. He peered back out of the window. Racing in the opposite direction was a woman; dressed in black with her hood pulled down over her eyes. George sat bolt upright. His drowsy eyes snapped open. He twisted in his seat and tried to catch a glimpse of her face as they glided past. She turned to cross the street. Blonde – long blonde hair. It wasn't her. He slumped back down into his seat.

"Dad – one more question," he said, as their cottage came into view.

"Yes, George."

"There was a woman at the vault, I think she was trying to stop Victor."

Sam slowed the van and glanced over at George. "A woman?"

"Yeah, I thought maybe she was one of yours – you know – an officer."

"Hmm," Sam's frown-lines deepened. "What did she look like?"

George described her as best he could. Sam's expression didn't change.

"She tried to help us out, she was on our side – I'm sure of it," George said.

"It's possible, but Victor has made plenty of enemies over the years … leave it with me, George – I'll look into it."

With that, they pulled up to the cottage.

George had never been happier to lay eyes on the creaky metal gate that greeted you at the threshold of their home. The sound of his dad's van crunching onto the gravel drive had never sounded more welcoming and reassuring. He would never look at his dad's van in the same way again. It had gone from an embarrassment to something George couldn't be prouder of, not that he could ever let anyone know. But he didn't care. Sam pulled the keys from the ignition and looked over at his son.

"I'm proud of you, George," he said. He paused, looked down at his hands in his lap and cleared his throat. "Your mum would have been exceptionally proud of you too. You're just like she once was: brave, impulsive, determined. Not sure you get any of that from me." He looked back over at George and smiled. It was the best smile George had ever seen.

"Thanks, Dad."

"Shall we go in? Gran will be hopping around, dying to see that you're OK."

"Yeah. Might need a whole pot of hot chocolate if we're gonna' tell her the whole story."

"Yeah, and maybe a whole fudge cake – with any luck. But, you know, we can't tell her everything, right?"

"Yes – of course – does she really not know?"

"No, and she mustn't, George."

They hopped down from the van, headed up the path and could hear the TV and the radio blasting out as usual. George's eye was still swollen, his head throbbed and his neck was stiff and encrusted with blood. He sorely needed a long bath, a decent meal and a deep, dreamless sleep.

As they approached the front door, Sam threw out his arm, stopping George in his tracks.

"Stop there!"

George looked down. The front door was slightly ajar; the wood around the lock splintered. Sam drew his gun and slowly entered the hallway. George crept in behind him, his heart pounding. They passed the lounge door, and George could see Marshall hiding under Gran's footstool. Expecting his regular frosty welcome, he was shocked when Marshall scampered from under the stool and threw himself into George's arms.

"What the – Gran!" George said, panic rising up from his gut. "Dad, where's Gran?" He tried to push his way deeper into the hall.

"Wait, George! Stay behind me," Sam said.

They slid along the corridor. Sam pushed the kitchen door open with his toe, his gun leading the way. The door peeled open, but the room was empty. George couldn't take it any longer.

"Gran?" he called out, pushing past Sam.

"Careful, George," Sam warned, moving towards the bathroom.

The radio was even louder than usual. George gently placed Marshall down on the counter top and turned the radio off. He dashed towards the back window to look out into the garden but stumbled over a broken plate. He could feel the fear tearing at his insides.

"Where is she?" he screamed, dashing back out into the hall.

"Wait for me, George!"

But George was already leaping up the stairs, two at a time. He checked every room. Gran was nowhere to be seen.

"She's gone, Dad!" he cried. But as he descended the stairs, something caught his eye – something was pinned to the back of the front door. "Dad, look," he said, pointing at the small piece of crumpled paper.

Sam turned, grabbed it and read aloud:

"I am Victor Sokolov,

Seven years I have waited,
Waited to get my revenge,
Waited to take back what you stole from me,
Waited to re-build that which you destroyed.

I have sent the Falcon to flight,
I have hit you where it hurts the most,
I have snatched the thing you hold dearest,
I will make you beg for lenience.

I am Victor Sokolov.

If you follow me, you will never see her again.
If you drop the tail, I will let her live.

I am Victor Sokolov."

End.

Thank you for reading **The Undergrounders and the Flight of the Falcon**.

If you enjoyed this adventure, and want to find out what happens to George and his friends, please head over to Amazon and grab yourself a copy of the next instalment:

The Undergrounders & the Deception of the Dead

The Undergrounders & the Malice of the Moth

In the meantime, I would love to hear your feedback, so please leave a review on Amazon and follow me on:
Website: ctfrankcom.com
Twitter: @ctfrankcom
Facebook: CT Frankcom
Instagram: CT Frankcom

Printed in Great Britain
by Amazon